I0761293

BURIED IN A BOOK

Also by T.C. LoTempio

The Cozy Bookshop Mysteries

MURDER ON THE BOOKS *

The Tiffany Austin Food Blogger Mysteries

EAT, DRINK AND DROP DEAD *
A CRUST TO DIE FOR *
A DISH BEST SERVED DEAD

The Nick and Nora Mysteries

MEOW IF IT'S MURDER
CLAWS FOR ALARM
CRIME AND CATNIP
HISS H FOR HOMICIDE
MURDER FAUX PAWS
A PURR BEFORE DYING
BELL, BOOK AND CORPSES

The Cat Rescue Mysteries

PURR M FOR MURDER
DEATH BY A WHISKER

The Urban Tails Pet Shop Mysteries

THE TIME FOR MURDER IS MEOW
KILLERS OF A FEATHER
DEATH STEALS THE SPOTLIGHT
CATS, CARATS AND KILLERS
A SIDE DISH OF DEATH

* *available from Severn House*

BURIED IN A BOOK

T.C. LoTempio

SEVERN
HOUSE

First world edition published in Great Britain and the USA in 2026
by Severn House, an imprint of Canongate Books Ltd,
14 High Street, Edinburgh EH1 1TE.

severnhouse.com

Cover and jacket design by Piers Tilbury

British Library Cataloguing-in-Publication Data
A CIP catalogue record for this title is available from the British Library.

ISBN-13: 978-1-4483-1528-4 (cased)
ISBN-13: 978-1-4483-1923-7 (paper)
ISBN-13: 978-1-4483-1529-1 (e-book)

All Severn House titles are printed on acid-free paper.

Typeset by Palimpsest Book Production Ltd., Falkirk, Stirlingshire, Scotland.
Printed and bound in Great Britain by TJ Books, Padstow, Cornwall.

The manufacturer's authorised representative in the EU for product safety is Authorised Rep Compliance Ltd, 71 Lower Baggot Street, Dublin D02 P593 Ireland (arccompliance.com)

Praise for T.C. LoTempio

"A fast-paced mystery with lots of twists and turns . . . I look forward to reading more about Charley and her adventures"
Kings River Life Magazine on *Murder on the Books*

"If you've ever wondered what it would be like to read a Hallmark Mystery movie in book format, wonder no more. *Murder on the Books* . . . is as close as you will ever get"
Cozy Crime Mystery on *Murder on the Books*

"Captivating characters and plenty of intrigue . . . Delightful"
Publishers Weekly on *Eat, Drink and Drop Dead*

"An exciting mystery . . . I was hooked from start to finish!"
Laura Childs, *New York Times* bestselling author of the Tea Shop Mysteries, on *Eat, Drink and Drop Dead*

"Entertaining . . . Cozy fans will be satisfied"
Publishers Weekly on *The Time for Murder is Meow*

About the author

T.C. LoTempio is the award-winning, nationally bestselling author of the Nick and Nora Mysteries, the Urban Tails Pet Shop Mysteries, the Cat Rescue Mysteries, the Tiffany Austin Food Blogger Mysteries, and the new Cozy Bookshop Mysteries. Born in New York City, she now resides in Phoenix, Arizona with her two cats, Maxx and Rocco. Rocco prides himself on being the inspiration for her Nick and Nora series.

www.tclotempio.net

To the Master of Horror himself . . . the late Vincent Price

Acknowledgments

As always, thanks go to my agent, Josh Getzler, and my editor, Tina Pietron! And to all the fans who buy my books and keep me writing, my heartfelt thanks and appreciation. Just to clarify: some of the facts about Vincent Price in this book are fictional for storytelling purposes, but that "black cat contest" actually happened! I hope readers enjoy reading this story as much as I did writing it!

Characters

The Regulars

Charlotte "Charley" James, aka C.J. Barrett – ex-thriller writer, now owner of the Mainely Mysteries Bookstore

Poe – Charley's black cat

Ian Grant – detective at Philadelphia PD

Zane Adams – Charley's friend and business partner, bakery store owner

Barbara Jeanne "Barbie" Donaldson – homicide detective in training at Austin PD and former high school nemesis of Charley and Zane

Randy Zucker – new homicide detective at Philadelphia PD

Phyllis Wooster – owner of the Jumpin' Beans café

Betty Stubing – owner of the Frozen Spoon, the local ice cream store

Mandy Thatcher – clerk at Mainely Mysteries Bookstore

Masie Hanson, Anna Fisk and Braedon Ohlmeyer – bookstore and bakery clerks working for Charley and Zane

Max Molenaro – Charley's agent

New Characters

Jeffrey Thomas – book dealer

Gordon Knight – late scientist

Peter Bridges – retired drama professor

Gil Sullivan – author of a book on Vincent Price

Jake Rodgers – Mandy's new beau

Maddie Elster – wealthy heiress and rare book collector

Edmund Elster – Maddie's brother

Amanda Elster – Maddie and Edmund's late sister

Douglas Winchell – Amanda's husband, formerly employed by Gordon Knight

Jewell Winchell – Amanda and Douglas's daughter

Efram Winchell – Amanda and Douglas's son

Janice Rutger – Maddie's former maid

Riley May Connor – new local reporter

David Trent – FBI agent

ONE

"Part of me wants to get the next book in the series, but a little voice inside me is protesting 'no, no' so I can get to sleep before two a.m."

I glanced up from my computer and smiled at the woman in front of my counter. Betty Stubing was the owner of the Frozen Spoon, the one and only old-fashioned ice cream parlor in my hometown of Austin, Pennsylvania. She'd been in my bookshop ever since it opened, spending most of her time leafing through the cookbooks and books on fancy desserts. The last time she'd been in, she'd expressed an interest in diversifying her reading material, and I'd introduced her to the J.D. Robb series, which, judging from her reaction, had been an excellent choice. "I know. I love the dynamic between the two main characters. There's plenty of suspense and a dash of romance. Something for everyone, right?"

"Right. Who knew I'd get hooked on a futuristic police procedural." Betty gave her head a brisk shake, causing her gray curls to bob to and fro. "I may just have to give in and get the next two. I just don't want to read them too fast."

"Considering there are over sixty books in the series, it'll take you a while to work your way through them," I said. I tapped my keyboard and looked at my computer screen. "I do have book two in stock but not book three. Do you want me to order it for you?"

Betty hesitated, then shook her head. "Better not. If I take my time, the second book should last me till Christmas. I'll put the third and fourth on my gift list. I'm sure one of my brothers will get them for me. And speaking of brothers . . ." Betty reached into her tote bag and whipped out a slip of paper, which she smoothed out on the counter. "I nearly forgot," she said. "My brother wanted me to ask if you could check to see if there's a new Steve Sheppard book coming out this year? He hasn't heard anything and he's getting a little concerned."

My hand stilled over my keyboard. "I haven't heard about a new release in that series," I said. "I'm not sure if there is one scheduled for this year." Well, that was a lie. I knew for a fact there weren't any Steve Sheppard books scheduled for release anytime soon. And just how did I know that?

I knew because I hadn't written a new one.

In another life I, Charlotte "Charley" James, was also C.J. Barrett, thriller author. I'd enjoyed a successful career writing a series about an intrepid secret agent until a few months ago, when I'd been struck with a horrendous case of writer's block. I'd sat at my computer in my New York townhouse for hours, staring at a white screen, willing words to come that never did. Whereas in my last fifteen books, the ideas had flowed freely, now there was . . . nothing. No inspiration of any kind came to mind. After all these years it appeared the well, as they say, had run dry.

My solution to this problem? Since my contract with my current publisher was completed, I pulled up stakes and ditched the bright lights of New York City for my hometown of Austin, Pennsylvania. I'd reconnected with my BFF from high school, Zane Adams. After I'd helped to clear her of the murder of her business partner (a long story, recounted elsewhere for anyone interested), she'd managed to talk me into going into business with her in the double storefront she'd rented. My side was a bookstore, specializing in mysteries (what else?). I'd kept the name her partner Sheila had registered the business under, Mainely Mysteries, because it just seemed to suit. Zane ran her bakery, Zaney's Sweet Treats, on the other. I'd agreed to give it a whirl for a six-month trial period to see how it went. So far things were going well—aside from the daily texts from my agent, Max Molenaro, trying to coax me back into writing. Yesterday's text had been: PHR willing to pay big buckos for the return of Steve Sheppard. How about it? Ready to give it a whirl?

I texted back: Not interested.

Max's reply: At least think about it.

I did—for all of two seconds before I texted back: Still not interested.

Less than five seconds later came this: Well then, what about a new series? How about doing a cozy based on that recent adventure of yours? We can do it under another pen name. How about it? It might be just the spark you need to get those creative juices flowing. Any interest?

I sighed. As I recalled, Max had been very interested when I'd revealed my role in solving the aforementioned murder. He'd immediately zeroed in on the cozy genre. *C'mon, Charley! It's so Jessica Fletcher! I bet it'd be a big hit!*

Unfortunately for Max, I had no desire to write cozies or anything else at the moment. I was, believe it or not, perfectly happy selling other people's books. I hadn't answered his text, and today, when I checked my messages, there was nothing from Max. I had no doubt his feelings had been hurt by my lack of response and now he was waiting for me to make the next move.

Sorry, Max. You're in for a long wait.

"That's a shame." Betty's nasal voice interrupted my thoughts. She stuffed the note back in her bag. "He'll be disappointed. C.J. Barrett is one of his favorite authors—maybe even his very favorite."

"Tha—I mean, that's nice," I said. I'd almost said thank you. No one in Austin knew I was C.J. Barrett, and I wanted to keep it that way. I peered at the computer screen. "Does he like Clive Cussler? There's a new book of his coming out next week."

"I'm not sure. I'll ask him. He's coming over to the shop later to help me plan a few special treats for the big day—speaking of which, are you planning to do any decorating?"

She cast a disparaging look around the shop and I bit down on my lower lip. The "big day" Betty was referring to was Halloween, and of course I was decorating—if I didn't, the good citizens of Austin would probably boycott my bookshop or worse still, haul me out to the town square and tar and feather me—and I wasn't kidding. I personally had never considered Halloween a holiday, but the residents of Austin did. Here it was just as big, if not bigger, than Thanksgiving or Christmas. I nodded toward the large plate glass window. "Mandy has some ideas for the window. She was thinking maybe something in the Hitchcock vein—a hand gripping a shower curtain, a mannequin covered with black birds, another mannequin in a chair with a leg cast and a camera. I looked, and we have a pretty good selection of books about Hitchcock we can put in the window too."

Betty gave a nod of approval. "*Psycho*, *The Birds*, *Rear Window*. I like it." She paused and glanced significantly around the store. "How about inside?"

"Mandy set up a display of Halloween cozies yesterday, and I started another display in Aisle Six." My hand fluttered toward the aisle where the classics were located. "I pulled out some books on Edgar Allan Poe. I thought he'd be quite appropriate for the season."

No sooner had the author's name left my mouth than a large black cat jumped up on the counter, causing Betty to gasp and take a step back. He widened his golden eyes and swiveled his head in the direction I'd indicated. "Meow?"

"Not you, Poe, although you are the embodiment of the quintessential Halloween cat," I said. I ran my hand down the cat's back and his tail curved slightly. "I was talking about the actual author." I grinned at Betty. "For my money, you can't get any scarier than Poe—the author, not my cat. I remember reading *The Pit and the Pendulum* in high school and having nightmares."

"I felt the same way when we had to read *The Raven*," Betty said. "I dreamt about a black bird following me home and croaking 'nevermore' for weeks."

At mention of the word "bird," Poe's ears flicked forward, and his pink tongue darted out and licked his lips.

I snapped my fingers. "That's a thought. I'll look online and see if I can find a stuffed raven. He'd look good perched on a stack of books."

"Oh, you don't have to bother looking," said Betty. "I have an extra I can loan you."

I looked at her. "You have an extra raven? You're kidding."

"Nope. They were having a sale at Gilley's a few years ago. I made sure I got there early and got first pick of the Halloween and Christmas decorations." She rubbed her hands together. "You'd have to put him up high, though, so the kids can't reach him. They love to press the button that makes him talk."

I barked out a laugh. "The raven talks?"

"Yep. He's a very wordy raven unlike the one in the poem. He says 'Nevermore,' and 'once upon a midnight dreary,' and something else. I just can't remember what." She reached out and grabbed my arm. "Oh, maybe you could get one of those Halloween trees? That big box store out on the highway has a lot of them. They look like a Christmas tree, but they're black or orange. As a matter of fact, I think they even have one that's both colors."

"That's not a bad idea," I said. "I could get a small one—three feet, four tops—and put it in the center of the table and perch the raven on top. That would look pretty cool."

"It definitely would." Betty's voice rose as her excitement mounted. "You know what else would be cool? Scattering some DVDs of the movies they made from his works in with the books."

"That would be cool, but we don't sell DVDs," I said. "And I don't have any of my own." I'd had a DVD player in New York, but my ex-boyfriend had taken it with him when we'd broken up, and I'd never bothered to replace it.

She waved her hand carelessly. "Oh, I can loan you some. Just mark 'em display only, not for sale. I have all the ones with Vincent Price in them." She let out a sigh. "I just loved him—he was such a terrific actor. I have *House of Wax*, but that's not a Poe title." She started to tick off on her fingers. "Let's see, I've got *The Black Cat*, *The Masque of the Red Death*, *House of Usher*, *The Tomb of Ligeia . . .*"

"Quite an impressive list, only Vincent Price wasn't in *The Black Cat*."

Betty and I both turned. Neither of us had heard the shop doorbell tinkle once again or noticed the stranger who now stood behind Betty. I took a moment to study him. He looked to be mid to late thirties, tall and lean, with brown eyes, a strong jaw, chiseled cheekbones, and a mass of dark hair that curled around his ears. He was dressed in what I'd always thought of as elegant casual: Italian leather loafers, pressed Dockers, a checked shirt peeping out from a navy V-necked sweater that looked like cashmere. I'd seen guys dressed like him nearly every day going up and down Park Avenue in Manhattan. In short, he reeked of money.

"Price wasn't in *The Black Cat*," he repeated without waiting for either of us to answer him. He looked directly at Betty and said, "At least, not if you're referring to the 1934 version. That one starred Boris Karloff and Bela Lugosi. He did, however, star in a segment of the 1962 film *Tales of Terror* entitled *The Black Cat*."

"That must be the one I'm thinking of," Betty said, a little confused. "I remember Vincent Price was in it, and I believe Peter Lorre was as well."

"Then that's definitely *Tales of Terror*," said the man with a confident smile. "You know the story about the black cat auditions for that segment of the movie, right?" When we both shook our heads, he went on. "Price auditioned over a hundred and fifty cats for the role. Most of them were dismissed at the initial audition because they had a tip of white on the lip or the nose. He kept at it until he found the perfect all-black cat. It was quite a big deal back in 1961—oh my!"

The stranger stopped speaking as Poe jumped up on the counter. He regarded the man for a moment with a fixed yellow stare, then, with a flick of his tail, jumped down and sauntered off toward the rear of the store.

The man reached up and swiped at his forehead. He inclined his head toward the rapidly disappearing Poe. "Now that's one good-looking cat. Too bad he's not totally black, or I bet Price would have hired him for sure." He turned to me and added, "I'm assuming he's the shop cat."

"Yes, but he's also my cat," I said. "And oddly enough his name happens to be Poe."

The man laughed. "Well, that is appropriate." He tapped his chin with his finger. "I must say, I do like your display. Poe personifies Halloween, and Vincent Price was superb in all of those Poe films. Did you know that he was also an avid art collector and critic?"

"Yes," Betty and I both chorused. "And a gourmet cook," Betty added.

"That's right, he was," I said. "He wrote several cookbooks, and they're still in print. I'm pretty sure there might be one over in the Cooking section."

Betty let out a reminiscent sigh. "My mother had the first one he and his wife Mary co-wrote. It has photos and recipes from restaurants all over the world. It's a thick book too. I still have it. I'm pretty sure she said it's a first edition."

The stranger's eyes widened. "Really? What sort of shape is it in?"

Betty's nose wrinkled. "Not that great, I'm afraid. The spine is cracked and some of the pages are loose. My mother put it through the wringer. I think she must have tried nearly every recipe in the book. She was a good cook, and so am I. I'm always on the lookout for a new recipe."

The stranger clucked his tongue before replying, "Too bad. A first edition in good shape could go for several hundred dollars. I've seen one in pristine—that's nearly new—condition go for five hundred. And if it had been autographed by Price, why, it would have sold for much more."

"If that cookbook had been autographed by Vincent Price, my mother would never sell it, and neither would I," said Betty, tapping her nails on the counter for emphasis.

"Are you sure about that?" the man asked. "An avid collector would pay big bucks for an item like that, especially a first edition." He turned to me and jabbed a finger in the air. "You should get a copy of *The Price of Fear*. It chronicles all of his films and would make a nice addition to your display."

Betty angled her face so the stranger couldn't see her and rolled her eyes, then raised her hand and tapped at the watch on her wrist. "As interesting as this discussion is, I've got to get going. I'll look for that raven when I get home." Betty squeezed my hand, gave the stranger a brief nod, and was gone. After the door closed behind her, the man looked at me.

"Interesting woman. Always looking for new recipes, huh? Does she like to cook?"

"You could say that," I said with a grin. "She runs the Frozen Spoon. It's an old-fashioned ice cream parlor."

"Ah, I'll have to stop by. Nothing I like better than a good black cow." He held out his hand. "Forgive me, where are my manners? I never introduced myself. Jeffrey Thomas. I take it you're the manager of this shop?"

"Manager and owner. Charley James."

His eyes widened slightly. "Really. Allow me to compliment you, Ms. James. You have a very nice store here. A very large mystery section, but I guess considering the name of the store, that's to be expected."

"We specialize in mysteries—cozies, thrillers. The other genres seem to be selling well too. It's been my experience that a truly successful store has a well-stocked variety of subjects."

"Quite true." He paused and then added, "I didn't see a section on used books."

"We have a small selection. It's right before the children's reading nook," I said. "There are a few Agatha Christies, some Raymond Chandlers if you like oldies but goodies, Louise Penny and Gillian Flynn, James Patterson for the thriller fans, and I know there are some vintage Stephen Kings there—I'm pretty sure *Carrie* is one of them. There's a bunch of cozies too, by Laura Childs, E.J. Copperman, and Lorna Barrett. And there are about a dozen romance novels and a few children's books, *Harry Potter*, Dr. Seuss. If you're looking to score a first edition, though, I'm afraid you're out of luck. What I have came from garage and library sales."

"I see." He stared off into space for a few moments, then swung his gaze back to me. "Then I doubt you'd have what I'm looking for. It's a book that was published by a small press back in the eighties. I believe it had a very small print run. It details all of Poe's works, with an emphasis on those which translated into film. The author paid special tribute to Price in the book. Apparently he was a huge fan of both the author and the actor. It is supposed to be quite rare."

"I'm positive I've never seen a book like that," I said, "but it does sound fascinating. Have you tried some of the antiquarian online dealers? Maybe they have a copy."

He shook his head. "It's a book that doesn't often come up for resale. I did hear, though, from a reliable source, that there might be a copy of that book for sale floating around this little burg somewhere. So when I saw your Poe display, I thought maybe . . ." His voice trailed off and I saw a faraway gleam come into his eyes.

"I could make some inquiries," I offered. "What's the name? Who's the author and the publisher?"

He looked a bit sheepish as he responded, "I'm not certain about the exact title. It has something to do with the complete works of Poe, I think."

I raised an eyebrow. "You're looking for a book, but you don't know the title? What about the author? Or the publisher?"

"I'm afraid my client didn't give me many specifics, other than a vague title. And he's out of town right now, somewhere abroad. He didn't leave contact information."

I stared at him. "Did you say your client? So you're not looking for this book for yourself?"

"No." He cleared his throat. "I should have mentioned I'm a rare book dealer. When I got the tip about a Poe–Price book being for sale, I decided to come out here and take a look around, hoping I might get lucky and it was the one my client wanted."

"So you would have bought it, not knowing if it was the right book or not?"

"Sure, if the price was right. I'd have found a buyer for it."

I was tempted to comment on what I thought was bad business practice, but Jeffrey Thomas reached into his shirt pocket and pulled out a square of cream paper, which he pressed into my hand. "If you should come across a book like the one I described, I'd appreciate a call."

I took the card, but before I could look at it, the shop bell tinkled and a tall, gangly girl dressed in blue jeans and a plaid flannel shirt hurried in. She bustled right up to the counter and addressed me, ignoring Thomas, who politely stepped to one side. “Hey, Charley. My mother wanted to know if that Heather Morris book she ordered is in yet.”

“Got it right here.” I reached underneath the counter and pulled out one of the lilac plastic bags that had Mainely Mysteries emblazoned on it. As the girl fumbled in her purse for her wallet, I slid Thomas’s card into my pocket without looking at it. As I glanced up, I saw him going out the door. He paused, waved, and then he was gone.

The morning passed rather quickly after that. I did an Internet search for books on both Poe and Vincent Price and ended up calling my distributor to order a copy of *The Price of Fear*. A few more customers came in, and then I felt in need of a break. Mandy wasn’t due for her shift for another hour, so I put the “Back in 20 minutes” sign in the window, locked the front door, and ducked through the connecting door to Zaney’s Sweet Treats. I settled into my favorite table, a small one tucked into the corner, and after a minute Zane herself bustled out from the back and over to the table. In one hand she held a steaming teapot, in another a delicate mug, which she set before me.

“I was hoping you’d come in,” she announced. “I’m dying for you to try this new tea my distributor insisted I take. It’s called Blooming Green Tea.”

“Yeah?” I eyed the steaming teapot. “What’s blooming about it?”

Zane’s smile broadened. “When it steeps, it blooms and reveals a gorgeous red and gold blossom inside. I served it to a few people, and they loved it.”

“Sounds . . . different. I’ll try some,” I said, rather unnecessarily, as Zane was already pouring the blend into my cup. The rich, full scent rose up to caress my nose and I breathed it in. “It smells good, anyway.”

“How about some chocolate mousse to go with it? It’s made with vanilla tea.”

I patted my stomach. “I’m trying to keep my figure, which is getting harder and harder every day,” I said. In New York I’d worked out at the gym every day before settling in front of my computer. Not so anymore.

She looked me over with a critical eye then placed a hand on one ample hip. "Your figure looks fine to me. What are you, a size two?"

"I used to be." I snapped at the waistband of my jeans. "They're getting snug. I've probably graduated to at least a four." Zane rolled her eyes, and I sighed. "I really should skip the sweet."

Zane folded her arms over her chest. "But you won't. How about a nice strawberry macaron?"

"Lo-Cal?"

Her smile turned wicked. "But of course?"

I sighed. "You're a terrible liar, and I have no willpower. OK, sold. One strawberry macaron."

Zane hurried off and returned a few minutes later with a plate on which rested not one, but two macarons. "One for you, one for me," she said, setting the plate in front of me. She flopped into the chair next to mine. "I deserve a break too." She grabbed a macaron, took a bite, chewed, swallowed, and said, "So, what's up? Mandy told Masie she's doing Hitchcock for your window Halloween display, so now Masie wants me to decide on a theme for the bakery window." Masie Hanson was Zane's assistant at the bakery and fast friends with my assistant. "I was thinking something Hansel and Gretel-ish?"

"That might work. You do make a mean gingerbread." I took a bite of the macaron, set it down, and took another sip of tea. "Something odd happened this afternoon. A man came into the store."

"A man, huh?" Zane chuckled. "And what was odd about him? Did he have two heads?"

I stuck my tongue out at her before replying, "No, just one and the one he had was quite good-looking. But there was just something, oh, I don't know . . . off about him. He said he was a rare book dealer, but he didn't look like one."

"Yeah? And just how would you know what a rare book dealer would look like?"

"I met quite a few book dealers when I lived in New York, and trust me, this guy looked a lot more affluent than they did. He struck me as more the stockbroker type. His clothes reeked of money."

"Maybe he sells a lot of expensive books," Zane said with a shrug. "So what was he doing in your store?"

"He said he was searching for a particular book for a client, but he didn't know much about it. He didn't know the title, author, or publisher."

Zane's eyes popped. "He didn't know any of that and yet he called himself a rare book dealer? Seems to me any sort of book dealer should know that."

"My thoughts exactly. All he could say was that it was a book about the works of Edgar Allan Poe that have been made into movies, with an emphasis on the ones starring Vincent Price." I leaned back in the chair, fiddling with the edge of my napkin. "I did a quick online search, but I couldn't find any books that combined a detailed analysis of Poe's works and the films made from them—and none that cited Price's films specifically."

"So then the book that guy wants must be pretty rare." Zane leaned back in the chair and crossed her arms over her chest. "But if you don't know the particulars, how could you hunt something like that down? Leave it to luck or chance?"

"Apparently that's exactly what he's doing. He heard a rumor a book like that might be for sale around here and he came himself to scout it out," I said. "He gave me his card and asked me to advise him if I found out anything, but . . ."

"But you don't feel comfortable doing that?"

"I'm not sure. He struck me as a bit of a know-it-all. I'm not entirely sure I buy that story about a client, either. He could be looking for the book for himself, you know, buy cheap sell high, maybe on eBay."

"Maybe he's trying to beat out someone else after the same book," suggested Zane. "In any event, I'd be careful dealing with him if I were you. I mean, if you think there's something fishy about the guy, well, you've got pretty good instincts when it comes to this sort of thing."

"Gee thanks." I reached into my pocket and pulled out the card Thomas had given me. I looked at it, frowned, then turned it over. My frown deepened. "Well, I'll be!"

Zane leaned forward. "What's wrong?"

"See for yourself."

I held out the card so Zane could see. The front read:

Jeffrey Thomas
Rare Book Dealer

I flipped the card over, and Zane let out a gasp. The back of the card was blank. No address, no phone, no email.

"Holy Moses," cried Zane. "How are you supposed to get in touch with him—look him up in a crystal ball?"

"An excellent point," I said. "How on earth can he do business if no one can get hold of him?" I slapped my forehead with my palm. "I just knew that guy was no whiz at business."

The door to the bakery opened and three women came in, lugging shopping bags. Zane immediately jumped up. "Gotta go. Customers."

I gulped down the rest of my tea. "I should go too."

Zane hurried off and I slid the card back into my pocket, thinking that Zane was right about my instincts. There was something definitely off about Jeffrey Thomas, and I wondered idly if I would ever find out just what that was.

TWO

I returned to my store, took down the “Back in 20 minutes” sign, and settled in behind the counter. Mandy Thatcher, my clerk, came in to start her shift at one. She divided her time between working in my store and the Bite Me Diner, which is where I'd first met her. Around one fifteen the customers started to roll in. I'd just finished ringing up a sale of the latest Laura Childs cozy and two early Alex Crosses when I noticed a woman lingering at the counter's edge, a sour expression on her face. She held one of our small wire baskets in one hand and kept glancing at her watch as if she were in a great hurry. I bagged the books for my customer, and once she'd gone I stepped to the other end of the counter and addressed the woman with a smile. “May I help you?”

“You certainly may.” Irritation was evident in her tone. “My nephew wants some books about dinosaurs and mummies for his birthday, and for the life of me I can't seem to find any such books. I tried the big box bookstore up on the highway and the sales clerk there looked at me like I'd lost my mind.”

“Dinosaurs and mummies, huh? Is it a series?”

The woman shook her head. “I think so, but I'm not sure. You know kids. All he could tell me was that he read one in the school library and now he wants to read them all.” She let out a sigh. “Nine-year-olds, right?”

I frowned. I didn't have any kids, or any nieces or nephews for that matter, so my education on children's books was sorely lacking—unless, of course, it was a mystery series. I glanced over at the counter and motioned to Mandy to join us. I knew she had a five-year-old niece and a ten-year-old nephew. When she approached I said, “Mandy, have you ever heard of a children's series that has dinosaurs and mummies in it? This lady is looking for books like that for her nine-year-old nephew.”

Mandy thought for a moment and then said, “How about

the Magic Tree House series? My nephew is ten and he loves that series. If I'm not mistaken, the first book is called *Dinosaurs Before Dark*, and there are others that feature mummies and pirates too."

The woman's eyes lit up. "That sounds perfect," she cried. "Do you have that series in stock here?"

"As a matter of fact, I think we might have one box set left."

Mandy took the woman's arm and led her over to the children's section. I resumed my place behind the counter, and a few minutes later Mandy and the woman returned. I saw a box set bundle nestled inside the wire basket. The woman fairly beamed as she transferred it to the counter. "Your clerk is just fabulous," she gushed. "She's saved me a lot of trouble; I can tell you that. Such excellent service. I'm going to recommend your shop to all my friends!"

I started to ring up the sale, and when the woman began fishing inside her purse for her credit card, I gave Mandy a quick thumbs up. After the woman had gone with her purchase, Mandy came up to me with a wide grin on her face. "Good thing I have a nephew who prefers reading to video games," she said with a chuckle.

I grinned back. "It sure is. I have to say you handled her beautifully."

"Thanks. Working at the diner has certainly honed my people skills." She placed both her hands on the counter. "So has anything else exciting happened here this morning? Or was the dinosaur mummy conundrum it for the day so far?"

"Funny you should ask."

I related the story of Jeffrey Thomas and his search for the rare Poe book that he didn't know either the title or author of. Mandy listened, and when I finished she tapped her finger against her chin. "Hm—I wonder . . ." She straightened. "I'll be right back."

Mandy vanished into the back room, returning a few minutes later with a thick book tucked under her arm. She walked over to the counter and set it in front of me with a dramatic flourish. "I found this when I was cleaning up the back room the other day. It was in a box shoved under that old table."

I looked at the cover. "*Catalog of Rare Books.* This must have been Sheila's," I said. I ran my finger along the edge of the book. "Wow, this baby is thicker than King's *The Stand.*" I flipped to the first page. It was copyrighted four years ago, so fairly recent.

A woman approached the counter with a stack of books, and I motioned to Mandy. "You take care of her," I said. "I'll be OK here." Mandy hesitated, then left. Once she'd gone, I turned to the index and ran my finger down the list. Midway down I saw: *A Compendium of Poe—Complete Works, plus Stories Adapted for the Screen.* "Page three hundred and twenty."

I turned to that page and pored over the book. There was a thumbnail picture of a book cover, done entirely in black, with a rather grainy likeness of Poe on one side, a large raven on the other. Beneath the photo the caption read:

> *Edgar Allan Poe was one of the greatest suspense writers of all time. This book chronicles all of his works but pays special attention to the ones that Hollywood has made into movies over the years that feature the actor, art historian and gourmet cook Vincent Price. Have they done justice to "the man with the tomahawk" or merely exploited his darker side for money? You, dear reader, be the judge.*

Beneath that was another caption that read: *Author: Gil Sullivan. Publisher: Trilby Press.*

I'd never heard of them. I also noted the book was published over thirty years ago.

I turned to the computer, called up a search engine, and typed in the name of the book. Plenty of sites came up on Poe, but nothing for that particular book. Then I typed "Trilby Press" into the search engine. A website came up, but when I clicked on it, I was redirected to another site, Living the Dream Books. There were sixteen tabs at the top of the page. I clicked on the one marked "Our story" and waited for it to come up. I got an "Oops—that page can't be found" notice. I clicked on the other tabs, each with the same result.

"Looks as if this Living the Dream Books might be out of business," I murmured.

I went back into the storeroom and shot off a quick text to Max, asking if he knew anything about either Trilby Press or Living the Dream Books. Since I hadn't responded to his text from the other day, I had no idea if he'd even answer me or not. Max could be quite the drama queen when he wanted to be.

Phyllis Wooster came in around a quarter to four. She was the owner of Jumpin' Beans, the local coffee shop that was located a short walk from mine. She walked over to the counter and leaned an elbow on it. "Betty came by and said nice things about your planned window display," she said. "Too bad the Chamber doesn't do that Halloween window decorating contest anymore. You'd have had a good shot at first place."

"They had a window decorating contest? Why did they stop it?"

"Suffice it to say that the competition got a little . . . heated five years ago. Some windows were broken, props stolen, and the council voted to discontinue the contest to restore peace and harmony."

"Wow, well, maybe enough time has passed for the villagers to come to their senses," I said. "Maybe I should bring up reinstating the contest at the next town meeting."

"This town gets crazy enough over Halloween as it is. No need to fan the flames." Phyllis leaned in closer to me and said in a low tone, "Speaking of crazy, Betty also mentioned that an interesting guy was in here earlier."

"Jeffrey Thomas, the rare book dealer—or at least, he said he was a rare book dealer." I explained about the Poe slash Price book and showed Phyllis the card he'd given me. "So even though there's a good chance I may have found out the name of the book and the author, I have no way to contact him. The whole incident was just . . . odd."

Phyllis reached up to scratch her ear. "I'll say, although . . ." She was quiet for a few minutes and then said, "I've heard of that book. More to the point, I've seen it."

I goggled at her. "You're kidding? You have? Where?"

"In a private collection," she said. "I don't think that Maddie Elster wants to sell it, though."

I frowned. "Maddie Elster? Why does that name seem familiar—oh, wait." I snapped my fingers in the air. "Wasn't that the name of the female lead in *Vertigo*? Kim Novak's character?"

"Right. These Elsters are old money, from Philadelphia. I have to admit, in her younger days, Maddie did resemble Kim Novak. As for her family, well, they could have come out of a Hitchcock movie for sure."

"Meaning they're a bit eccentric?"

"That's putting it mildly." Phyllis raised her hand and started to tick off on her fingers. "There's her brother Edmund. He's a lazy sloth with a degree in archaeology and another in botany. Never married and lives with her in the mansion. Then there was the younger sister, Amanda. She was a pretty thing, smart as a whip. She died in an auto accident ten years ago last July. Her death near broke old man Elster's heart. Amanda was his favorite. If she'd lived, she'd have gotten everything instead of Maddie, I'm sure of it. Anyway, Amanda was married to a guy named Douglas Winchell. Elster never thought he was good enough for his daughter. They had two children, a daughter, Jewell, and a son, Efram. Jewell lives in the mansion with her aunt and uncle."

"And the son?" I asked as Phyllis paused. "He doesn't live there?"

"No. Efram was a sort of . . . problem child," Phyllis said carefully. "Anyway, the Elsters have about as much money as Zuckerberg or Musk, maybe more. Old man Elster had a large library of books, and most of 'em were rare first editions. Maddie inherited that from him, and she's an avid collector herself. I remember when I told her I had first editions of the first ten Nancy Drew books and one that was autographed by the author, she went nuts. Offered me three grand for 'em, but I told her heck no. They were my mother's. I couldn't part with them."

I huffed a curl out of my eyes. "Getting back to the Poe book—was that also part of her inheritance?"

"No, she lucked into that. Got it at an estate sale auction. It was in an old trunk that belonged to Gordon Knight."

I wrinkled my nose. "Gordon Knight? Who's he?"

"He was one of Austin's more prominent citizens. He was a scientist, worked at Axitrom Chemicals. Most people thought he was strange."

"Was he?"

"I suppose it would depend on your definition of strange. He was a bit of a recluse, but every so often he'd come into town and stop by the Frozen Spoon. He loved ice cream, and he'd spend a few minutes talking to Betty about her flavor of the day. Anyway, he retired and passed away six months later—from what I understand, he'd been sick for a while. The reason I know all this is because we were both at that estate sale. His only niece, who inherited his estate, decided to put some of his things up for auction. One of them was that trunk. It was a nice one too—black leather, brass-bound. I thought it would look nice in my home office. Maddie nosed me out on the bidding by two hundred dollars. Once she paid for it, she wanted to open it right away. It was full of all sorts of odds and ends—beakers, chem books, only things a scientist like Knight would appreciate. She picked up an old sweater and what should fall out but that book! I thought she was going to start doing jumping jacks when she saw it. Apparently she's a big fan of Poe and did her college thesis on him." Phyllis paused for a breath. "Do you know Peter Bridges?"

"The retired drama professor from Penn State? Sure. He's come in the shop a few times and purchased some books."

"He travels around now, giving lectures at various schools and clubs around the tri-state area on drama, cinema, the arts in general. He's been known to purchase bits of memorabilia to use in various talks." Phyllis waved a finger in the air. "One of his most popular lectures is on Edgar Allan Poe, and the role of his poetry and prose in film. He desperately wanted to buy that book from Maddie to use when he gave that particular lecture. He offered her a thousand dollars for it. She laughed in his face, said she wouldn't part with it for less than twenty-five . . . thousand."

"Twenty-five thousand! That's absurd," I cried.

"Of course it is," replied Phyllis. "Maddie threw out a ridiculous amount so Peter wouldn't keep bugging her about selling him the book. She'd never part with it, not for a million bucks. I mean, it was autographed by Vincent Price."

Now my jaw did drop. "Vincent Price? The actor?"

"No, the quarterback for the Philly Eagles," Phyllis said with a scornful look. "Of course the actor. Boris Karloff signed it too, on one of his photos in the book—you do know who Boris Karloff is, right, Charley?"

"Of course. He's the voice of the Grinch on my favorite Christmas special."

"Well, that too, but he's also—oh, you're kidding!" Phyllis tossed me a baleful look as I started to laugh. "Anyway, Maddie had a handwriting expert authenticate both signatures. They're the genuine article." Phyllis chuckled. "And on the off chance she has changed her mind and is trying to sell it, she may not ask for twenty-five thousand, but rest assured it's not going to go cheap."

I shook my head. "Well, that would be Jeffrey Thomas's headache. If he ever finds out about it, that is."

"Maybe he'll come back, and you can tell him to contact Maddie." The door to the shop opened and she gave me a poke in the ribs. "Maybe this is him now."

Alas, it wasn't. A group of women poured inside. They were chatting and laughing, and they all looked pretty much the same: around five foot four or five, late forties to early fifties, a mixture of thin and chubby builds, dressed in capris and t-shirts, in deference to our fall heatwave. Some carried light jackets over one arm, others voluminous totes. I looked outside and saw a tour bus parked at the curb.

Phyllis patted my arm. "Looks like you've hit the mother lode of customers," she said. "Almost makes me want to go back and open up my shop—almost." She wiggled her fingers. "I'm heading home to watch my soap. Tootles."

Phyllis exited with a smile as the women descended upon my shop. One wandered down Aisle Six and I heard a shout. "Come look at all this Edgar Allan Poe stuff! I just love reading his poems, especially this time of year." She cleared her throat. "Once upon a nighttime dreary . . ."

"No, no," another woman cut in. "Isn't it midnight dreary? Once upon a midnight dreary?"

"I'm sure it's nighttime," said the first woman.

"Forget all that," still another barked out. "Come look at this cozy display. Goodness, I didn't know there were so many with a Halloween theme."

While they bickered back and forth, Mandy sidled over to the counter. "Looks like we're going to have a productive afternoon," she said.

For the next hour we were delightfully busy. The visitors picked up everything, put items back in the wrong places, giggled and laughed as they showed their finds to each other. But, fortunately for us, most of them were buyers.

I'd just finished ringing up three cozies for the woman who'd gotten so enthusiastic about my Poe display when another approached the counter. I paused and took a moment to study her. She was short—not even five feet tall—and very thin, with a prominent chin and a beak-shaped nose. The dark pants and long-sleeved shirt she wore hung on her frame, as if they were a size too large, and she wore heavy-soled loafers on her feet that looked as if they might be orthopedic. Her dark hair was pulled back into an untidy bun, and she wore no makeup. She looked tired, as if all the life had been sucked right out of her. She had no purse; a white plastic bag dangled from one wrist. Her eyes darted all around the room, and she tapped a finger impatiently against the bag. As my customer turned away, hugging the bag containing her Harry Potter purchases to her chest, the newcomer stepped up and laid one hand on the counter.

"You have some very interesting things in here," she said. Her gaze flicked to the Poe display, then back to me. "Very interesting," she said again.

"Thank you," I said. "Is there something in particular you're looking for?"

Her eyes narrowed and her expression darkened for a fraction of a second, and then was gone. She shifted her bag from one hand to the other. "No. I'm just window shopping right now."

"Thank you. Feel free to browse, and if you need help, my name is Charley."

Her eyes darted around the shop again, and then circled back to me. "Do you have a restroom?" she asked.

"Yes. It's right through there in that alcove," I said, pointing.

"Thanks," she murmured and moved away, her plastic sack dangling from her wrist. I turned and saw a small line beginning to form in front of the register, so I hurried over and started ringing up purchases. I'd just finished with a customer when I saw the white-bag woman (as I'd nicknamed her) out of the corner of my eye. She was standing off to one side, staring out the picture window at the street beyond. She turned her head and saw me looking at her, then quickly turned and moved off toward the shelf of used books. I was tempted to walk over and ask her again if she needed help, but at that moment a woman in a sweatshirt and tight jeans hurried up to the counter, an armload of Oz books in her arms. She dumped them unceremoniously on the counter and declared, "My niece will be thrilled when she finds this under the Christmas tree. She's been wanting the whole set for a while now."

I started to ring up her purchase when the shop door opened and I saw a familiar figure enter—Jake Rodgers, Mandy's current beau. She'd met him at some club, and they'd only been going out a few weeks, but she was pretty starry-eyed over him. I could see why. He seemed likeable enough and took her out at least twice a week to fancy restaurants for dinner. He gave her presents, too. Last week it was a pearl necklace. The week before, it had been a silver and amethyst cuff bracelet. The pieces had looked expensive to me, certainly not costume. According to Mandy, he was some sort of freelance consultant, and the job obviously paid well!

Mandy emerged from the rear of the store carrying an armload of books, which she nearly dropped when she caught sight of her beau. "Jake! What are you doing here? I thought I wasn't going to see you tonight," she gushed.

"I thought I'd stop by and say hello. I missed you," he responded. He touched the tip of her nose with his fingertip then glanced up, saw me, and tipped his head. "Hello, Charley."

"Jake."

Mandy reached up and tugged his head down to hers. They huddled together a few moments, and then Mandy hurried over to help a customer while Jake made his way to the rear of the store. I saw him linger for a few moments at the Poe display.

I noticed the white-bag woman had returned and resumed her post near the picture window. I was tempted to go over to her, but two more women toting books arrived at the counter and put a halt to that idea. I spent the next few minutes ringing up their sales and had just finished bagging them when a loud whistle rent the air, and the room grew still. "All right, ladies." The tour group leader, a young shaggy-haired boy who looked like he should still be in high school, clapped his hands. "The bus will be leaving in twenty minutes. Please finish your purchases and make your way to the end of the street where the bus is located."

There was a flurry as everyone rushed to grab a final item, and I had a brief glimpse of the white-bag woman hurrying out the front door before the crowd descended on us. For the next twenty minutes, Mandy and I rang up and wrapped purchases. When the door finally closed behind the last tourist, we looked at each other and then started to laugh.

"What a day," cried Mandy. "I think we might have sold out of some books."

"Those Oz ones for sure," I said. "The cozies are half gone."

"Halloween books too," said Mandy. "And a lot of the Poe books. That exhibit garnered a lot of attention today."

"It did, didn't it." I glanced at the clock on the wall. It was just a few minutes after six. I turned back to Mandy. "I know we're supposed to close at seven tonight, but what do you say we close now? I think we made a pretty good haul with those tour bus ladies. Maybe you and Jake can catch a movie after dinner—where is he, anyway?"

"Oh, he left right before those women did. He said he

promised some friends he'd hang with them tonight, so I'm free to stay and help clean up."

I smiled at my assistant. "Well, if you're sure, that would be great."

Mandy headed into the Children's section, which had taken the brunt of the tour bus women. I headed for the mystery aisle. Feline Poe, who'd been taking refuge under the counter ever since the tour group had appeared, now emerged and sauntered along beside me. I noticed right off that several books had been put back in the wrong places on the shelf, and a few jammed in backward. I was just about to slip a book back in its proper place on the bottom shelf when I saw Poe stick his head in an open space on the shelf.

"You silly cat," I chided him. "What are you doing?"

Poe lifted his head and looked at me. "Meow," he said. He raised a paw and seemed to point toward the opening. I bent over and caught sight of something white sticking out. I reached down and my fingers touched something soft. I bent over for a closer look and saw a white plastic bag wedged in tightly behind a thick book.

"What on earth?" I looked sharply at the cat. "What did you find here, Poe?"

The cat looked at me, blinked, then turned and sauntered away, tail flicking to and fro as if to say, "My job is done. Figure it out, human."

I reached down to pull it out. The bag was surprisingly heavy, and it took two tugs for me to pry it loose. It was a white bag, just like the one that woman had carried on her wrist. I cleared a space on a nearby table and peered inside. There were a few odds and ends—some cards from various stores on the square, a few brochures, and . . . I stared at what was nestled at the bottom, hardly daring to believe what I'd seen. I shook my head to clear it, and then peered inside the bag again. Then I pulled the article out and laid it on the table on top of the bag.

I'd seen a picture of this cover only hours before, with Poe on one side, a large raven on the other. *A Compendium of Poe—Complete Works, plus Stories Adapted for the Screen.*

But it couldn't possibly be the same book Phyllis had told me about—could it?

I opened the book and flipped to the title page. There was an inscription there, and my eyes widened as I read it:

To Gordon,
With much appreciation for a flattering profile and your support of my career.
Vincent Price

Then a hand came down on my shoulder, and I screamed.

THREE

"Geez, Charley, chill! I didn't mean to scare you."

Mandy looked contrite as she said that. I waited for my heart to stop hammering in my chest before I answered her. "You shouldn't sneak up on someone like that," I said. "Cough, clear your throat . . . let someone know you're there."

"Sorry. These shoes squeak so much, I thought you heard me." Her gaze wandered down to the book I held in my hand. "Oh, wow, is that a book about Poe? What a cool cover." She reached for it. "Jake would love this. Maybe I should buy it for him for Christmas."

I held the book out of her reach. "I found it shoved in the back of the shelf. I'm not sure that it's one of ours."

Mandy's eyes narrowed. "What, you think someone might have put it there? Why would they do that?"

Why indeed, I thought. Maybe because it was stolen goods? Aloud I said, "I'd just feel more comfortable researching it, to see if it might have been part of an order. I'm sure you could find another book on Poe for Jake for Christmas."

Mandy wrinkled her nose. "Maybe, but I haven't seen one like this, that lists all of his works plus ones made into movies. It just seems like the perfect gift for him." She looked at me. "If it does turn out you ordered it, could I buy it?"

"We'll see," I said. I slid the book back into the plastic bag and tucked it under my arm. "Why don't you get going? There's not much left to do, and I can handle it myself. I'll see you tomorrow."

Mandy's eyes narrowed. "You know, if I didn't know any better, I'd say you were trying to get rid of me, Charley."

"I am. I'm trying to give you the rest of the night off. You worked hard today and don't forget, you're going to start on the window display tomorrow, so you should get plenty of rest."

"Plenty of rest? I'm twenty, not seventy. Besides, I know what's going on here." She screwed her lips into a pout. "You're still mad at me because I scared you. I said I was sorry."

I walked behind the register and put the bag and book on the shelf beneath. "I know you did. I'm not mad, Mandy."

She gave me a long look then turned on her heel and vanished into the back room, emerging a moment later with her jacket and purse. She gave me a brief salute and headed for the door. As she flung it open, she gasped as she nearly collided with Zane, who was standing on the other side, her hand on the knob.

"Whoa," Zane cried. She put out both hands to steady Mandy. "Where's the fire?"

"I didn't expect anyone to be standing there. Sorry." She tossed me a rueful glance over one shoulder. "Looks like it's my night to scare people," she muttered, then pushed past Zane and hurried out onto the street.

Zane stood in the doorway and jabbed her thumb at Mandy's retreating form. "What's got into her?"

"She thinks I'm mad at her," I said. "She came up behind me earlier and I wasn't expecting it."

Zane cocked a brow at me. "Are you mad at her?"

"No, of course not. She wanted to stay and help clean up, but I told her she should leave and rest up. She's going to start putting up the window display tomorrow."

Zane snorted. "Twenty-year-old girls don't need to rest up for something like that. I'm surprised she's not going out with her honey."

"My thoughts exactly."

I flipped the switch to shut off the lights in the back of the store. Zane frowned. "Isn't tonight your late night?"

"It is, but a tour bus came in and cleaned us out of a lot of stock," I said. I went over, flipped the sign from Open to Closed, then turned the lock. I crooked my finger at her. "Follow me," I said. "I want to show you something."

"Ooh—that sounds mysterious," she said. "Does it have anything to do with that mystery book dealer?"

"It might." I gave Zane's arm a tug. "Come on in."

Zane entered, and I reached underneath the register and handed her the plastic bag. She took it, peered inside, and almost dropped the bag. "Holy moly! Is that the same book that Jeffrey Thomas was interested in?"

"I think so. It fits his description of the book he's looking for, but . . . I think this particular volume may have been . . . stolen."

Zane let out a squeal. "Stolen! What makes you think that?"

I related what Phyllis Wooster had told me about Maddie Elster and her book. "This book fits the description of Ms. Elster's book. It appears to be in pristine condition, and it's got Vincent Price's signature. Phyllis thought it might have Karloff's too. I was about to check when Mandy came up behind me."

"So Mandy saw the book?"

"Yes, and she wanted to buy it for Jake for Christmas. I had to talk her out of it."

Zane waved her hand in a circle. "So, we're alone here, what are you waiting for? I'm dying to know if Karloff signed it too."

I opened the book and showed her Price's signature on the title page, then flipped quickly through the book. It wasn't very thick, under ninety pages, but most of them were photos and illustrations. In the center there was a large section containing black and white and color stills from the Poe movies. I recognized several I'd seen—Price in *The Pit and the Pendulum* in a scene with actress Barbara Steele, and in one of my favorites, *The Tomb of Ligeia*. Zane's hand suddenly shot out. "Look at that photo, bottom right corner," she said. "Doesn't it look like something's written there?"

The photo in question was a still from a 1960s film, *The Raven*, which starred Price, Karloff, and Peter Lorre. I'd seen that movie years ago on Thriller Theatre. It had been a black comedy, loosely based on Poe's poem, about a magician who gets turned into a raven and seeks out a sorcerer's help. I peered at the photo. Sure enough, something was written there in a silver marker. "It looks like 'Regards, Boris Karloff,'" I said.

"Wow. If that's his real signature, then I bet an avid collector of this type of memorabilia would pay a fortune for this book," cried Zane.

"Maybe so," I said. I flipped through a few more pages, then paused. "That's odd," I said.

Zane cocked her head. "What's odd?"

"It looks like there's a page missing." I held the book out so Zane could see. "Right here in this section about Ligeia. There are a few loose threads as if a page has been carefully pulled out."

"That sucks," said Zane. "It would probably diminish the value of the book too. I wonder what was on it?"

"It might have been a blank page, or maybe it had a photo on it. From what I can see, its removal doesn't appear to have interfered with the book copy."

"That's a good thing, right?" Zane ran a hand through her hair. "So what now?"

"Well, I'm definitely not going to leave this book in the store," I said. "I haven't gotten around to getting that alarm system fixed, and if this is Maddie Elster's book, I don't want it just lying around here. I'd take it to my safe deposit box in the bank, but I have the small size one and this book is way too big to fit in there."

Zane put a finger to her lips. "Well . . . I suppose we could put it in the safe at my house."

I looked at her. "You have a safe in your house?"

"My aunt had it put in. She kept important papers and her jewelry in there," said Zane. "It's in the den, behind that picture of the lake with the ducks."

I flashed a grateful smile. "That sounds like a plan."

"Don't mention it. You can buy me dinner at O'Doul's as a reward."

"Done. An O'Doul's burger sounds more appetizing than a frozen TV dinner or ordering pizza. I'm afraid the delivery guy at Antonio's is going to start calling me by my first name soon."

"Naw, I've got dibs on that honor. So, what do you plan to do with the book?" Zane asked. "If it's stolen, shouldn't you notify the police?"

"If I knew for sure it was stolen, of course. But I have no proof that this is Maddie Elster's book."

Zane goggled at me. "How many of those books do you think there are that have both Price and Karloff's signatures in it? It's got to be hers."

"Maybe," I said. I tapped my chin. "I saw that woman look out the window a few times, like she was looking for someone."

"Who, a buyer for the stolen book? She was supposed to meet them at your store and do one of those—what do you call them in your books, Charley? A covert exchange?"

"If she did have something like that planned, and the person didn't show, why hide the book here? Why not just take it with her? It doesn't make sense."

"I don't like it," Zane said. "I still think you should notify the police. If nothing else, it's a good excuse for you to see Detective Hottie again."

I felt my heart flutter. Detective Ian Grant and I had butted heads the last time we'd come in contact, which was when he'd suspected Zane of murdering her business partner, and he'd made it clear he hadn't appreciated my well-intentioned "interference" in his case. In the end, we'd reached an understanding—sort of. As it turned out, we both shared a love of cooking. The last time I'd seen him had been at the grand opening of Mainely Mysteries. He'd hinted at a get-together, but since then I hadn't heard a peep from him, although I suspected between overseeing police duties in Austin, his own in Philly, and his lecturing at the university, he'd probably been too busy to give me a second thought.

"Ian—Detective Grant—wouldn't handle something like this," I said. "He's homicide, remember? I'd most likely have to deal with Barbie."

Barbie was Barbara Jeanne Donaldson. She'd been my nemesis in high school, and when I'd returned to Austin, I'd been surprised to find out that the former cheerleader had become a police officer—and a pretty good one at that. Currently she was the acting lead homicide detective here while the town council and the mayor debated over whether or not to replace the former homicide detective who'd retired. I personally thought they were stalling, hoping that Ian Grant might show some interest in taking the job, but I doubted he'd give up his position in Philly for a much smaller venue. I had an idea, though, that Barbie wouldn't be one bit disappointed if they gave Ian that job, since she seemed to have a big crush on him.

Zane made a face. "We sure don't want Barbie poking her big fat nose in," she said. "She'll probably think we're making too much out of it—or else find a way to make it seem like we're involved with the theft."

"True. Besides, I want to talk to this woman first. She seemed more frightened than anything. If I approach it the right way, maybe I can get the truth out of her."

"Or maybe she'll pull a gun on you and demand the book back," said Zane.

I eyed my friend. "Are you sure you're not a closet thriller writer yourself?" I teased.

"Aw, heck no," Zane replied. "Anyway, how are you gonna talk to her? You have no idea who she is or where you can find her."

"That's true, I don't." I sighed. "Let's put the book in your safe and then go over to O'Doul's. I'm starving. Maybe a good dinner will spark some ideas."

"Sounds like a plan."

I shut the book and started to slide it into the bag. As I did so, a square of paper fluttered out of the bag onto the floor. I snatched it up. It was a scrap of stationery, pale blue in color. It was stamped at the top of the page, *Austin Inn.*

Zane chuckled. "Let me guess. You want to make a stop at the inn after dinner."

"You're partially right," I admitted. "I was thinking *before* dinner."

My friend groaned and rubbed her stomach. "I was afraid you'd say that. OK, then. Let's get moving."

I gathered up the book and Poe and we all went back to Zane's house, where I refilled Poe's water bowl and scooped out a generous helping of tuna for his dinner. While he slurped away in the kitchen, Zane put the bag containing the book into the safe, and then we left for the Austin Inn. As we pulled out of the driveway, Zane remarked, "Barbie or not, I still think we should call the police."

"I will, once I speak to this woman. After all, if it is Maddie Elster's book, it could be worth a considerable amount of money. I can't chance Barbie getting donut crumbs and stains all over it."

"She wouldn't—oh, you're kidding," Zane said as my lips curved upward. "Very funny."

The Austin Inn was only fifteen minutes away. They rented rooms by the week, and I'd considered staying there until Zane had offered me an empty room in the house her aunt had left her. The inn was in a prime location not far from the business district. I located a spot under a shady elm not far from the front entrance, and then we hurried into the lobby. We sidled over to the reception desk, where a bored-looking clerk was just handing a key over to a family that consisted of Dad, Mom, and a whining toddler.

"Your room is on the third floor, fourth door on the left. Enjoy your stay."

The man accepted the room key and then he and the rest of the fam proceeded over to the bank of elevators at the far left. I stepped up to the desk and flashed the clerk what I hoped was a sunny smile. Zane, right beside me, did the same.

"Good evening," I said. "We're not checking in, but we're looking for someone who might be a guest here."

The clerk, an overweight man with a shiny bald pate and a handlebar moustache, looked at us curiously. "Might be a guest?"

"Yes. She's short, about an inch or two less than five feet, slight of build. She has dark hair worn in an untidy bun, and she had on dark clothes, slacks and a long-sleeved shirt. I run the bookstore here in town and she was in there earlier. I think she may have left something in my store, and I'd like to talk to her about it."

He hesitated and then said, "A woman fitting that description checked in here early this morning and then went out. I'm not sure if she's back or not." He held out his hand. "If you have something to return to her, you can leave it with me. I'll make sure she gets it."

"I'm not one hundred percent sure she left this item," I said. "That's why I would like to talk to her."

He pulled a pad and pen out from underneath the counter. "OK. Then leave me your name and a number where you can be reached, and I'll see she gets it."

I bit down hard on my bottom lip. "Wouldn't it be easier to just phone her room? If she's there, you can announce us, and if not . . . well, then I'll just leave a message."

He looked from me to Zane and then back to me. "OK," he said finally. He picked up the phone and punched in some digits. After a few seconds he replaced the receiver and shook his head. "No answer. The machine isn't even going on." He pushed the pad and a pen in front of me. "Write down your info, and I'll make sure she gets it."

I took the pad and pen and wrote down my name and the store's number along with a short sentence: *I believe I have a book that may or may not be yours. Please call me.* I ripped the page from the pad and handed it over to the clerk. He took it, glanced at it, and then lay it down beside the computer. "I'll see she gets it," he said.

He turned away with an air of finality. We moved away from the counter and Zane dug her fingers into my arm. "Ten bucks says that woman never sees your note," she hissed. "That guy was super cautious."

"He probably got in trouble once by giving out information on a guest," I remarked. "It happens."

Zane started to turn back toward the main door, but I grabbed her elbow and steered her over to the bank of elevators. "While he isn't looking, we can just go up to her room and see whether or not she is there," I whispered.

Zane looked at me. "Go to her room? But we don't know where it is?"

"I do," I said smugly. "Third floor. Room three-seven-eight."

My friend narrowed her gaze at me. "Now how on earth do you know that?"

"I haven't spent the last fifteen years writing suspense stories for nothing. I watched the clerk push the buttons on the phone when he dialed the room."

The elevator doors opened, and we stepped inside. I punched the button for the third floor and a few seconds later we arrived at our destination. The doors slid open, and I hurried out first to look at the sign showing where the rooms were located. Room 378 was located all the way down at the end of the corridor, next to the door marked "stairs." As we approached the door, I frowned.

"This door's not closed all the way," I said.

Zane plucked at my sleeve. "Come away, Charley. I don't have a good feeling about this. Let's call the police and be done with it."

I set my jaw and rapped my knuckles on the door. "Miss? It's Charley from the mystery bookstore in town. I found the bag you left in the store. If you've a few moments, I'd like to speak with you."

We waited a few moments, and nothing. No sound whatsoever. I pushed on the door, and it swung wide.

Zane grabbed my arm. "Oh, no, we can't just walk in there. That's illegal. It's breaking and entering."

"Not when the door's open."

I pushed the door open all the way with the toe of my sneaker and stepped boldly inside, leaving Zane little choice but to follow. The room was dark, so it took my eyes a few seconds to adjust. Once they did, I could see the room was typical of a budget hotel: a double bed, a worn and scratched dresser, a nightstand with a lamp and phone. A large-screen TV sat on top of the dresser. A cheap flowered print hung above the bed. Thick green floral curtains covered the windows. The curtains were closed, and the table lamp was off. The drawers on the dresser and the nightstand were all open, their contents tossed on the floor. A suitcase lay open on the floor between the bed and the bathroom, its contents strewn about. "Looks as if someone was looking for something," I murmured.

"Or she's just a slob," remarked Zane. She grabbed my arm and pointed. The bathroom door was partially closed, but we could see a sliver of light emanating from beneath the door. "She's probably in the bathroom. For God's sakes, let's get out of here."

I shrugged Zane's arm off and started toward the door. My gut was telling me that something was off, and I wasn't leaving without finding out just what that was. As I approached the bed, I looked down and froze.

"Zane," I called over my shoulder. "I've found her."

Zane was at my side in an instant. Behind me, I heard her sharp intake of breath.

The woman lying on the floor was definitely the woman who'd been in the shop earlier. Her arms were thrown wide, and her lips formed a perfect O. Her eyes were wide and staring, but I knew that she couldn't see us.

I also knew that she wouldn't be able to answer any of the multitude of questions I had, because she was stone-cold dead.

FOUR

Zane let out a little squeal, I clapped my hand over her mouth, and together we backed out of the room and back into the hallway. Zane immediately sagged against the wall, gasping for breath.

"Easy does it," I said. I rubbed my hand in a circle across her back. "Take deep breaths," I advised. "In and out."

Zane inhaled and then exhaled deeply. "I'm OK now," she assured me. The look she shot me was skeptical. "But how on earth can you be so calm? In case you haven't noticed, that's a dead body in there."

I didn't feel calm. My heart was pounding so hard inside my chest I thought it would surely explode. I could feel drops of sweat starting to form at the back of my neck. I took a deep breath myself and exhaled slowly. "You find one dead body for real, you kind of get used to it—sort of."

Zane let out another breath, and then turned to me. "OK. So what do we do now? We can't just walk away from this."

"You're right, we can't. Call 911. I'm going back inside."

"WHAT!" Zane grabbed my arm and dug her fingers in. "Are you crazy?"

"No. I just . . . I need to take a look around before the authorities get here. They won't tell us anything, especially if it's Barbie who shows up."

Zane made an exasperated sound, and then whipped out her cell phone. I pushed the door back open with the toe of my shoe and slid noiselessly back into the room. I whipped out my own phone, switched to camera mode, and started snapping photographs. I took a full view of the room, then a few of the dead woman. I zoomed in for a few close-ups. Her lips and tongue had a blue tinge to them, and there were a few red marks across her neck.

I turned my attention to the suitcase lying open on the floor and the contents beside it. I felt in my pocket, pulled out a tissue, and wrapped it around my fingers. It wasn't ideal, but it would suffice to prevent my leaving fingerprints. I bent over to examine the strewn contents. A pair of faded green trousers, a plaid shirt, some underwear, a toothbrush and toothpaste, a comb. That appeared to be the sum total—or was it? I turned my attention to the suitcase. There was still a pile of underwear inside, and something seemed to bulge beneath the floral cotton panties. I carefully pushed them aside and beheld a medium-sized teakwood box. I lifted it up for a closer look. It reminded me of another box I'd encountered not that long ago. I poked and prodded at the box, and sure enough, a portion of the top slid open. I peered inside and gasped aloud at the contents.

Diamonds and rubies winked at me from a pair of gold dangle earrings that, if they weren't real, were a darn good imitation. There was a necklace made out of gold interlocking rings, and a bracelet comprised of diamonds and rubies. One piece in particular, a brooch in the shape of a jungle cat with a sapphire eye, winked up at me. There had to be at least a dozen varied pieces there, and even to my untrained eye, I knew these gems had to be worth a small fortune. Whoever had tossed the room had missed this—possibly something had interrupted their search? I swiftly took pictures of all of the contents, replaced the lid on the box, then shoved it back underneath the panties. Outside I could hear the murmur of Zane's voice, so I knew she was still on the phone; however, I was betting it wasn't going to be long before the police made an appearance.

I saw a tote bag lying on the floor, half under the bed. I picked it up, set it on the dresser, and spilled the contents out. The bag contained typical items: tissues, a key ring, a small notepad—blank—and some pens. There was also a lip balm, a small compact, and a wallet. I grabbed the latter and opened it eagerly. The first thing I saw was a Pennsylvania Driver's License in the name of Janice Rutger. It gave an address in Comstock, a small town some twenty miles south. I thumbed through the wallet. Its contents consisted of one credit card, a few bills amounting to less than seventy dollars, and a handful of coins, mostly pennies.

I picked up the tote bag and shook it, and a letter-sized envelope fluttered out. It was unsealed, so I lifted the flap and pulled out the contents. There was another driver's license there, this one in the name of Jane Radcliffe. There were also photocopies of three articles. Two were about Vincent Price: one on the cookbooks he'd written, and one on acting in general. The third article was an interview with Boris Karloff. The dates on the pages indicated the articles had been published in the late sixties/early seventies, ostensibly taken from an old movie magazine. Each article had a photograph of the actor accompanying it. They appeared to be the standard eight by ten glossy that was sent out by the studios to fans who wrote letters to the stars. The photographs had the actor's signature scrawled across the bottom of the photo. I spread the articles out on the dresser top and snapped pictures of them.

I'd just replaced everything back in the tote bag when I heard a timid knock at the door. It opened a crack, just enough for Zane to stick her head in. "Hurry up," she hissed. "The dispatcher said a car was in the area. The police will be here any minute."

"I'm done."

I tossed the bag back where I'd found it, stuffed the Kleenex back in my pocket, and joined Zane in the hall just as the elevator doors slid open. Two EMTs rushed out and came right over to us. The taller one asked without any preamble, "Where's the victim?"

I inclined my head toward the door. "In there. On the floor between the bed and the bathroom."

The EMTs hurried inside and then the second elevator opened. This time a man and a woman emerged. I recognized Barbie instantly and felt a pang of disappointment as I realized the man accompanying her definitely wasn't Ian Grant. He was fairly young, with thick blond hair and a smattering of freckles across his nose. They walked right over to us, and I saw Barbie's eyes narrow when she caught sight of us. She planted herself in front of me and fisted a hand on one hip. "Well, well, Charley James. Fancy meeting you here."

I smiled sweetly at her. "Nice to see you again, Bar—Detective Donaldson," I amended quickly as Barbie's eyes narrowed.

Barbie turned to the man. "Go inside, Randy, and get a look at the body," she directed. "Tell the EMTs not to move it until I have a look."

Randy nodded. "Yes, Detective," he mumbled and hurried inside like his pants were on fire.

Zane glanced over at Barbie. "You've got him trained well," she said.

Barbie shot Zane a withering glance. "That's Randy Zucker. He just graduated the academy. Ia—Detective Grant assigned him here, figured it would be a good place for him to ease in slowly. Who knew he'd catch a corpse the first day on the job." She whipped a pad and pen out of her pocket and brandished them in front of us. "So, who called this in? As if I couldn't guess."

"I did," Zane began, but I stepped in front of her and looked Barbie right in the eyes. "Zane called it in, but I'm the one who found the body," I said.

"Of course you are," Barbie muttered. She scribbled in her notepad. "So tell me, Charley. How did you happen to come across this one? Were you acquainted with the deceased?"

I shook my head. "Not exactly. She was in my store earlier today and . . . left something. I wanted to return it to her."

"I see. And what did she leave?"

"A plastic bag."

Barbie's head jerked up. "A plastic bag?"

"Yes."

She stared at me as if I'd just been caught escaping from a mental ward. "A plastic bag," she repeated. "That's it? Nothing else?"

"There were a few odds and ends," I said. "I wanted to make sure that she did indeed leave the bag, so I came here to talk to her about it."

"O-K." Barbie scribbled on her pad again. "You wanted

to return her property. How did you know where to find her?"

"There was a piece of inn stationery in the bag, so I just deduced she was staying here."

Barbie's eyes narrowed to mere slits. "You deduced it, huh?" She shook her head. "Just because you own a mystery bookstore doesn't mean you're a detective." She paused as a shout sounded from inside the room. "You two wait right here," she said and then turned on her heel and disappeared inside the room. She gave the door a backwards kick as she went in, but it didn't close all the way.

"Tsk, tsk," I said. "Barbie's losing her touch."

"Yeah, and she's as pleasant as ever too," muttered Zane. "Are you going to tell her about the book?"

"Definitely not," I said emphatically. "I'd rather share that information with Detective Grant." I walked over and gave the door a push. I saw the EMTs over in the corner by the bed, shaking their heads. Randy held the tote bag in one hand and was talking to Barbie while making gestures with his other hand. Barbie stood listening, then fished her phone out of her pocket, punched in a number, and turned away, phone to her ear. Was she calling Grant? I wondered.

Barbie finished her call and started to turn toward the door. I immediately jerked my head back and scurried back to stand next to Zane, and not a second too soon. Just as Barbie emerged from the room, the elevator pinged, and the doors slid back to reveal another man. I bit back a gasp as I recognized the tousled dark hair, the cleft chin, the nose with the slight bump that kept him from being movie-star handsome. Ian Grant's gaze fell upon me and Zane, and his eyes widened. He walked right over to us and paused, hand on hip. "Well, Charlotte. We meet again," he said softly.

I swallowed. "Detective Grant," I said primly. "We really have to stop running into each other like this."

His gaze pierced through me. "I take it you found the body?" Without giving me a chance to answer, he went on, "You do seem to have a knack for finding corpses, don't you?"

Barbie cleared her throat loudly, then turned to Ian. Her

voice dripped honey as she said, "When you said you'd be right here, you really meant it," she said.

Ian shrugged. "I just happened to be in the area. What have you got?"

"Victim's driver license indicates her name is Janice Rutger of Comstock, Pennsylvania. The COD is undetermined so far."

Ian swung his gaze back to me. "You first, Charlotte. I'm interested to know how the two of you happened to be here."

Before I could answer, Randy poked his head outside the door. "The EMTs are nearly done." His gaze fell on Ian, and he actually smiled. "Good evening, Detective Grant," he said.

Ian inclined his head. "Randy. Some first night for you, huh?" Without waiting for an answer, he said, "Get some crime scene tape and cordon this area off. But before you do that—" His gaze swept over Zane and me. "Find these two ladies a comfortable place to sit until I can question them."

"Great," Zane mumbled to me. "There goes dinner."

I saw Ian's lips twitch slightly. "Sorry for the inconvenience," he said, but from the look on his face, I doubted he was sorry at all. "I'll try to keep it brief." He turned back to Barbie and said, "Detective, let's go inside. I want a look at the body before the EMTs remove her."

"Of course, Detective Grant." Barbie couldn't resist tossing me a smug smile before she followed Ian inside. This time when she kicked the door shut, we heard an audible click.

Randy gestured to us. "Ladies, if you'd follow me."

"I wonder if she calls him Ian when they're alone," hissed Zane. "Could she be any more obvious with those moonstruck stares she gives him? Sheesh. And anyone with eyes in their head can tell he's not interested in her—not that way."

"How can you be so sure?"

Zane shot me an impish grin. "Because I see the way he looks at you, dummy. And the way you look at him."

"Oh yeah? And just how do I look at him?"

Zane grinned. "Like he's the cherry on top of a hot fudge sundae. And he looks at you the same way."

"Ahem—ladies, if you'll follow me?" Randy gave his foot an impatient tap.

"Natives sure are restless," muttered Zane. She shot me another look and then we fell into step behind Randy. He led us to a door at the opposite end of the hall. He pushed the door open and ushered us into a room with a small table, three chairs, and two large vending machines inside. "Break room," he said. "Believe it or not, I used to work summers here when I was in college. Have a seat, and Detective Grant will be with you shortly." He turned and pulled the door shut, leaving us alone.

We sat in silence for a few minutes, then Zane leaned across the table and plopped her chin in her hands. "Swell. Who knows how long we'll be stuck here with your boyfriend."

I slumped in the chair. "He's not my boyfriend."

"Yeah, well, with a little effort on your part, he could be," Zane asserted. Her stomach let out a low growl. "Today was super busy, what with that tour bus and all. I haven't eaten since I grabbed a yogurt at lunch. My stomach thinks my throat's been cut."

"Come to think of it, I just had some crackers for lunch. I could do with some food myself," I admitted. I got up and walked over to the vending machines. One had a selection of soft drinks, the other different snacks. I looked over my shoulder at Zane. "Want a candy bar?"

Zane shook her head. "Too much chocolate bothers my stomach. I'll hold out for dinner, thanks."

"Suit yourself—but don't think you're going to poach any of my Snickers."

I fished in my purse for a dollar bill, shoved it in the machine, and pressed the button for a Snickers bar. The candy bar wavered in the air and then . . . nothing. It hung there, suspended. I groaned and gave the machine a sharp kick with the toe of my shoe. Still nothing.

"Hey," I cried. "This machine stole my money."

"Charley, calm down," Zane said.

"I can't calm down," I replied. "I paid my money, and I want my candy, darn it."

I raised both my hands and started pounding on the glass. The Snickers bar wiggled a little, looked as if it were about to drop, then stopped.

"Hey! Give me my candy!" I yelled. I raised both hands and balled them into fists. I'd just started to pound on the glass when I was suddenly jerked back, and I found myself staring into a very familiar pair of storm-gray eyes.

"Hunger pangs getting the better of you, Charlotte?" Ian Grant asked softly.

I'd never cared for my given name—Charlotte—and I always hated it when anyone said it. Somehow, though, when Ian said it, it sounded different—almost seductive. I stared into those mesmerizing eyes for a full minute before I took a step back and pointed at the machine. "That—that machine stole my money. It didn't give me my Snickers."

He regarded me thoughtfully, then shook his head. "It didn't? Well, now, we can't have that, can we?"

Ian went over, jiggled the handle of the coin return, and then pressed the button for the Snickers bar. This time the candy bar fell neatly out of its slot. He bent, retrieved the bar, and handed it to me. "Sometimes a little patience goes a long way," he said. "Shall we get down to it? I promise this won't take very long. I know that you and your friend are . . . hungry."

I jammed the candy bar into my pocket and returned to the table. I eased myself into the chair beside Zane. "What do you want to know?"

"Detective Donaldson said you came here to return something to the deceased?"

"Sort of," I said.

Ian frowned. "Sort of? What does that mean?"

"It means that that woman was in my shop earlier today, at the same time as a tour bus group. After they'd all left, I found a bag that resembled one I'd seen her carrying jammed into one of the low shelves in the store. I—ah—came here to find out if it was indeed hers."

Ian drummed his fingers on the table. "OK. Where is the bag? I assume you brought it so she could identify it."

I shook my head. "I—ah—no, I didn't bring it with me."

"You . . . didn't . . . bring it?" Ian leaned back in the chair, closed his eyes, and reached up to massage his temple. After a few moments he lowered his hand, opened his eyes, and said,

"You said you wanted to find out if the bag was hers. How could you do that without showing it to her?"

Before I could answer, the door to the break room flew open and Randy thrust his head inside. "Detective Grant, Detective Donaldson needs to see you—right now. It's important." He was struggling to keep from hopping up and down, and I figured they must have found the jewels. Between the two of them, my money was on Randy.

Ian frowned. "Can't it wait? We should be done here shortly—I hope."

Randy shook his head. "Detective Donaldson said no, this can't wait. It's very important," he added, stressing the word "very." He glanced over at us, then back to Ian. "She also said it might take a while, so . . ." He glanced over at us again and wiggled his eyebrows.

Zane moaned audibly and put a hand over her stomach, which took that particular moment to let out a loud growl. Ian hesitated, then put both hands on the table and rose from his seat. He pinned Zane with a piercing stare. "I can take a hint," he said. "Far be it from me to have you two ladies starve on my watch. You're free to go . . . for now." As we both scraped our chairs back, he held up his hand. "There are a few conditions," he said.

"Don't worry, we're not leaving town," Zane said.

Ian's gaze lingered on me for a moment and then he said, "I'd appreciate it if the two of you could stay available tonight. I'd like to get your official statements."

"Fine. We'll be at O'Doul's chowing down," said Zane. She didn't even try to keep the snarkiness out of her tone. "Anything else?"

"Yes. Please do not repeat anything we discussed here with anyone else."

"Well, duh, that goes without saying," Zane said. "Who would we tell anyway?"

With that she turned and stalked out of the room. I paused for a moment and looked at Grant. "She's right. We certainly aren't going to gossip about this. We're just going to have a nice quiet dinner at O'Doul's and then go home. If you need to speak to us tonight, Detective, that's where you can find us. I know that you know where we live."

"That I do, Charlotte," Ian said softly. "That I do."

I nodded curtly and left the room, aware of his gaze boring into my back the whole time.

FIVE

O'Doul's was located in a single-story redbrick building. It boasted pine-plank floors that got covered most nights in peanut shells from the complimentary bowls of nuts that graced the bar and all of the tables. The tables themselves were carved out of dark pine, to match the walls that were covered with beautiful framed photographs of various scenic spots in Ireland. Behind the bar were plaques with different Irish sayings: *A Cold Pint and Another One*, *If you're lucky enough to be Irish . . . you're lucky enough!* and *Sláinte!* which, when translated, was the Irish equivalent of "Cheers." As far as actual food, their menu was pretty varied. The house specialty was shepherd's pie (of course—it was an Irish tavern, after all), but they also did a mean jalapeño popper and kick-butt chili. Zane and I settled ourselves in a booth near the bar and ordered mugs of Guinness stout. When the apple-cheeked waitress returned with our drinks, we gave our orders: a cheese-steak sub with extra onion and peppers for Zane, corned beef and sauerkraut sliders for me, with extra mustard.

Zane raised her mug once the waitress had departed. "So, here's to what? Getting away from the crime scene unscathed?"

I smiled. "I'll drink to that."

We clinked glasses and took a deep sip of our drinks. Zane looked at me over the rim of her mug. "So, are you going to tell Detective Hottie your suspicions about that book?"

I ran my finger around the rim of my glass. "I was going to, but now that I've had time to think about it . . . I'm not sure."

Zane frowned. "What do you mean, you're not sure? Why not?"

I leaned across the table and lowered my voice. "What if that book isn't stolen property? What if it doesn't belong to Maddie Elster?"

Zane stared at me for a moment, then shook her head. "What are you talking about, Charley? That has to be her book. There surely couldn't be two of them with Price and Karloff's signatures floating around, could there?"

"No, of course not. But how do we know the Price and Karloff signatures in this particular book are genuine?"

"Oh." Zane's lips formed a perfect O. "I think I see where you're going with this. You think that this Janice Rutger somehow got her hands on a copy of that book and forged Price and Karloff's signatures, right?"

"It does seem a possibility, particularly when you consider she had copies of articles about those two actors that showed their signatures on photographs. Then there's the second driver's license. I found another one under the name of Jane Radcliffe."

Zane whistled. "Wow, so she had two identities?"

"It appears so." I leaned in closer. "Either she knew Maddie Elster, or she knew someone else who did. They could have been the ones who planted the rumor Thomas heard about the book being available for sale, hoping to attract a buyer."

Zane's brow puckered. "But why make a duplicate book?"

"If someone took it outright, Maddie would know instantly it was missing. Substituting a duplicate would buy them time to sell the original and make a clean getaway." I paused. "And if this book isn't Maddie's, then perhaps the substitution wasn't made yet, and she got cold feet—decided not to go through with it. It's possible that whoever she was in league with could have been blackmailing her."

"Gee, I never thought of that," cried Zane. "Over something in that Janice Rutger's past, right? That's brilliant." She lowered her voice and added, "It's the kind of thing a seasoned thief would think of . . . or a top thriller writer."

I wiggled my fingers in the air, brushing Zane's compliment away. "I think for whatever reason, she decided to back out of the deal. I think she must have arranged to meet her partner in my store, maybe turn the book over to him or her, and that's why she kept looking out the window and seemed so nervous. Either she bolted or the other person didn't show, and that's when she decided to hide the book in my store. She probably thought it'd be safe there, and she could return at a later time and retrieve it."

Zane chuckled. "She didn't count on you having a curious cat."

"Her partner probably came to her room," I went on. "They must have argued, one thing led to another, the argument escalated and . . . they killed her. Then they searched her room for the book, which of course they didn't find." I paused. "They missed the jewels too."

Zane sat up straight. "Jewels? What jewels?"

"I didn't get a chance to tell you." I related what I'd found in the box. "I'm betting that Randy and Barbie found the box and one of them—I'm thinking Randy—figured out how to open it. That was why he came to get Detective Grant."

"Wow," said Zane. "So she was a jewel thief too? Maybe that book wasn't the only thing she was getting cold feet about. Do you think they belong to Maddie Elster too?"

"I think it's a very good possibility." I drummed my fingers on the scarred tabletop. "I can't exactly ask either Detective Grant or Barbie about the jewels, and now that Janice Rutger is dead, I can't question her—not that she'd have answered any of my questions, but I might have been able to get a sense of whether or not she was telling the truth." I took a sip of my beer and set the mug down. "This has all the components of being an inside job."

"An inside—you think a member of Maddie Elster's family was in on this?"

"Judging from the description Phyllis gave me of them, it's possible," I admitted. "Of course it's also possible the partner could be someone who works or has worked there—a staff member, a maid, a cook. For all we know, maybe she and her partner were both employees."

The waitress came and deposited our dinners in front of us. Once she'd left, Zane picked up her cheesesteak, took a large bite, chewed, and swallowed before saying, "So spill. I can see the wheels turning in your brain, Charley. You might be on a sabbatical from writing, but I'm betting you've got an idea on how to find out about that book."

I set down my half-eaten slider and dabbed at my lip with a napkin. "The most direct way would be to pay her a visit, but I can't just walk up to her door and say, 'Hello, Ms. Elster, you don't know me, but I may have something that belongs to you. Oh, and by the way, are you missing any jewelry? Have you fired any staff members lately, or more specifically one named Janice Rutger?'"

Zane barked out a laugh and then started to talk very fast, her words almost running into each other. "Heck, you sure can't do that. That would be crazy. Maybe you could pretend to be collecting donations for some charity? Or how about selling something? Then again, maybe not. Do people still go door to door selling stuff, other than Girl Scout cookies? And if so, what would a wealthy woman be interested in? Magazine subscriptions? Do they even still do that?" She paused, breathless, and looked at me wide-eyed.

"I have no idea. Most people subscribe and read magazines online nowadays. The charity angle might work, but I'd have to find out what charities she's interested in—if any." I started to take a bite out of my slider, then stopped. It dropped to my plate as I snapped my fingers. "Wait, let's go back to the selling angle. Phyllis mentioned that Maddie collected first editions."

Zane frowned. "How is that helpful? You don't carry first editions in your shop."

"I don't, but I know someone who has a small collection Maddie might be interested in."

I whipped out my phone, but before I could make a call, a shadow fell across our table. We both looked up to see a tall blonde woman hovering there. She leaned over and said, "Hello. You're Charley James, aren't you? The bookstore owner?"

I nodded. "I am." I gestured toward Zane. "This is my friend Zane."

The woman turned toward Zane with a wide smile. "Right. Zaney's Sweet Treats. I bought a croissant in there the other day. It was delicious."

"Thanks," Zane said. "And you are . . .?"

"Oh, forgive me." Her hand fluttered near her throat. "I'm Riley May Connor from the *Austin Bugle*." When neither of us reacted, she added, "I replaced Derek Proust."

"Ah yes, Derek," I said. Derek Proust had been a reporter on the *Austin Bugle* and a real pain in the butt, although in his quest for a big scoop, he had helped to save my life, and for that I'd always be grateful. As a result of his doggedness, he'd landed a cushy job on a Philadelphia newspaper. "So what can I do for you, Ms. Connor?"

She shot me another smile. This one reminded me of a crocodile getting ready to strike. "May I join you? I promise this won't take long."

Without waiting for either of us to answer, she plopped down on the edge of the bench beside Zane, leaving my friend no choice but to move over. "Thanks," she said. "I'll get right to the point. I heard you two were over at the Austin Inn earlier."

I picked up another slider. "What if we were?"

"I was just curious if you knew anything about the body that was discovered there."

Zane and I exchanged a glance. I figured she was thinking the same thing I was—had Ian been thinking of Riley when he'd cautioned us against speaking to anyone? "Sorry," I said, looking her straight in the eye. "I'm not at liberty to discuss it. Police orders."

Zane bobbed her head up and down. "Me too."

That disclaimer wasn't enough to stop Riley May Connor. She leaned forward and said, "Oh, I'm not looking for much, just a hint. Surely you can tell me something that's off the record."

I took a bite out of the slider, set it down, then dabbed at my lips with my napkin. "Such as?"

"Well, for starters, how did you happen to be there? Did you know the deceased?"

"Not at all," I said. "She was a customer. She'd been in my bookshop earlier."

"I see. Is that a habit of yours? To track down people who have been in your shop for no reason?"

"I had a reason," I said. "She'd left something in the store, and I wanted to ask her about it. That's all."

"So you tracked her down because she left something in your store? It must have been a pretty big something."

"Big or small, someone left it in my store, and I wanted to return it. I wanted to speak with her to make sure what was left there was indeed hers."

"I see." Riley fished in her pocket and pulled out a small pad and a pen. "You said she was a customer. Would you happen to know her name?"

"I'm sorry, I've said far too much already," I said. "Now if you don't mind, I'd like to finish my dinner in peace."

"OK, OK, I can take a hint." Riley pointed the tip of her pen at me. "Derek was right. You are a cagey one. He said I should keep an eye on you. That if anything exciting happened in this town, you'd probably be in the middle of it."

"He said that, did he?" I mumbled. "I'm sorry you think that trying to return someone's property qualifies as something exciting."

"Not in itself, but couple that with the police advising you against discussing it, and two and two add up to four." She paused and reached into her jacket pocket. She whipped out her cell phone, looked at the screen, then rose, shoving the phone back into her pocket. "Ladies, I've got to go. I'm sure we'll see each other again . . . soon."

After Riley marched away, Zane picked up her mug and raised it. "Well, if you ask me, Riley May Connor reeks of trouble. I didn't think anyone could be more annoying than Derek Proust, but it appears I was wrong."

I'd been typing on my phone and now looked up. "Yeah, it wouldn't surprise me if she starts her own investigation into that woman's death. Wait until she crosses paths with Barbie."

"Now that I'd like to see." Zane chuckled.

"Me too." My phone pinged. I picked it up, looked at the screen, and smiled. Zane looked at me as she picked up her sandwich. "You look pleased. Was that Grant, texting you to stay put and he's coming right over to finish his interrogation?"

"No, actually it was Phyllis," I said. "I asked her if I could drop by later—pick her brain about Maddie Elster."

Zane's eyes twinkled as she lifted the remaining portion of cheesesteak to her lips. "Tell the truth, Charley. You're disappointed. You'd love Grant to corral you, wouldn't you?"

I dropped my gaze to my half-eaten slider. "No comment."

SIX

We finished our dinners and then Zane opted to return home. She had to get up earlier than usual tomorrow because she had a big order to fill for the public-school assembly. I dropped her off and then continued onto Phyllis's house, which was located at the other end of town. I found it without any trouble. It was a small bungalow tucked in a shady corner on a quiet street lined with huge elm trees and flowering shrubs. I parked in front, got out, and locked the car, then walked up the neatly trimmed walkway to an enclosed porch. I went up to the front door, rang the bell, and waited. A few minutes later Phyllis appeared, and for a moment I didn't recognize her. I was used to seeing her at the coffee shop—perfectly groomed, not a hair out of place. Now her hair was tousled and the ends stuck out at a raking angle. Instead of the crisp white shirt and skirt I was used to seeing her wear, now her attire consisted of frayed jeans with a hole in one knee, and a black and white striped sweatshirt that looked as if it had seen better days. The pang of guilt I felt at disturbing her vanished as she smiled widely at me. "Well, well, Charley. Welcome to my humble abode."

"Thanks for seeing me, Phyllis," I said as I stepped inside. "I know it's late, and I really hate to disturb you at home."

"It's not all that late," Phyllis responded. "To be honest, I got a little worried. Your text sounded a bit . . . desperate."

"Did it? I didn't mean for it to sound that way," I said quickly. "It's just as I said. It's a dilemma I feel only you can help me with."

"Only me, eh? Well, you've got my attention." She rubbed her hands together. "Let's get comfy and you can tell me all about this dilemma." She closed one eye in a wink. "I even made refreshments."

She wiggled her fingers, motioning for me to follow her. A

few moments later she led me into a large room that boasted a white damask upholstered sofa and matching loveseat, positioned in front of a fireplace. She walked over to a small table and flicked on a lamp with a fringed shade. I noticed a copy of the latest Miranda James cozy lying there, a bookmark tucked into its pages midway through. She wiggled her fingers again and I settled down on the sofa and scooted to the edge of the seat. There was a mission-style cocktail table positioned between the sofa and loveseat, on which rested a tray with two tall glasses and an iced pitcher that I figured had either iced tea or lemonade in it. Phyllis leaned over and picked up the pitcher. "How about some iced tea?"

I wasn't all that thirsty after two mugs of beer, but I wasn't about to be rude, either. "Sure. I like iced tea."

Phyllis poured the tea into the glasses, handed one to me, and then took the other for herself. She settled herself on the loveseat across from me and took a long sip of her drink before setting it down on a coaster on the coffee table. She leaned back and folded her hands in her lap. "OK, Charley. It's your dime. Talk."

I took a sip of the iced tea, which was delicious. I leaned forward, set my glass down beside Phyllis's, then took a deep breath. "I need a reason to visit Madeleine Elster, and I think you're the only one who can help me with that."

Phyllis raised an eyebrow. "And just why do you need to visit Maddie Elster?"

I looked her right in the eye. "I can't go into detail, Phyllis, but trust me, it's very important."

"It is, huh?" Now the eyebrow reached Spockian proportions. "Would this sudden urge to visit Maddie have anything to do with the body that was found at the Austin Inn earlier tonight?"

My jaw dropped—literally. "How on earth did you know about the body?"

"Charley, Charley, Charley. Surely you've lived here long enough to know that nothing stays a secret in this town for long, and there's nothing in Austin that I don't know about." Phyllis settled back in the loveseat with a cat-ate-the-canary smile. "A good friend of mine heard it over her police scanner, and she called me."

I shook my head to clear out the cobwebs. "Well, since you're obviously so well informed, I'll tell you the whole story—but please, please, promise me that you won't say a word till I'm done, and you won't repeat any of it to a soul. Detective Grant would have my head. He specifically ordered me and Zane not to talk about it."

Phyllis made a crossing motion over her heart. "OK, I promise not to breathe a word of this to another living soul. Spill."

I exhaled a deep breath. "You remember the man I told you about earlier, the one who was in my store today?"

"The book dealer slash Vincent Price expert? Yeah, I remember—oh gee!" She gasped. "Don't tell me—is he the one who's dead?"

I waved my hands back and forth. "No, not him. And remember—not a word till I'm done."

Phyllis leaned back against the loveseat cushions again and I proceeded to recount the day's adventure, from my conversation with Jeffrey Thomas about the Poe book, to the strange woman and the bag containing said book that Poe had found jammed in the shelf, to Zane and me coming across her body and my search of her room. "The book was inscribed by Price," I finished. "And Zane and I did find a photo of Karloff in the book that also appears to be autographed, but . . . I have no way of knowing if those are really Price and Karloff's signatures, or a clever forgery." I whipped out my phone and called up the photos of the articles I'd taken, then passed the phone to Phyllis. "Why else would she be carrying those around?"

Phyllis had sat silently through my dissertation, but I could tell from her body language she'd been itching to speak. Now she passed my phone back and held up a finger. "Permission to speak?" she asked. At my nod she leaned forward. "That is one fantastic story. To be honest, I'm having trouble wrapping my head around the fact Gordon Knight was a fanboy when it came to Vincent Price."

I arched a brow. "That's what you take away from all this?

That it's hard to believe a scientist could have idolized an actor?"

"Among other things." Phyllis cleared her throat. "So you think that this woman—Janice what's her name—somehow got her hands on a copy of that Poe book, then forged Price and Karloff's signatures so she could substitute it for Maddie's and sell it?"

"In a nutshell, yes. She might also have helped herself to some of Maddie's jewelry as well. I'm not a jewelry expert by any means, but those gems sure looked real to me."

Phyllis reached up to scratch her head, making the tufts of hair stick out. "Do you think that Poe book is that valuable?"

"Well, it was signed by two popular actors. And according to Jeffrey Thomas, diehard fans will spend big bucks for something that they really want. And it's possible that what might seem like small change to us maybe seemed like a fortune to Janice Rutger and her partner."

"I guess," Phyllis said again. She reached for her tea and took a long sip before she said, "What did Detective Grant have to say about all this?"

"Nothing. I haven't told him about the book yet."

"You haven't—good Lord, girl, what are you waiting for?"

"I do intend to tell him, but first I wanted to find out if the book in my possession is Maddie's or a fake. How often do you think she actually looks at it? And by look at it, I mean really look at it. Go through the book, look at all the pages—particularly the ones with signatures."

"A very good question," Phyllis replied. "I doubt Maddie's looked at that book—really looked at it—since she put it on display. If she did, and a substitution was made, I'm sure she'd be able to tell. She's rather anal about things like that."

"That's exactly what I'm counting on," I said. "I need to get inside that house and get her talking about that book so that she'll take it out of the case and show it to me. That's the only way I'll know if it's the same book."

Phyllis ran her finger down the side of her glass. "I'm a little puzzled, though. You said you needed a reason to visit her, and I was the only one who could help. I honestly don't know how I could. It's not like we're best buds. We haven't seen each other in years."

"That is true, but . . . you do have something she wants."

Phyllis goggled at me. "I do? What?"

"Well . . . you told me earlier today how interested Maddie was in your Nancy Drew collection."

"Yeah, that she was, probably still is—oh no!" Phyllis's eyes widened. "Get that idea out of your head right now," she shrilled. "I am not going to sell her any of my Nancy Drews so you can get inside that mansion!"

"Relax, Phyllis. I don't want you to sell her any of your Nancy Drews," I said in as calm a tone as I could muster. "I just need her to think you're willing to part with one or two of them. I thought I might go there and act as a sort of . . . intermediary between you—a middleman. After all, I am in the business of selling books. I thought I could tell her that you decided to part with a few, and you hired me to do the transaction."

Phyllis closed her eyes for a few moments, then they flew open, and she trained her gaze on me. "As nutty as that sounds, it might work," she said slowly. "Maddie sure was hot to trot about my collection. I imagine you'd get a lot farther faster, though, if she thought I were going to put the whole shebang up for sale—all ten first editions, instead of one or two."

I fought the urge to do a fist pump in the air. "If you're willing to do that, Phyllis, that would be great," I said. I reached into my bag and pulled out my cell phone. "I can take photos of the books right now if that's OK with you."

Phyllis fluttered her hands to and fro. "Now just hold on a second, girl," she said. "If I'm going along with this nutty scheme of yours, I have a few conditions."

I let out a groan. "Conditions seem to be the thing tonight. OK, what are they?"

"For one thing, when you go to see Maddie and deliver this proposition, I go along." I opened my mouth to protest, but she held up her hand. "Maddie's no dummy. She knows darn well I'd rather die than give up that collection. If I'm considering parting with it, then the reason has to be something really big—something I'd only share in person."

"Like what?" I put a hand to my mouth. "You mean like . . . you're dying?"

"Of course not. Well, at least not me," Phyllis said. "Maddie knows I'm very close to my cousin Fred and his wife Jessie in Omaha. I could say that either he or Jessie needs a major operation and there's only one specialist who can do it, and he's in New York. It's gonna cost mucho dinero, which they don't have. I'm thinking of selling my collection to help them out and I wanted to know if she was still interested."

I frowned. "That all sounds a bit dramatic, don't you think? Like something you'd see on a soap opera."

"Exactly like that—and they call them daytime dramas now. Maddie will fall for that hook, line, and sinker," Phyllis said confidently. "She's got a real sense of the dramatic, plus she's a sucker when it comes to family. I mean, look at all the losers she's got living with her."

"Speaking of her family—do you think any of them might be behind this? Janice Rutger could have been partnered with one of them, or maybe a staff member?"

"I've heard she treats her staff extremely well, so I doubt that. The family, though—now there are possibilities there." She tapped her finger against her chin. "I'll call her tomorrow, try and set up something. What time is good for you?"

"You get the appointment, I'll make sure I'm available, even if I have to close the shop for a few hours," I said. "Now, since you're going to make the sales pitch in person, I can't very well say I'm your intermediary. I'll need an excuse for tagging along."

"Well, I could say you're an expert on books—that I had you appraise the collection, and I brought you along to verify their worth so she'd know I wasn't trying to pull a fast one with pricing." She closed one eye in a broad wink.

"Just don't make the asking price too outlandish and scare her off," I cautioned.

"Oh, don't worry. I know how to handle Maddie. I'm

curious, though. Just how do you plan to get her to show you that book?"

"I have no idea," I admitted, "but I'll think of something." I took a final sip of my tea, set the glass down, and rose. "I can't thank you enough, Phyllis. I really owe you."

Phyllis chuckled as she walked me to the door. "Don't worry, sweetie. I'll find a way to collect. I'll call you tomorrow after I talk to Maddie."

I left and returned to my car. I turned the ignition on and then pulled out my phone to check my messages. One from Zane: All is well here. Poe sleeping. And three from Ian Grant, the first one being: Charlotte: Went by O'Doul's. Just missed you. Please call me so we can finish our conversation. Second text: Charlotte, where are you? Didn't I tell you to stay available? Answer me please. And the last one: WE NEED TO TALK.

"Sorry, Detective Grant," I said as I pulled away from the curb. "I'm shutting my phone off for the night. I'll catch you tomorrow—after Phyllis and I talk to Maddie Elster."

I pulled into Zane's driveway and went into the house. Only the lamps Zane kept on at night were on, so I figured my pal had gone to bed. I wondered if she'd gotten any frantic texts from Grant and figured she hadn't. I was probably the lucky one. As I walked in the door, Poe came out of the kitchen and rubbed his head against my ankles. I bent down to give him a scratch behind his ear.

"Miss me?" I asked him. "Zane said you were snoozing. I imagine you're hungry again?"

Poe gave a meow of assent, and I turned in the direction of the kitchen. As I did so, Poe suddenly stopped. His head angled toward the front door, and his tail bristled and stuck straight up. His lips peeled back, and he let out a low hiss.

I paused. "What's wrong, Poe?" I cast a glance toward the front door, and my heart leapt into my throat as I saw a shadow outlined there. I looked around for something I might use as a weapon when a familiar voice called out.

"Open up, Charlotte," Ian Grant called back. "I know you're in there. We have to have a talk . . . now."

SEVEN

"Curses," I hissed in my best Snidely Whiplash imitation. "Foiled again." I shot Poe a meaningful look, then went over to the door and opened it. Ian Grant stood there, hands on hips, the expression on his face as dark as a thundercloud.

"Don't you look at your phone?" he barked. "I sent you several texts."

"I don't like to be a slave to the phone," I said loftily. "I shut it off when Zane and I were having dinner, and I forgot to turn it back on." I widened my eyes at him. "You texted me?"

He shot me a look, then, without waiting for an invitation, pushed past me and into the hallway. "I distinctly remember telling you and your friend to keep yourselves available," he said.

I smiled sweetly at him. "That you did," I said. "But you never did mention a definite time."

Ian raised his hand and ran it through his thick head of hair. He looked as if he were having a hard time keeping from screaming his frustration out loud. "Well, I'm here now," he finally ground out. "There are a few things that need clarification."

"Of course." I inclined my head toward the doorway. "Did you want me to get Zane up? She has an early day tomorrow, so she's most likely asleep, but you did tell her to stay available so . . ."

"Not necessary," he said. "You're the main one I need to speak with. I can catch up with Zane tomorrow."

"How good of you," I murmured. I made a sweeping gesture with my hand. "I was just about to make a pot of coffee. Would you like a cup?"

His eyes narrowed. "This isn't a social call, Charlotte, but since you offered—yes, I would like a cup."

I groaned inwardly. I hadn't been about to make coffee; I'd just been stalling for time. I was betting he knew that, too. I turned on my heel and headed to the kitchen, both Ian and Poe behind me. Ian took a seat on one of the stools at the island while Poe went over to his water bowl at the opposite end of the room and hunkered down. A moment later the sound of contented slurping reached our ears.

I opened one of the cabinets and pulled out a jar. "Instant all right?" I asked.

"Fine."

I filled the kettle with water and set it on the stove to boil while I spooned instant coffee into two mugs. Mine had the Mainely Murder logo on it—the state of Maine—and my name. The other had been a promotional mug from the local hardware store. "Low Price But Not Quality" was emblazoned on one side, "Jenks Hardware" on the other. I glanced over my shoulder and saw that Poe had abandoned his water bowl and was sprawled at Ian's feet. Ian had leaned over and was petting him.

"Traitor," I mumbled as the kettle whistled.

Ian glanced up. "Did you say something, Charlotte?"

"Nothing important," I replied. I filled the mugs with water, then stuck a spoon in each and transferred them to the island along with a small pitcher of milk and some sugar packets. Poe cast a hopeful look at me and then back at his food bowl, but I ignored him and hopped up on the stool beside Ian. I raised my mug as a disappointed Poe slunk away. "Cheers."

Ian added milk and two sugars to his coffee, stirred, took a sip, and set the mug back down. "Strong," he commented.

"I figured I'd need it strong," I said. I took a small sip because I really didn't want the coffee anyway and pushed the mug off to one side. "OK, so . . . you need my statement?"

He pulled a small notebook and a pen out of his jacket pocket and set them down next to his mug. "Take me through exactly what happened at the Austin Inn earlier tonight," he said. "From the moment you got there to the moment you entered the room and found the body."

I took a deep breath and said, "I was closing the bookshop

early tonight. While doing that, Poe"—I looked down at the cat still sprawled at Ian's feet—"found a plastic bag jammed into one of the bottom shelves. I thought I recognized it as belonging to that woman. A slip of notepaper fell out of the bag, and I recognized it as stationery from the Austin Inn, so I thought I'd try and find the woman and make sure that this bag was indeed her property."

I paused for a breath, and Ian's hand stilled over his notebook. "Why did you feel the need to verify that? You said you recognized it as belonging to her?"

"I *thought* I recognized it," I amended. "I could have been wrong. Zane stopped by after doing her daily cleanup, so we thought we'd go over to the inn together, then catch a late supper afterwards. We got to the inn, and the clerk wasn't exactly cooperative. He said that a woman fitting the description I gave him was registered there, but he wasn't too eager to do much more. Fortunately, I was able to ascertain the room number, so Zane and I decided to pay a call on the woman. We got to the room, and the door was unlocked, so we went inside and found her dead."

"I see."

There were a few awkward moments of silence, then Ian's hand dipped into his pocket, and this time he pulled out a small envelope with the inn logo on it. "There isn't anything else you want to tell me? About a message you left, perhaps?"

I swallowed. "Oh yeah. That clerk insisted I write a note for her, so I did. I figured she'd never see it. That's why Zane and I decided to pay her a call."

"Is that right?" Ian waved the envelope under my nose. "He gave us this. He had it in her cubbyhole reserved for messages." He opened the flap, tipped the envelope over, and my note fell out onto the counter. He flicked the paper over toward me. "What book are you talking about in this note, Charlotte? You told me the bag contained some odds and ends. I don't consider a book an odd or an end."

"No?" I shrugged. "It's not a big deal, but yes, there was a book inside the bag."

"I see. So was that the real reason you went to see this

woman? You thought she might have been trying to shoplift a book from your store?"

I set my lips. "I can tell you with certainty, Detective, that the book inside that bag was most definitely not from my store. I just wanted to ask her where she'd gotten it."

"Why did you want to do that?"

"Because . . . earlier in the day a man was in the store, a rare book dealer. He told me that he came to Austin hoping to acquire a rare book about Edgar Allan Poe. He saw my display and thought that perhaps I might have the book." I paused and then continued, "I had a good reason to think, though, that this book I found hidden in my shop might have been the same one this man was after. I just wanted to ask her about it, that's all."

"I see," Ian murmured. "And if it were the same book?"

I shrugged. "I was going to tell her about the man who inquired after it. His name is Jeffrey Thomas. He gave me his card, but alas it has no contact information."

Grant looked skeptical. "A business card with no number, no address? It doesn't sound like this guy is a very good businessman."

"I agree." I pulled the square out of my pocket and handed it to Grant. "So? Are you satisfied?"

He looked at me as he handed back the card. "All I wanted was to clear that point up," he said. "I didn't want to think you might be keeping secrets from me—not in a murder investigation. We've gone through this before, remember?"

I did remember—all too well. I could feel my cheeks searing with heat. I slid off the stool. "So I guess we're done here?"

Ian didn't answer, but he closed his notebook and slid it and his pen back into his pocket. He glanced around the kitchen. "I remember the last time I was here," he said. "You were making something that smelled delicious."

"One-pot parmesan garlic pasta," I replied. "As I recall, you were acquainted with the dish. You also took the time to toot your own horn. I believe your exact words were, 'I'm a pretty good cook myself,' right?"

"Yes, and I still am a pretty good cook," he said. After a

moment he added, “I’m still interested in a recipe exchange. I have a recipe for chicken scampi pasta that will knock your socks off.”

“Yum. I love chicken scampi. Shrimp scampi too. Do you like Thai food? Because I have a recipe for a sweet potato curry that is delicious.” I eyed him. “You really want to do this?”

“I really do. Unfortunately, it doesn’t look like I’ll be able to do it anytime soon.” Ian looked around the kitchen again then back at me. “You mentioned Thai food before. There’s a good restaurant that opened up over in Emporium—oh, sorry,” he said as his phone pinged. He fished it out of his pocket, looked at the screen, frowned, then slid it back into his pocket as he hopped off the stool. “I’ve got to go. Thanks for your statement, Charlotte. We’ll be in touch.”

He turned on his heel and was gone before I could say anything else. I stared after him for a moment, and then shook my head. “Well, that was abrupt. I wonder what that text said.” Poe glanced up and let out a soft meow. “Yes, your buddy had to leave,” I said. “But before he did, I wonder—was he about to ask me to go to that Thai restaurant with him?” I eyed the cat. “And if he asks me, should I say yes?”

Poe sat up and waved a paw in the air.

And at that precise moment, my own cell phone pinged. Thank God it hadn’t done that when Ian was here, after I’d made a point of saying I’d turned it off. I looked at the screen and saw it was Phyllis. I hit the answer icon and said, “Don’t tell me you got in touch with Maddie Elster tonight?”

“No, no, not yet.” Phyllis’s voice sounded strained. “I just thought you’d like to know this. My friend just called me with the latest item from her police scanner.

“Charley, your store—it’s been broken into!”

EIGHT

For a moment I just stood there, gaping at my phone. Then I found my voice. "My store? Are you sure?"

"Your store address is 311 Main, right? Of course I'm sure." Phyllis sounded hurt that I would have doubted her—or her friend's police scanner.

"Oh my gosh, Phyllis. I've got to go. I'll catch you later."

Phyllis was still talking, but I didn't hear a word she said as I disconnected and grabbed my jacket from the back of the chair. I hesitated briefly, wondering if I should wake up Zane or not, but in the end decided against it. It was bad enough that one of us was upset, and Phyllis hadn't mentioned the bakery being broken into as well. Poe let out a sharp meow as I raced past him.

"Sorry, boy," I said. I made a dive for the cabinet, grabbed a can of salmon, and spooned it into his bowl. Poe hunkered down eagerly. "You've got plenty of food and water, Poe. I'll see you later," I said and then I was out the door.

Less than ten minutes later I pulled up across the street from the store. There were two police cruisers parked outside, lights flashing. A dark, unmarked car was parked right behind them. I parked, hopped out of the car, and fairly flew across the street. The first thing I noticed was that the picture window was still intact—they hadn't broken that, at least. Before I could get to the door, though, Barbie appeared out of nowhere and grabbed my arm.

"Charley! What are you doing here?" she said.

"A little birdie told me someone broke into my store," I snapped. "I want to see it—now!"

Without waiting for Barbie to answer, I jerked my arm free and ran up to the door, which stood slightly ajar. I took one look inside and sagged against the doorframe. "Oh no," I moaned.

The store was the picture of chaos. A few glass cases had been smashed, and the contents were strewn across the floor. Shelves had been stripped bare, the books lying in a jumbled mass. I moved inside and went immediately to the register. So as not to smear any potential prints from the culprit, I pulled a tissue from my pocket, wound it around my fingers, and opened the register. All the money from the previous day looked to be intact.

"So robbery wasn't a motive," I murmured as I closed the drawer. "At least, not cash."

"If not cash, what?"

I whirled around to face Barbie, and the smug expression on her face made all my frustration and anger at the situation rise up and bubble out. "Just what are you doing here anyway?" I bit out, ignoring her question. "Aren't you supposed to be working homicide now? This is a bit out of your bailiwick, unless there happens to be a dead body here in my store."

"Relax, Charley, geez. There are no dead bodies on the premises," Barbie said in a much calmer tone than I would have. "We're just a bit shorthanded right now, so Detective Grant told me to come here with Randy so he could get some more experience."

"Detective Grant told you to come here." I frowned, remembering the text Ian had gotten right before he'd hightailed it out of Zane's house—had it been about the break-in? And why hadn't he come himself? Unless, perhaps, he was out following another lead, maybe on Janice Rutger's murder?

Barbie's voice broke into my thoughts. "You were lucky—at least they didn't break the store window. They just picked the door lock." She inclined her head toward a pile of books. "I don't suppose you'd be up to taking a walk through the store, see if anything's missing?"

"I greatly doubt that," I mumbled under my breath.

Unfortunately Barbie was standing close enough to hear me. Her gaze narrowed. "What makes you say that? Look at this place! Someone was after something, all right."

"Well, it wasn't cash," I said. I jerked the drawer open and pointed to the stack of bills. "I forgot to clean the register out before I left, and as you can plainly see, it's still here."

Barbie leaned over my shoulder to peer at the money. "How much cash are we talking about?"

I shrugged. "Not a lot. Fifty, sixty dollars at most."

"OK. Is there anything else here that someone might consider valuable enough to steal?"

My gaze flicked back to the ruined shop, then back to Barbie. I shrugged. "I can honestly say there's nothing in my store right now that's valuable enough to warrant this."

A young officer hurried up to Barbie. "No sign of forced entry anywhere," he said. "Whoever did this knew how to pick a lock like a pro."

Barbie swung her gaze to me. "I take it you have no burglar alarm?"

"It's been on the fritz. I've been meaning to get it fixed."

Barbie's phone buzzed, and she turned away to answer it. I moved off and walked deeper into the store. Every book section was a complete mess. Not one had been left unscathed. Nearly every book had been pulled off the shelves, and even the bin that held magazines had been upended, its contents all over the floor. The worst was the Poe display. Every single book had been riffled through, and two looked to have had their spines broken. I gritted my teeth as I realized the broken books had been brand-new copies of Poe's poetry. What a waste.

"Charlotte?"

I whirled, nearly avoiding bumping into Ian Grant. His hand shot out and gripped my arm to steady me. "Sorry. You OK?"

"Of course I'm not OK," I said hotly. "My store has been desecrated, and just look at this mess! It will take me a few days to set things right."

"I'm sorry," he said again. He actually sounded like he meant it.

I set the book I'd picked up back on the table and took a

few deep breaths to calm myself. "So was my break-in your emergency text?"

He eyed me. "No, it was something connected to one of my Philly cases. But I heard about the break-in on the scanner, and I sent Donaldson over here with Randy."

"How nice of you. Sorry, I forgot how in demand your services are." I noticed two men walking around the store. They appeared to be dusting with small brushes. Ian saw me looking and said, "They're from the crime scene unit. They're dusting for prints."

I let out a snort. "That's going to be a waste of time. There will be fingerprints all over the place. My customers don't wear gloves." I held up a hand. "But you don't have to tell me, I know. It's SOP—standard operating procedure."

He shot me a quizzical look. "You do seem to know quite a bit about police procedures, don't you? More than the average citizen."

I ducked my head. "Well, I do run a mystery bookstore, and I've been an avid reader for years. One does tend to pick up a few things."

One eyebrow rose, but he made no comment, just turned and walked back to where Barbie and Randy stood talking. After a moment I walked over too. Barbie saw me coming, nudged Randy, and leaned over and whispered something to Ian. The three of them all turned to look at me as I approached.

Ian moved forward. "We should be finished here shortly, Charlotte. You can go back home." His gaze strayed over to the doorway, where an officer was stringing up the yellow crime scene tape. "We'll need to keep that up for a day or two while we make sure we haven't overlooked anything, and then you can re-open the store."

"I'll need to do a major cleanup before that," I said, my tone sharp. "Do you think I should worry about a return visit?"

Ian met my gaze. "I imagine that would depend on if whoever broke in here found whatever they were looking for." His gaze bored into mine, and I knew he was thinking about the book.

Barbie let out a snort. "What could they possibly be looking for here? I bet it was a bunch of drunken teenagers, practicing for Mischief Night."

"If that's so, wouldn't they have taken the money?" asked Randy. "I know guys in my class in high school that wouldn't have passed any amount up, however big or small. They would have broken that plate glass window too. I also took a look around at the other stores. None of them seem to have been touched, not even the bakery next door. It seems to me as if whoever did this singled out the bookstore."

Ian clapped Randy on the shoulder. "Very observant, Randy."

Barbie's face flushed. She let out a sigh and lowered her gaze. "I guess you're right. Detective Grant, I still do have a lot to learn," she said, her tone contrite.

I turned my head away, and I couldn't help it—I rolled my eyes. Randy saw me, and I noticed the ghost of a smile flitter across his face. I fought the urge to grin back at him and instead switched my gaze over to Barbie. "I'm so glad, Detective, to have given you this learning opportunity," I said crisply. "Now, I suppose I may as well go back home. You'll let me know when I can come back into the store?"

I'd addressed the question to Barbie, but it was Ian who answered. "The crime scene techs will most likely finish up tomorrow," he said. "Detective Donaldson will confirm that and advise you when you can re-open."

I inclined my head toward the door that connected my shop with Zane's. "How about the bakery? If Zane's store wasn't touched, I assume she can open as usual tomorrow?"

"She can open," said Ian. "I'll need to come by at some point and speak with her. I still need her statement from your earlier encounter."

I smiled sweetly at him. "She'll be thrilled to see you—especially when she sees the yellow tape across my doorway. It'll bring back fond memories, I'm sure."

I started to move away, but Ian caught my arm. "We need to talk some more, Charlotte," he said in a low tone.

"About what? I thought we said all that needs to be said."

"About that book in your possession—the one you wanted to ask Janice Rutger about. Do you think that was what the thief was after?"

"I honestly have no way of knowing, Detective. I also have no idea if it's the same book Jeffrey Thomas was after or not."

He pursed his lips. "Any chance this Jeffrey Thomas could be responsible for this?"

I thought for a moment, then shrugged. "Anything's possible."

Ian put his hands on his hips and gave me a long, searching look. "Just what did you do with that book, anyway?" he asked at last.

I shifted my weight from one foot to the other, dropping my eyes to avoid his gaze. "It's in a safe place."

"Yeah? Well, maybe you should turn it over to me tonight. Just in case."

"It's in a safe place," I said defensively.

"How safe is safe?"

"A wall safe," I said. "Zane has one in her house."

Both his eyebrows rose. "In the house? Now I really must insist you turn that book over to me. What if this thief knows where you live?"

"I doubt that," I said. "Anyway, I don't know the combination, and like I said, Zane's got a real early day tomorrow. I really hate to wake her up."

"I'm sure she'd rather be woken up than have her house ransacked."

"Really, Detective, the chance of that happening is pretty slim. But if you're so concerned for our safety, you could have a squad car drive past our house every hour just to make sure."

He hesitated, then let out a giant sigh. "Fine, you win. I'll have a squad car cruise by Zane's house every hour on the hour, just to be sure there isn't another . . . incident." He waggled his finger in front of my face. "However, tomorrow . . ."

"I know." I held up my hand. "First chance I get, I'll have Zane get the book out of the safe and turn it over to you."

His stiff stance relaxed a bit, but his sour expression didn't change. "I guess that will have to do. Good night, then. I'll be in touch."

He turned and moved away to where Barbie and Randy stood. As they huddled together, I gave my store one final once-over before I walked out the door. Outside I caught sight of a familiar figure—Riley May Connor. She was standing across the street, scribbling in her notepad. I started to turn away when I heard her shrill out, "Ms. James!"

I halted in my tracks as she ran up to me. "Oh my gosh," she said. "Your poor store! That is your store that was vandalized, right?"

I set my lips. "It certainly looks that way."

"Who could have done this? Do you have any idea?"

"The police seem to think it might just be an act of vandalism—kids practicing for Mischief Night," I muttered.

"Oh?" She scribbled something in her notepad. "If that were the case, don't you think the bakery would have been vandalized too?" She turned and gave a swift glance up and down the street. "Plus, it appears that none of the other stores in the area were touched."

"That is true," I said. "Maybe you have a valid point, Riley. Perhaps you should share your theory with the police. I'm sure Detective Grant and Detective Donaldson in particular would be very interested to hear your viewpoint."

She shot me a sidelong glance. "You're mocking me, aren't you? You've already considered that, and you don't think it was vandalism, do you?"

I shrugged. "All I know for sure is nothing was taken from my store. As to whether or not it was an act of vandalism—I have no comment on that. You'll have to ask the police."

I started to push past her, but she caught my arm. In a low tone she asked, "Do you think this has anything to do with what happened earlier tonight? At the Austin Inn?"

I leaned in close to Riley and said in a confidential whisper, "No comment."

She shot me a lopsided smile. "I take it that's a yes?"

"You may take that as a no comment," I repeated. Then I turned on my heel and strode toward my car without a backward glance. I'd made up my mind about one thing, though.

That meeting with Maddie Elster couldn't come fast enough for me.

NINE

I was wide awake at six a.m., having spent a restless night tossing and turning. It had gotten so bad at one point that I'd knocked poor Poe off the bed. I kept replaying everything in my mind. Of course, I was certain that the thief had been after that book, whether it was the genuine article or not, and that only made me more determined than ever to find out the truth about it.

I also had to find some way to delay giving Ian that book. I wasn't willing to part with it until I'd had my chat with Maddie Elster.

I hauled myself out of bed, showered, then dressed in comfortable jeans and a green pullover sweater that matched my eyes. I fed Poe, than settled in at the table with some toast and a hot cup of coffee. I'd hardly taken a bite out of the toast when my cell buzzed with an incoming call. "Really, Detective? Before seven?" I muttered. I looked at the caller ID and almost dropped the phone when I saw Max's name on the screen. I hit the answer icon and said, "You're up early."

"As are you," said Max. From the tone of his voice, I had the feeling he'd been hoping my voicemail would have kicked in. "I got your text," he said after a brief pause. "Why the interest in those publishers?"

I said what I knew he'd want to hear. "I was just noodling around with some possible plots for a future book," I said. "And I needed some information."

Max's tone turned more upbeat. "That's great, Charley. What sort of information are you looking for?"

"Well, for example, those publishers I inquired about, do they charge some sort of fee for their services?"

"Actually—they're not two different publishers. They're the same company. Trilby Press filed for chapter eleven, but then they revamped and re-opened as Living the Dream Books.

Anyway, to answer your question—yes. Both incarnations charge fees for the actual publishing in addition to a host of other services they made available—the editing, cover design, things like that."

"I see. And roughly how much do you think it would cost to have your book printed by a publisher like that?"

"It depends on the number of pages, the binding, the paper—but I'd say that if an author wanted five hundred copies of a two-hundred-and-fifty-page paperback-sized book, it would cost him or her somewhere in the neighborhood of five thousand dollars—and that's just for the actual book, without any add-ons."

"That much?" I closed my eyes and visualized the Poe book. "What about a larger book? Let's say coffee table style—not more than ninety pages, with black and white and color photographs?"

"That's awfully specific," he remarked. There followed a period of silence, and I could just hear Max running numbers in his head. "Something like that would probably run five figures," he said at last. "Depending on the print run."

"A small run, say, maybe fifteen hundred?"

"I'd say around twenty thousand, give or take a few hundred."

I let out a low whistle. "Wow, that is some serious coin. You'd really have to want to see your book in print to do that."

"Agreed." He paused and then said, "This doesn't sound like much of a plot point to me. Care to share the real reason for your interest?"

"A book dealer came into my shop yesterday looking for a self-published book on Edgar Allan Poe, so it made me . . . curious about the whole process."

"Poe, huh?" Max said in a more mollified tone. "Well, he's always been popular around this time of year."

"The book is called *A Compendium of Poe—Complete Works, plus Stories Adapted for the Screen*. It was published in the nineties. Ever heard of it?"

"Can't say I have. Compendium, huh? Fancy word. Why not just say collection? That's what it means, right?"

"A collection of detailed information, and from what I gather, this book is exactly that," I said.

"About Poe? I didn't realize there was anything more to be written about him. Although the stories adapted for the screen part could be interesting. Who was the author?"

"Gil Sullivan."

"You're kidding? As in Gilbert and Sullivan?" He let out a chuckle. "If that's not a pseudonym, I'll eat my tie. So, what about the book itself? Did you check all the antiquarian sites, and eBay?"

"Yes, and there are no copies to be had anywhere. It was supposed to have a very small print run, and I believe it." I paused and then asked, "How much do you figure it would have cost to publish that book back in the nineties? A lot less than now?"

"I bet it's not that much of a difference." He paused. "You know, maybe this idea of yours would be better as a cozy mystery. You could do one that has thriller elements. I'm sure I could get you a good deal, but it would have to be under another pseudonym to distinguish them from your Sheppard series. I'm sure Parker Press might be interested. They've been thinking about expanding their cozy line and—"

I cut him off mid-sentence. "Thanks Max, but I'm not ready. Don't worry, though. When I decide to return to writing, whether it's another Steve Sheppard or something else, you will be the first to know. And now I've really got to go."

"Wait, wait. Just keep this in the back of your mind. That publishing house is still interested in another Steve Sheppard. They even upped their offer by ten percent. I really think with a little haggling I can get 'em up to twenty."

"I'll keep that in mind. Thanks for the info, Max." I disconnected quickly, glad that at least we were talking again, even if it was on shaky ground. "Ground that will probably never be entirely solid until I write another darn book," I muttered.

I mentally reviewed what Max had told me. Vanity publishing seemed very expensive, particularly for a coffee-table-style book like the Poe Compendium. I hadn't found any reviews of the book online, which made me wonder just how small that print run had been, and what had happened to the other copies?

I got out my laptop and called up the Living the Dream Books website. This time all the pages were accessible—it was possible there had just been some sort of glitch when I'd tried before. I went to the section marked "Contact Us" and typed in a brief message:

I'm looking for information on a book published in the nineties by Trilby Press entitled A Compendium of Poe—Complete Works, plus Stories Adapted for the Screen. *Curious if you might still have any copies available for sale, or know where I might locate one or possibly contact information for the author?*

I typed in my name and contact info, then hit the send button. I wondered if anyone would even bother replying—after all, the book had been published thirty-something years ago. But it was worth a shot. And at this point I was willing to grasp at any thread, no matter how slim.

It was a little after seven when I stepped into Zane's bakery, and there was already a long line before the counter. I eyed the display case and saw that there were still plenty of my favorite pastry there—bear claws. Good thing—I really needed one right now. My heart did a brief flip-flop when I saw Masie start to load some into a large box. I was debating calling out, "Save some for me," when I heard a sharp hiss behind me. I turned and saw Zane standing there. She crooked her finger and motioned for me to follow her. With a last longing look at the remaining bear claws, I turned and followed her into the kitchen. Once we were inside, she backed me up against the door and stuck her finger right under my nose.

"What happened here last night?" she cried. "I almost died when I got here at three this morning and saw that yellow tape stretched across your doorway. Does that mean that someone else was—"

"If there was another murder, it wasn't in my store," I said.

"It was broken into. They really trashed it too. Broke the spines on a couple of brand-new books. Fortunately my picture window was spared."

"Oh my God." Zane put her hand to her mouth. "You know as well as I do what they were looking for. That book," she whispered.

"No doubt they were. And I'm sure they were very disappointed when they didn't find it. I'm thinking the only reason the window was spared was because something interrupted their search."

Zane's eyes widened. "They might think you have it," she cried. "They could come to the house looking for it! We have to get it out of the safe!"

"Calm down," I hissed. "Grant was concerned too. He wants me to turn the book over to him for safekeeping."

"Oh, good, you told him," Zane breathed. "And that's a good idea, giving him the book. I've got that big order to get out, but I think I could manage to slip away around nine thirty."

"Not so fast," I said. "Before I hand it over to him, I really want to talk to Maddie Elster. Phyllis is going to try and arrange a meeting."

Zane rolled her eyes. "For today?"

"Hopefully," I said.

"So what? In the meantime we hang onto that book?" Zane shook her head. "I don't want my house broken into, Charley."

"I don't either. Give me twenty-four hours. If Phyllis doesn't get us a meeting with Maddie Elster by noon tomorrow, I'll turn the book over to Grant."

"Think Grant will wait that long?"

"Probably not." I sighed. "That's why I'm going to have to avoid him like the plague."

"Good luck with that." Zane blew out a breath. "Well, I have to get back to work. Keep me posted, will ya?"

I squeezed her arm. "Of course."

Zane went back inside the kitchen, and I resumed my place in the line. I'd barely taken five steps when my phone buzzed with an incoming text. It was from Barbie: Good news. The crime scene boys worked all night and finished up, so you can re-open your store whenever.

I remembered the look that had crossed Ian's face when I'd complained about having to clean up and wondered if he'd had anything to do with the speedy service. I typed back: Thanks. I'll call Mandy and we'll get on putting the store to rights so we can re-open.

I moved up in the line another two steps and then dialed Mandy. She answered on the first ring. "Charley! Oh my gosh, I read what happened in the paper! How bad is it?"

"Pretty bad," I said, "but the police have finished with their part, so I just got the word we can re-open. There's a lot of cleaning up to do first, though."

"I'll be right down," said Mandy. "Today's my day off from the diner, so I'm all yours."

"Thanks, Mandy, I appreciate that. I'm bringing coffee and donuts for fortification."

I disconnected and then called up the online edition of today's *Austin Bugle* on my phone. Apparently I wasn't considered big news because there was only a small mention, way at the bottom of page three: *LOCAL STORE RANSACKED*. There followed a brief account followed by a quote from Grant saying an investigation was currently underway. I sighed. The sooner I could get rid of that book, the better.

A pleasant surprise awaited me when I stepped into my shop a half hour later. I paused in the doorway, astonished at the transformation that had taken place. In just a short space of time, Mandy had somehow managed to put our Humpty-Dumpty of a store back together again. Nearly all the books had been taken off the floor and put on our rolling carts. Quite a few of the shelves had been restocked, and the glass from the smashed cases had been cleared away and put in large black bags stacked against one wall. I walked over to the counter to set the coffee and bakery box down and jumped back as Mandy's head popped up. "Like it?" she asked.

"Like it? Mandy, you're a magician! How on earth did you manage to do all this in less than an hour?"

She grinned at me. "I had some help," she admitted.

I shot her a questioning look. "Help?"

"Jake was with me when you called. He offered to help, and I figured the more hands on deck, the better, right?"

I turned around and saw Jake standing behind me. He had a bunch of books tucked under his arm, and I recognized them immediately. They were the books from the Poe display.

Jake saw me looking and held the books up. "I cleaned up the books from the floor in the front and stacked 'em on the carts, and then I saw the mess your intruder made of that Poe display. I've almost got it back together. Want to see?"

"I—ah—yeah, sure."

I followed Jake over to where I'd set up the display. He'd set the table to rights and arranged the books back on top, in a circular design that was far better than the stacks of books I'd done. "Mandy mentioned you getting one of those Halloween trees," he said. "I thought you could put that in the center of all the books, maybe get a raven or a skeleton or something to put on top of the tree. I arranged the books according to size, the smaller poetry books in front, the larger compilations of his stories and combined works in the back."

"It looks great, Jake. Thank you. But I feel bad about you spending your time here helping us clean up. I'm sure you have other things to do. What about your consulting job?"

Jake shrugged. "Oh, it's slow right now. Besides, Mandy was pretty upset about everything, so if this helps her feel better, then . . . it's worth it." He arranged the books he'd been holding on the display, then stepped back to survey his handiwork. "Not bad, if I do say so myself," he said with a grin. "If you want, I can go over to the big box store later and pick up one of those trees. What color do you want? Black, orange?"

"If they have a combo black and orange, that would be great. Otherwise just a plain black one. I can give you money out of petty cash, right now."

He waved me away. "That's OK, I've got money. You can pay me back later." He angled his chin toward the shelves behind the display. "That store doesn't open till ten, so in the meantime I could start restocking those shelves for you."

"Oh, you don't have to do that," I said quickly. "Mandy and

I can take care of that, and Anna and Braedon can help when they get here. You picking up that tree will be a huge help, believe me."

My phone rang. I fished it out from my pocket and my heart started to beat faster when I saw Phyllis's name on the screen. "Excuse me," I said, turning away. I hit the accept icon and said, "Good news, I hope?"

Phyllis's voice, tinged with excitement, floated over the wire. "Yep. I'll pick you up at your store at one. We've got a meeting with Maddie Elster today at two. Here's hoping it turns out to be a productive one."

TEN

I disconnected from Phyllis and shoved my phone back into my pocket. I turned and saw Jake still looking at me. "You're sure you don't want me to start restocking these shelves?" he asked.

Mandy called out from the front of the store. "Jake! If you're not too busy, I could use some help out here taking all this glass out to the curb. I forgot, today is garbage pick-up, and they'll be by any minute."

Jake chuckled. "Whatever milady wants," he called out, then gave me a half-smile. When he was halfway to the front of the store, the bell above my shop door tinkled, and a moment later my other two clerks, Anna Fisk and Braedon Ohlmeyer, came inside. I started forward with a wide smile.

"Hey, guys," I said. "I thought you had classes this morning."

"They got canceled," said Braedon as Anna stepped forward to embrace me in a giant bear-hug. A tall, good-looking blonde, her nearly six-foot frame towered over my five-foot-six one. "We just couldn't believe it when we heard," Anna mumbled against my neck. She released me and looked swiftly around the store. "It's not as bad as we thought."

"No, it isn't," said Braedon. He was tall too, only about an inch shorter than Anna. Both of them had won basketball scholarships to college. Braedon was a business major, while Anna was pre-med. She wanted to be a vet and had already assured me that once she'd set up her practice, I'd get a generous discount on services for Poe. Braedon winked at Mandy. "Someone started without us."

"Jake did most of the cleanup," Mandy admitted. "He's taking the bags with all the glass out to the curb, and then he's going up to Gilley's to get one of those Halloween trees for the Poe display."

"Jake did all that? Wow!" Braedon sounded surprised. "Well,

once he gets the tree I can put it together and then I'll start restocking all the shelves in the back. No need for him to waste his whole day here. I'm sure he's got things of his own to do." He smiled at Mandy. "You, Jake, and Anna can handle restocking the front, right?"

"Actually I was hoping Anna could handle it by herself," said Mandy. "I'd really like to do that Hitchcock window display. Jake said he'd help me set up the mannequins."

"I think that's a splendid idea," I said. "I have to go somewhere at one, but I can help with the restocking till then."

Jake came back inside, rubbing his hands together. "All the bags are out by the curb," he announced. "Just in time too. The garbage truck is down the street."

"Change of plans, Jake," said Mandy. "I'll go with you to get the tree, and Braedon and Anna will handle the restocking. When we get back, you and I are going to work on the window display."

Jake frowned. "I was going to set up the tree in the Poe display," he began, but Braedon waved his hand, cutting him off.

"No need. I can handle that, and then I'll just work on the shelves in that area. I think it's more important to get that window display up, right, Charley?"

"Yes, I think that's a good idea. People are asking about our Halloween decorations." I smiled at Jake. "It really would be a big help to Mandy, Jake. The window is her project."

His chin went up a bit, but then he nodded. "If it helps Mandy, I'm in," he said. He glanced at his watch. "What say we head out now? We can grab a quick bite to eat at the diner before the store opens. With your employee discount, I think I'll have Eggs Benedict."

Mandy giggled. "I'll settle for avocado toast. Those bear claws are filling."

"Well, now that's settled, go on, you two," I said, making a shooing motion with my hand. "Enjoy your breakfast. More bear claws for me." I smiled at Jake. "And thank you again for all your help."

He waved one hand in a careless motion and slipped his

other arm around Mandy's shoulders. "Don't mention it. Like I said, I'd do anything to help Mandy out."

Mandy swatted at his arm and looked at him with moon-struck eyes. "You're the best," she gushed.

He and Mandy left, and Braedon and Anna got busy in their sections, loading books back onto the shelves. I walked over to the cart that contained the books I displayed in the front of the store, mostly new releases. I'd only put back two books when my phone buzzed, signaling an incoming email. I fished the phone out of my pocket, intending to put it on silent, but my breath caught in my throat when I saw the name of the sender: Living the Dream Books. I opened the message eagerly. It was short and to the point:

Dear Ms. James

Thank you for your interest in our company. Unfortunately, we are unable to give out any detailed information on the book you inquired about without the author's permission. What we can tell you is that this book is no longer available on our website. I trust this answer is satisfactory.

Should you have any other questions or concerns, feel free to contact us.

Sincerely,

Chastity McAllister, Editorial Assistant

I frowned and read the message again. "Asking if you have copies for sale is considered detailed information? That's rich," I muttered. "They need the author's permission for that, huh? I wonder if they know where to find him. Sorry, Ms. McAllister, but your answer is not satisfactory, not at all."

I hit the reply button and typed another message:

Dear Ms. McAllister

Thank you for your prompt reply. I was inquiring about that particular book because it seems to be very similar to one that I myself am thinking of self-publishing. So, if you could possibly provide me with some information regarding that avenue, it would be greatly appreciated.

Sincerely,

Charlotte James

My finger hovered over the send button. They'd mentioned the book was "no longer available on their website" but had it been? And if so, who might have ordered it? A longshot for sure, but if they thought there was money to be made, I might be able to convince them to part with some info—like author contact information, perhaps? I held my breath and hit send—and then my phone rang! Without even thinking, I hit the answer icon. "Charlotte James."

"Good morning, Charlotte."

My stomach sank at the sound of Ian's voice. "Detective Grant. What a nice surprise."

"It can't be that much of a surprise, Charlotte. I told you I'd be in touch today."

"That you did, and while I have your attention, I want to thank you for rushing that investigation along. Detective Donaldson told me I could re-open, so my crew and I are here at the store trying to clean up so we can do just that tomorrow."

A pause and then, "So is that your way of telling me that you're too busy to hand over that book?"

I swallowed. "I don't know. Is it?"

Now he laughed. "Sometimes you're a real piece of work, Charlotte. I should think you'd want to get rid of that book. I'm betting your pal Zane doesn't want it around."

"I'm not taking that bet."

"Smart girl. Anyway, the reason I'm calling is to tell you that you're off the proverbial hook until tomorrow. I have to go out of town on an important errand I can't put off."

I bit back a sigh of relief. "So you won't be dropping by today?"

"No, but tell Zane I'm having a car patrol your street every hour, just in case. I don't want her to feel uncomfortable having that book around—or you either." He paused. "Don't you have a bank vault you could put the book in until I can get there?"

"Yes, but it's one of the small boxes. This book is too big to fit in there." I rushed on before he could say anything else, "Sorry to cut this short, but I really have to get back to work now."

"OK, Charlotte. I'll see you tomorrow. Just be careful," he added before disconnecting. I made a face at my phone. Like I needed him to tell me that.

I sent Zane a quick text letting her know that it wouldn't be necessary for her to meet me at the house at nine thirty. I also told her that Grant would be sending a patrol car past the house every hour. She sent back an answer: **Make sure you see him tomorrow. The sooner we get rid of that book, the better!**

Mandy and Jake returned around eleven thirty bearing a medium-sized box. "We were lucky," said Jake. "They had one orange and black four-footer left."

"Great," I said. "How much do I owe you?"

Jake pulled a slip out of his pocket. "It came to forty-two sixty-eight with tax," he said. "You can just give me forty-two even."

"I'll give you forty-three," I said. I went to the register, counted out the bills, then pressed them into Jake's hand. "Thanks again, Jake."

"No problem." He eyed the box. "I can start setting it up, if you want."

Braedon came over to us, pushing an empty cart. "All the books in the Classics section are back in their rightful places," he announced. His gaze fell upon the box. "Is that the tree?"

I nodded. "Sure is. Orange and black."

"Perfect. I already have an idea for some accompanying decorations." He leaned over to pick up the box, but Jake's hand shot forward.

"Are you sure you don't want me to do it?" he asked me.

"I'd much rather you helped Mandy with the front window, Jake. Braedon seems as if he's got the Poe display under control."

Jake hesitated, then let his hand drop to his side. Braedon picked up the box, put it on the cart, and started wheeling it to the back of the store.

Mandy stepped forward and put her hand on Jake's shoulder. "Come on, give me a hand with the mannequins in the back room," she said. "I've got a great idea for the scene I want to do from *The Birds*."

Jake gave her a lopsided smile. "Sure thing, sweetums."

Jake headed back toward our supply room. Mandy hung back and inched closer to me. "Don't mind him," she said. "He can get a little intense when he's working on something. We'll do a good job on the window. You'll see."

I watched her walk off toward the supply room.

I glanced at my own watch and saw that it was a little after twelve. Just enough time for me to grab a sandwich and get ready for my meeting with Maddie Elster.

One way or another, I was going to find out the truth about that book . . . today.

ELEVEN

Maddie Elster lived in an exclusive section of Austin called Austin Heights, situated at the farthest end of town, a good forty minutes from where my store was located. Phyllis had been a little late (darn gas station! All the pumps were occupied!) so it was a few minutes after two when we pulled into a gated drive on a quiet tree-lined street appropriately named Manor Lane. Phyllis rolled her window down just as the intercom beside the gate started to squawk. A male voice, thick with an English accent, floated out. "Whom shall I say is calling?"

Phyllis leaned her head out and said, "Tell Ms. Elster it's Phyllis Wooster and Charlotte James. She's expecting us."

"Very good, Miss."

There was utter and complete silence for about five minutes, then the intercom squawked to life again. "You may enter," the voice said as the heavy gates parted, revealing a winding circular driveway lined with overhanging elm and dogwood trees. At the very end was an exquisite residence built in the English Tudor style. It was large and appeared to be well-built, with a high-peaked slate roof with a façade of timbers and cross-hatching, symmetrically paned picture windows, and leaded glass sidelights. Handsome herringbone brickwork on the elegantly landscaped walkway led up to the entryway, where a pair of tall hammered columns rose to a balcony high overhead. The front garden boasted colorful blooms, lush greenery, and sculpted boxwoods.

I looked at Phyllis. "Wow! Her gardening bill must be tremendous."

"One would think, but gardening is another of Maddie's hobbies. She does most of this herself."

Phyllis parked the car, and we got out. She paused to remove a leather briefcase from the back seat, then we walked up the cobblestone walkway and up the short flight of steps to the main door. I rang the bell. We could hear the sound of soft chimes reverberating through the house, and a few moments later the door opened and a young girl in a black dress, a white apron knotted at the waist and white cap perched atop her russet curls, swung the door wide. "Ms. Wooster and Ms. James?" she asked. She looked at Phyllis, then at me, then back to Phyllis.

"Yes," Phyllis said. "We're expected."

"Actually," the maid said, her tone reproving, "you're a bit late. But please, follow me."

Phyllis and I exchanged a look, then followed the maid down a long hallway into a room that at first glance seemed to be both warm and inviting. A classic white marble fireplace graced one end of the room, set against walls that appeared to be beautifully hand painted in a soft mauve color. The furniture consisted of a sofa and loveseat combo upholstered in pale pink velvet and a cherrywood mission-style coffee table positioned between them. A high-backed Queen Anne chair, upholstered in the same pink velvet, sat just off to the left. The walls held floor-to-ceiling bookshelves, and they were filled with books, many of which were leather-bound and probably expensive first editions. Over in the far corner was a large bar area, with shelves containing dozens of bottles of liquor positioned behind it. Just off to the right of the bar sat a substantial lighted display case, the lone occupant of which was a large book, set on a wooden stand.

Phyllis gave me a soft nudge in the ribs and inclined her jaw toward the case. "See," she whispered. "There's a book in that case."

"Right. *A* book," I whispered back. "But is it the right book?"

The maid turned toward us. "Please make yourselves comfortable. I'll tell Ms. Elster you are here."

She turned on her heel and exited the room. She'd barely been gone a second before I crossed the room over to the glass case. I peered at the object within. The familiar black book cover featuring Poe and the raven stared back at me. It looked identical to the one I'd found in my shop, no mistake about that. I was half tempted to lift the book out of the case, to see what, if anything, was on the title page, but the sight of the large lock attached to the case's side put an end to that idea. That, and the keypad that was attached to the base of the case.

"Charley!" Phyllis's sharp whisper broke into my thoughts. "Hurry back here. I hear footsteps. She's coming."

I hurried back to the seating area and settled down just as the parlor door opened and a young girl entered. She was very attractive, with long blonde hair held in place by a black velvet ribbon and flawless skin that didn't need the slightest bit of makeup. The distressed jeans and blue cashmere sweater she wore were definitely designer, as were the blue suede ankle booties on her tiny feet. "You're not Maddie Elster," I blurted out.

The girl rolled her big blue eyes. "Heaven forbid. That's my aunt." She gave her head a toss, and I noticed there was a vibrant violet streak in her hair.

Phyllis leaned forward. "You must be Jewell, Maddie's niece," she said.

Jewell nodded. "Yes, I am. Are you here to see my aunt? Did Dottie announce you?"

"Is Dottie the maid?" I asked. At Jewell's nod, I went on, "Then yes, she went to tell Ms. Elster we're here."

"Auntie Dearest should be here soon, then." She crossed the room to the bar, reached underneath, and pulled out a bottle of vodka. She poured a generous amount into a glass, took a sip, and then set the glass down on the bar. Her lips twisted into a crooked smile. "Don't worry, I'm twenty-one as of last month," she said.

I cleared my throat. "This is a lovely room," I said.

Jewell wrinkled her nose. "You think? I've always thought it was rather stuffy myself. I'm not much of a reader, unless it's *Cosmo* or *Glamour*. Too many books for my taste."

"I own a bookstore," I said. "Maybe that's part of the appeal."

"A bookstore. Yeah, that would probably do it." She raised

her arm and pointed at the bookshelves. "This room is a combination parlor library. My aunt has a rather extensive collection. Most were left to her by my grandfather, but she's added to it over the years." Her gaze traveled to the glass case. "Have you seen the prize of her collection? Why she sets such store by this ugly thing is beyond me." She raised the glass again, took another swallow, and shrugged. "No accounting for taste, I suppose."

The parlor door opened again, and another woman appeared in the doorway. "Jewell. There you are." She looked pointedly at the glass in Jewell's hand. "It's a mite early for that, don't you think? Put the drink down and go to the kitchen. Consuela could use some help prepping for dinner."

Jewell raised the glass to her lips, took a sip, and then frowned. "I'm twenty-one, Aunt Maddie. You can't tell me what to do. As for my drink, well, it's five o'clock somewhere in the world, right?" She turned her face toward us and closed one eye in a wink.

Maddie's eyes flashed. "There's no need to be flippant, Jewell."

"Sorry, Auntie." She turned to us and flashed a smile. "I should go help Consuela, though," she said. "I'm actually a much better cook than she is. We're going to be having coq au vin later. Nice meeting you." She turned and stalked out of the room, glass clenched firmly in her hand.

Maddie Elster made an exasperated sound deep in her throat before turning to us. "I apologize for my niece. She's been more difficult than usual lately. I really don't know what's gotten into her. I swear she spends hours thinking up various ways she can annoy me. Oh, well . . ." She shook her head and then extended both her arms toward Phyllis, who had risen from her seat. "It's so lovely to see you again, Phyllis. It's been too long."

Phyllis sidestepped Maddie to avoid the hug. "No hugs necessary, Maddie. I know why you're happy to see me."

Maddie paused, then slowly lowered her outstretched arms. "I'm sorry about the circumstances, but I won't deny I was thrilled to hear you're considering selling your Nancy Drew collection."

"Considering being the operative word, Maddie," Phyllis said.

"Of course, of course," Maddie murmured. Her gaze shifted to me, and she glanced at Phyllis. "This is the friend you mentioned? The book expert?"

I rose, and Phyllis gave me a little push forward. "This is Charlotte James," said Phyllis. "She just opened a bookstore in Austin."

Maddie let out a squeal. "I read about the opening in the paper. Austin desperately needed a good bookstore. I've been wanting to drop in, but . . . it's been very hectic around here."

"Charley is quite astute when it comes to the value of books," put in Phyllis. "I brought her to validate the price I'll be asking for the Drews—if I decide to sell, that is."

Maddie waved her hand. "That wasn't necessary, Phyllis. You know I'd be glad to pay any price you asked to get my hands on those books. First edition Drews are a real treasure."

"I haven't decided if I'm selling the entire set or just the autographed ones," Phyllis said hastily. "It depends on a lot of factors."

"Of course, of course," Maddie murmured. "How are your cousin and his wife doing?"

While Maddie and Phyllis chatted about Phyllis's cousin, I took a moment to study Maddie Elster. I had no doubt that in her younger days she could probably have been Kim Novak's twin. Even now, in her late fifties, she looked well-preserved. Her build was slight, but she was curvaceous in all the right places. Her white-blonde hair was cut in a short, flattering style that emphasized her high cheekbones and slender neck. She regarded me with snapping hazel eyes with flecks of gold in the center of the irises, and her wide, full-lipped mouth was curved in a welcoming smile. She wore a black tunic and dove-gray slacks, simple in their lines but which spoke of understated elegance. The thick, gold braided chain around her neck, though, screamed old money.

Maddie and Phyllis had finished their conversation and now Maddie's gaze shifted to the briefcase Phyllis had brought. "You brought some of the books with you?" she asked hopefully.

"Yes." Phyllis sat back down and hoisted the briefcase onto her lap. "I brought the two that were signed by Mildred Wirt Benson, the original author of the Nancy Drew books, numbers eight and ten. Unfortunately they aren't the ones with the blank endpapers, but I have photos on my phone."

Phyllis opened the briefcase and carefully lifted out the two books. I leaned over for a closer look myself. While I'd read the Nancy Drew books and seen pictures of the original ten that contained the internal illustrations, I'd never seen any up close and personal. The books looked to be in remarkable shape for their age. The dust jackets were pretty near perfect (or as a true collector would say, pristine). They boasted colors that were still bright and hardly any chips, probably due to the thick mylar jackets they were swaddled in. Phyllis opened each book, and you could see the binding was nice and tight, the pages still white. I reached out and lightly touched number eight, *Nancy's Mysterious Letter*, which had always been one of my favorites. There was just something about seeing Nancy in a raccoon coat that got me every time. It made her seem more like an eighteen-year-old girl than the remarkable sleuth she was.

Phyllis flipped to the title page and pointed to the signature. *Regards and happy reading. Mildred Wirt Benson* was scrawled there. "I had the signature authenticated, but I imagine you'll want to do the same—if I do decide to sell?" asked Phyllis.

Maddie was staring at the books as if they were the Holy Grail. "Of course, of course," she murmured. "I have a very reliable person I can call upon." She reached out toward *The Password to Larkspur Lane*, but Phyllis shifted her position, putting the book out of her reach while at the same time jabbing her knee into my leg.

"Speaking of signature authentication," I said, "I understand you have in your possession a book that was signed by one of my favorite actors—Vincent Price?" I inclined my head toward the glass case. "*A Compendium of Poe—Complete Works, plus Stories Adapted for the Screen.*"

Maddie's face brightened. "Yes, I do. It's the centerpiece of my collection. I'm quite a fan of Poe's works—and a movie buff too."

I inclined my head toward the overflowing bookshelves. "So you collect books on movies too?"

"Yes." She ran one hand through her short crop of hair, making the ends spike up even more. "At first it started out as just a lark—I began collecting Kim Novak memorabilia. I have the same name as one of her characters in *Vertigo*, you know."

"Yes, I do."

"Well, I started out collecting her memorabilia, and then I branched out into Hitchcock memorabilia—I have a script of *The Birds* signed by him—and then I developed a fascination with horror films in general. I loved the old classics that Vincent Price and Boris Karloff starred in—ones like *House on Haunted Hill*, *Frankenstein* . . . and then I found myself becoming interested in the movies made from Poe classics. I'd studied Poe in English class in college, and I was always fascinated by his Gothic style of writing. He managed to weave in elements of fear, horror, death, and gloom so beautifully with the high emotion associated with romance." She let out a sigh. "I've always been a romantic at heart."

"Fascinating, to be sure," I murmured. "It was my understanding that the Poe Compendium had a very small print run. How did you come to acquire that volume?"

Maddie let out a tinkling laugh. "I'm surprised Phyllis hasn't told you the story," she said, tossing a wink in Phyllis's direction. "It was fate, right, Phyllis?"

"If you say so, Maddie."

"I do." Maddie turned back to me. "I got it at an estate sale. It was sheer luck, actually. The book was inside a leather trunk that both Phyllis and I were bidding on. I won out by two hundred dollars." She rubbed her hands together gleefully. "When I opened that trunk and found that book hidden inside that ratty sweater, I was ecstatic, let me tell you. It was the best two hundred dollars I'd ever spent."

"An estate sale, you said?"

"Yes. The trunk belonged to Gordon Knight. The man lived here in Austin, and he was a bit of a recluse, I guess you could say. He'd worked as a scientist at Axitrom Chemicals for many years. Imagine my surprise when I found that book in Knight's trunk. Who would ever have thought this man, an award-winning scientist who worked on many government programs, was a Poe fan, let alone one of Price and Karloff! And he somehow managed to get them to sign his copy! I tell you, when I saw all those signatures, I thought I'd died and gone to heaven."

"It sounds like a fabulous keepsake," I said. "I'm surprised that Mr. Knight's heirs let it go."

"Gordon never married and had no children. He had a sister who died, and her daughter was his heir. To be honest, I thought about trying to get in touch with her after I saw the Poe book, but I had so much going on at the time I forgot to ask the gallery for her contact information. By the time I thought about it again, so much time had elapsed . . . I just figured she'd seen the book when she opened the trunk and decided to include it." She shrugged and looked again at Phyllis. "Fate, right? I was meant to have that book."

"It would appear so," I murmured. "So the book is in perfect condition? No pages missing?"

"Pages missing? Why no. All ninety-two pages are there."

"And you mentioned you had the signatures authenticated?"

Maddie's hazel eyes snapped. "Well, duh! That was the first thing I did. And once I found out they were all genuine—well, I stuck this baby right here in my parlor, under lock and key, where I could take it out anytime in privacy and just simply drool over it."

I looked her right in the eyes. "So you do take the book out from time to time and flip through it?"

She flushed guiltily. "Well—I did in the beginning. I have to confess, though, the past few months I haven't given it the loving attention I used to. Maybe because of all the chaos around here."

I'd noted how Maddie's eyes fairly glowed with pride as she talked about the book. I sort of hated to burst her bubble, but it had to be done. I once again inclined my head toward the case. "You haven't taken the book out to look at it for several months. Are you certain the book that's in that case now is the same book you bought at that estate sale?"

Her rapturous expression faded, replaced by one of puzzlement. Her brows drew together, and her lips peeled back a bit, revealing teeth so white even I was certain they were caps. "Of course I'm certain. Just what are you getting at?"

"I can't explain fully, but certain events have transpired recently that make me question whether or not your copy of the Poe Compendium is authentic."

The puzzled expression morphed into anger. Her hazel eyes became two slits. "What do you mean, you can't explain fully?" she growled. "And why would you think my copy isn't authentic?"

I decided to tell part of the story. "A man named Jeffrey Thomas came into my shop recently. He said that he was looking for a copy of a book chronicling Poe's works as well as the movies made from them. He said the book was very rare and hard to come by, and that he'd heard it was part of a private collection that was being offered for sale."

Her angry expression faded, replaced by one of relief. "Well, I can tell you it most certainly isn't mine. I'm not putting up any of my private collection for sale, let alone that book!"

"You didn't, but maybe someone else did. Who else has access to the book?"

The angry light came back into Maddie's eyes. "What are you suggesting? That someone in my household is making plans to sell my book? That's preposterous." She waved her hand in the air. "No one in my household would even think of doing such a thing."

"Humor me," I said pleadingly. "Who, besides you, has access to it—or rather, who would have access to the key to the case? And the alarm code?"

Maddie's lips screwed up into a pout as she thought. "Well, the servants of course," she said at last. "The maids, in particular. They're supposed to dust it from time to time."

"Anyone else?"

"Well—there's my brother Edmund, but he'd never touch the book. Then there's my niece whom you met, my late sister's daughter, Jewell. She'd never touch it either. Has no interest whatsoever in that sort of thing."

"Yes, she mentioned she wasn't a reader," I said. "But how about having an interest in the money a sale would bring?"

"Hmpf." She sniffed. "It wouldn't bring enough for any of them to go against me. I repeat—no one in this household would touch that book. Not even Jewell would have the nerve."

"Are you sure?" I pressed on doggedly. "Are you absolutely certain the book sitting in that case is the same one you bought at the estate sale?"

"Oh, for goodness sakes." Maddie threw up both hands. "Come. I'll prove it to you."

We all walked over to stand in front of the glass case. Maddie punched in a five-digit code onto the keypad, then reached into the pocket of her tunic and pulled out a keyring. She fitted a small key into the lock at the side of the case and lifted the lid. Then she went over to a drawer in a nearby desk, whipped out a pair of latex gloves, pulled them on, and carefully lifted the book off its stand.

"This is utter nonsense," she muttered. She took the book over to the desk and laid it carefully on top of the blotter. I stepped in close to peer over her shoulder. First she flipped to the title page. There were the exact same signatures as in the copy I'd found in the store, in the exact same places on the page. I sucked in a breath. If either copy were a forgery, it was a master job.

"Well, there are two signatures. As I knew there would be, because this is the book I bought at the estate sale. And if you want more proof . . ."

Her fingers grazed the dust jacket, and she lifted up the front flap. Suddenly she let out a gasp. She dropped the flap and stepped away from the book as if her fingers had been burned.

"Oh my God." Maddie whirled to face me, her eyes over bright. "You–you're right, Charley. This isn't my book."

TWELVE

I felt a little thrill that my theory had been correct. I looked at Maddie. "You're certain, Ms. Elster, that this isn't your book?"

"Of course I'm certain," Maddie snapped. Two spots of red appeared in her cheeks. "Someone took my book and substituted a copy. And a good one, at that." She leaned over to peer at the book. "It's in just as good condition as mine—and the signatures on the title page, why, they look authentic. But they can't be—can they?"

I remembered the articles I'd found in Janice Rutger's possession and shook my head. "I'm guessing the chances of that are slim," I said. "I'm curious, though. How did you know for certain the book in the case is a forgery?"

"Why, it's simple. I—" Maddie stopped speaking and looked at us, her eyes narrowed. "Wait a second. Why should I tell you anything? Now that I think on it, it seems very odd to me that you'd part with any of your precious Drew books, no matter what your family crisis. How do I know this isn't some plot both of you are in on?"

Phyllis let out a moan of exasperation. "Oh, Maddie, really!"

"Don't act innocent with me, Phyllis Wooster," Maddie cried. She waved her finger in front of Phyllis's face. "You were pretty hot to get that trunk. Maybe you knew what was inside!"

Phyllis shook her head. "I wanted to get the trunk for my office, but I didn't want it bad enough to outbid you. And I was just as surprised as you when I saw the contents."

Maddie folded her arms across her chest and inclined her head at me. "Your friend here could have clued you in as to the worth of the book," she said stubbornly. "Maybe the two of you plan to sell it and make a tidy profit."

"And you think that we concocted some grand scheme to get it? Honestly, Maddie, you can be such a drama queen."

Phyllis shook her head in disgust. "I haven't been here recently, and this is Charley's first visit. When would either of us have had the chance to switch it out?"

Maddie's lower lip thrust out. "You could have bribed someone on my staff to do it for you," she said petulantly.

"Madeleine Elster!" Phyllis's voice was both reproachful and stern all at once. "You stop this ridiculous talk right now. You know darn well that I would never be a party to a theft of anything, and neither would Charley!"

Maddie's bluster vanished, and she dropped into a nearby chair and put her head in her hands. "Oh, I know," she wailed. "I apologize. I–I'm in shock, not thinking straight."

Phyllis put her hand on Maddie's shoulder. "I know, dear," she said in a soothing tone.

Maddie raised eyes that were quickly filling with tears to us. "It's just . . . what am I to do now? What am I to think? Apparently now I cannot trust anyone who lives in this house with me."

I knelt down beside her. "Have you had any visitors recently? Anyone who might have been in here, seen the book?"

"No one—wait!" Her head shot up abruptly. "I had some shelves replaced a few weeks ago. The man they sent came from a very reputable service. Mara down at the Clip N Curl recommended it."

"Do you remember the name of the service? Or the man they sent?"

Maddie snorted. "Man? More like a boy. Slender, dark hair, early twenties. He didn't do all that good a job. The name of the service was BuildPro, I think."

"BuildPro?" Phyllis looked at me. "That's Howard Ellis's company. Howard is very reputable. I'm surprised he would have sent you someone that would do a less than stellar job."

"Well, he did, and I fully intend to complain. I just haven't had a chance," Maddie huffed. "Anyway, I came in here and saw that handyman just standing here, staring at the book. When he saw me looking at him, he hotfooted it out of the room."

"Do you remember this handyman's name?" I asked.

"No, sorry. They usually have their name on their coveralls, but he didn't." She pursed her lips. "I'll admit, there seemed to be something familiar about him, though. I thought I might have seen him somewhere before, but I couldn't quite place it."

"OK. Anyone else you can think of that showed an interest in that book?"

"Well, Jewell was looking at it a few times," she said. "Edmund too. Then there was Peter Bridges," she added. "He dropped in unexpectedly just last week. Wanted to know if I'd changed my mind about selling him the book. Edmund let him in, and I found him right here, looking at it, his tongue hanging out."

"Would he have had enough time to make a switch?" Phyllis asked.

Maddie gave her head an emphatic shake. "No. Edmund got me immediately. Peter was only in there for five minutes alone, but if he had inside help . . ." Her voice trailed off, and then she squared her shoulders. In a more determined tone she said, "Let me tell you—Bridges, Ellis, my staff—they'll all have a lot of explaining to do."

I held my hand out, traffic-cop style. "I don't think confronting people right now is a good idea, Ms. Elster."

Maddie stared at me like I had three heads, and then she nodded. "You're right. I should leave that for the police."

She dug into her tunic pocket again and this time pulled out a large iPhone, the newest model. Phyllis and I exchanged a glance, and I stepped forward. "You should definitely notify the police," I said. "But then they'll come here, asking a lot of questions."

Maddie paused, hand poised to hit the buttons. "Well, that's the idea, isn't it? Isn't that how detectives catch thieves? By asking questions and interrogating witnesses?"

"Yes, that's true, but remember, that book dealer who came to my shop said that the potential sale of your book was only a rumor. Maybe nothing has been finalized yet. So, if the thief *is* someone in your household, you don't want to tip them off that you know about it—at least, not yet."

Maddie frowned. "Why?"

"Well . . . let's say whoever has the book is fielding offers from several different sources. If they get wind that you know, and the police are on their tail, they might rush the sale of the book, and you'll never get to see it again."

"If I do nothing at all, I definitely won't ever see it again," Maddie protested. Her eyes lit up and she snapped her fingers. "Should I hire a private eye? Someone to investigate?"

"I don't think that's necessary." I cleared my throat. "I have a few ideas. Why not let me handle it?"

Maddie's jaw dropped. "You? But you're not a detective."

"Maybe not, but Charley has a flair for that sort of thing," cut in Phyllis. "Why, she only recently assisted the police in solving a puzzling murder."

Maddie looked at me with wide eyes. "You did?"

I didn't answer, just stepped forward and laid my hand on Maddie's arm. "Look, Ms. Elster, all I'm asking for is forty-eight hours. After that, you can, and you should, notify the authorities."

Maddie looked from me to Phyllis and then back to me. Then she threw up both hands. "OK, fine. Forty-eight hours, no more. And I hope to God I'm not making a colossal mistake."

I hope not either, I thought, but I smiled at the woman and said, "Good. Now would you mind if I took some photos of the book and some of the pages?"

She hesitated briefly, then shrugged. "I suppose not. After all, it's not my book. Snap away."

I took a few quick photos of the exterior of the book and then flipped to the page that I'd found missing in what I now knew to be Maddie's copy. It had a drawing of Ligeia lying in her tomb on one side and a still from the movie showing Price standing in front of her tomb on the reverse. I snapped a photo of that and a few other pages for good measure. As I started to turn away, Maddie called out, "Wait." She moved forward and removed the front part of the dust jacket. She pointed to the corner of the book's cover. "You wanted to know how I knew this book wasn't mine? Well, I'll tell you. See that corner there?"

Phyllis and I leaned forward and looked at the spot Maddie

pointed to. "Yes," I said. "It's the top right edge of the front cover. There's nothing there."

"Exactly," Maddie said triumphantly. "On my copy, there's a white dot right at the edge of the corner, like someone spilled a dollop of liquid paper onto it. That's how I knew this wasn't my book." She let out a deep sigh. "I guess my copy wouldn't qualify as being in what collectors refer to as pristine condition, right?"

Even without the liquid paper mark, the missing page would surely affect the condition of the book. I shrugged and said, "I'm not an expert, but I would imagine it wouldn't qualify as pristine. Excellent, perhaps, or at the least very good."

"All of which lower the value. Oh well. I'm not going to sell it, so I guess it doesn't matter."

Maddie replaced the dust cover and then she put the book back in the case, closed and locked it. She thrust the keys back into her pocket with a sigh. "This isn't going to be easy. I'm not a phony person by nature. The only saving grace is none of my family gives a whit about that book—or so I always thought." She dropped her gaze to the briefcase. Phyllis had put the Drew books back in it and now held it in her arms. "You never intended to sell those books, did you, Phyllis? It was just a way to get to see my Poe book."

"Sorry, Maddie," said Phyllis. "But I promise you, if I ever do decide to sell them, you'll be the first one I'll call."

Maddie's lips drooped down. "Thanks. I won't hold my breath, though."

We walked down the long corridor to the front door. In the entryway I paused. "One last thing, Ms. Elster. Do you know a woman named Janice Rutger?"

"Her!" Maddie hissed. "I should say so. She was employed as a maid. Up and walked out on me about a week ago, at around the same time I found a lot of my jewelry was missing."

Phyllis inhaled sharply, and I gave her a soft jab in the ribs as I turned to Maddie. "That's terrible. Was the jewelry valuable?"

"All of my pieces are valuable," Maddie said loftily. She opened the front door and held it open as we walked through.

"I don't own a piece of costume jewelry. There were some very valuable pieces that witch took, some I had made just for me. One piece in particular was my favorite. A tiger with sapphire eyes." She let out a low moan. "It's not the first time staff has made off with some of my pieces. It happened a few years ago and none were overly valuable or my favorites, so I didn't report it. This most recent theft I did, and so far they've come up empty-handed, but let me tell you, if I find out Janice Rutger took my book along with my jewels, the police had better get to her before I do, because I just might not be able to restrain myself. If I get to her first, I just might kill her."

Maddie shut the door, and I looked at Phyllis. "She's a bit late with that sentiment," I said. "Someone else has already taken care of that."

Phyllis let out a low whistle as we got back into her car. "I think the sooner you turn that book over to Ian Grant, the better, Charley. And you should tell him about our meeting with Maddie today too," she added as she pulled out of the driveway.

"I intend to, but he's away doing an errand today," I said.

"You'd better hope that whoever is working with that woman doesn't know where you live," she said.

"We already thought of that," I said. "Detective Grant is having a patrol car go by Zane's house every hour. Hopefully if someone is planning an unscheduled visit, seeing the patrol car will scare them off."

"Maybe," Phyllis said doubtfully. "So, what's next?"

"For starters, I need to find out more about this Janice Rutger," I said. "I'm thinking there is more to her than meets the eye. When I was going through her things, I found a second driver's license in the name of Jane Radcliffe."

"That is interesting," said Phyllis. "I wonder which of those names is her real one—or maybe neither of them are!"

"I doubt she was in this alone," I said. "She had a partner. I'm thinking that she might have been planning to double cross said partner and take off. That could be why she stole Maddie's jewels, but—" I reached up to scratch my head.

"But what?" asked Phyllis when I remained silent.

"Maddie's copy has a page missing," I said. "Page seventy-seven. I looked in the copy she has and it's there. It's a drawing of Ligeia lying in her tomb on one side, and a still of Vincent Price standing in front of the tomb on the other. Janice must have taken it out of the book for some reason, but why?"

"It's a puzzle, that's for sure," remarked Phyllis. Suddenly she snapped her fingers. "Do you think Peter Bridges could be the partner? He dropped in here, after all this time . . . Maybe he wanted to check up on Janice's progress? Finalize details for the theft? What do you think?"

My stomach let out a loud growl. "It's hard to think on an empty stomach. All I had today was coffee, a bear claw, and a BLT." I made a face. "But the bacon was burnt and the tomato was tasteless, so it ended up being just an L on toast."

"I only had some toast and tea," said Phyllis. She made the turn onto Main Street. "What do you say? Got time for a late lunch at O'Doul's?"

"Lunch?" I glanced at my watch. "At this hour it's more like an early bird dinner. How about the diner? They have a good meatloaf special today, and the service is pretty fast. I'd like to get back to the store before five, see how it's coming along."

"OK," said Phyllis slowly. "It's just that O'Doul's has something the diner doesn't."

I looked at her. "What would that be? Beer?"

Phyllis's eyes twinkled. "That and one particular customer who usually stops in at O'Doul's for his afternoon Heineken. A customer whose initials are PB."

I stared at her, then my face broke into a wide grin. "You know, I've suddenly acquired a hankering for O'Doul's shepherd's pie. Lead the way."

THIRTEEN

I sent a quick text to Mandy, saying that I'd been delayed and wasn't sure what time I'd make it back to the store, then Phyllis and I headed straight for O'Doul's.

At four in the afternoon, the dining area of the pub was practically deserted, not so the bar area. As we entered, I looked over and saw that nearly every stool was filled. It took me a few minutes, but I finally spotted Peter Bridges. He was seated on a stool at the far left of the bar, nursing a bottle of Heineken. His eyes were glued to the soccer game playing on the flat-screen TV above the bar.

"Why don't you get a table?" I suggested to Phyllis as the hostess approached us. "Order me a shepherd's pie and get yourself whatever you want. It's my treat. Hopefully I won't be long."

Phyllis went off with the hostess and I made my way over to the bar. The man sitting beside Peter rose just as I approached, and I wasted no time claiming the stool. Peter glanced idly over, and then did a double take as he recognized me.

"Charley James! Fancy seeing you here," he said. He gestured toward his near-empty bottle. "How is my favorite bookstore owner? Can I buy you a drink?"

"Allow me," I said as the rosy-cheeked barmaid approached. I smiled at the girl, whose nametag read *GRETCHEN*. "I'll have a Coke, and my friend here will have another Heineken."

Peter looked amused as the barmaid turned away. "A Coke, eh? Live a little, Charley. It's five o'clock somewhere."

"I am living dangerously, Peter. I didn't order Diet."

Peter barked out a laugh. "My dear, you have such a sarcastic wit. I like it."

The barmaid set our drinks in front of us, and I reached into my purse and laid a ten-dollar bill on the bar. I raised my mug of Coke and Peter raised his beer, and we clinked them in the air. Peter took a long swig of his beer and set his bottle back on the bar. "I understand that you visited Maddie Elster recently," I said.

Peter raised one eyebrow. "Oh? I wasn't aware you were acquainted with her."

"I'm not. I only just met her today. I went there with Phyllis Wooster. She was thinking about selling Maddie a book."

Peter snorted. "Was she now? Well, it can't be just any book for Maddie to be interested. It's got to be a rare one."

"Like her Poe book?"

He shot me a look over the rim of his bottle. "Yes. Like that."

"I heard that you visited her hoping to get her to sell her copy."

Peter rolled his eyes. "The gossip chain has been working overtime, I see. Yes, I went there and made another attempt, and I was summarily shot down. I knew Gordon Knight for years and I never knew he was such a Poe fan. If I had, I might have been able to get that copy before he died. Now it just sits there in its glass case when I could be using it in my talks to inform and educate. It made my blood boil to see it just languishing away in that case. To be honest, I toyed with the idea of stealing it."

"You did!"

"I did—but only for a moment. It probably would be easy to figure out the alarm code, but the glass is very thick, and the lock is an EVVA MCS—one of the hardest locks to break."

"Really? Why is that?"

"It's rarely used, and each key has a complex rounded shape. To get access, the key would have to be cloned, which would require the services of a master locksmith. And of course, one would have to get their hand on the original key, which Maddie keeps under tight security." He grinned. "Maybe a professional thief could do it, but not me."

"I have to tell you, you're not the only person around here

with an interest in books on Poe," I said. "A book dealer came to my shop yesterday. He heard that there was a rare Poe book being offered for sale from a private collection around here."

Peter's eyes narrowed and he drummed his fingers on the counter. "So Maddie decided to sell after all, and not to me?" He let out a sigh. "I guess I shouldn't be surprised."

"Maddie didn't know anything about it," I said. "She's not selling her copy."

"No? Then that must mean . . ." His whole face lit up. "Someone else has a copy of that book for sale!"

"It would appear so," I said. "The dealer didn't know who was selling the book. As far as I know, he hasn't been able to track it down."

The elated look vanished from his face, and Peter's brows drew together. "I wish I could find out more about it. As I said, that book would be perfect as a prop for my talks. I've looked everywhere possible with no luck." He scrubbed his hand over his jaw. "I tried to locate the author. That was a waste of time. When I did a search, sites on Gilbert and Sullivan kept popping up. It was obviously a pseudonym." He paused and then added, "I contacted a friend of mine who's pretty tight with some people in the publishing world. He couldn't find out anything about either the book or the author, only that the book was pay to publish." He raised his bottle. "I really don't know why Maddie was so hot over that book. Oh, sure, she's a Poe fan, but her real love is Hitchcock. And that doesn't surprise me, with that weirdo family of hers."

"I've heard that," I said casually. "Are they really that weird?"

"They're definitely an odd bunch." He tapped his beer bottle with one finger. "Maddie is the oldest of the three Elster kids. She wasn't the favorite, though. That honor went to her late sister Amanda. Amanda married a nice guy, Douglas Winchell. Unfortunately, he wasn't cut from the same social cloth as the Elsters and he found it hard to adapt to that lifestyle. He managed to stick with her after their son was born, but he left Amanda shortly after she gave birth to Jewell."

"Yes, we met Jewell today," I said. "So her parents divorced?"

Peter shook his head. "No. Maddie pushed her sister to file for divorce, but they decided on a trial separation. Douglas couldn't live with Amanda, but he couldn't live without her either. She felt the same way about him too. Maddie, though, banned Douglas from the premises when he left her sister. He and Amanda often arranged little trysts, usually at night. Amanda was sneaking out to meet him on one of them when she was killed in that auto accident."

"How terrible!"

"Yes, Maddie felt horribly guilty. That's when she took in Amanda's children." He made a face. "Jewell, a spoiled brat if ever there was one, and then there was her older brother Efram. He became a real problem child after his mother's death, though. So much so that Maddie had him sent off to boarding school. That didn't turn out well either. The kid split one day, and just up and vanished. No one, not even his father, has heard from him in years. There was a rumor floating around that he was killed in Italy in a freak motorcycle accident, but it was never substantiated as far as I know."

"You seem to know a great deal about Douglas Winchell and his family," I said. "Which makes me think that you yourself might have been friendly with Douglas?"

Peter smiled. "Nice deduction, Charley. Yes, Doug and I were tight at one time. We met when he attended a few of my movie lectures. Over the years, though, we have drifted apart."

"I see. Would you know if he keeps in touch with his daughter?"

"I think he'd like to, but Maddie made it clear that if Jewell has anything to do with him, she can kiss any inheritance goodbye. Maddie thinks that Doug would be a less than positive influence on Jewell."

"She did seem rather resentful of her aunt," I said thoughtfully.

"Maddie spoiled Jewell right from the get-go. The kid

dropped out of college and doesn't do a damn thing except shop and spend her monthly allowance. She got a reputation as being quite the party girl, until Maddie put a stop to that a few months ago." Peter let out a sigh. "From what I understand, the kid's a pretty good cook. She wanted to go to culinary school, but that wasn't dignified enough for Maddie. She wants Jewell to go to Vassar and get a business degree."

"Poor Jewell. She could probably use a parental role model right about now."

"That she could, but trust me, it isn't Doug. Last I heard, he'd fallen on pretty hard times—the firm he was working at had to downsize and he lost his job, started drinking again. He'd been sober for a while, but . . . unfortunately it doesn't take much for him to slip back into his old ways."

"What about Maddie's brother?" I interjected. "Phyllis said he was lazy."

"Edmund?" Peter let out a snort. "Edmund certainly personifies the word irresponsible. He's what one calls a perennial student—the quiet, studious type. He's studied at more colleges and gotten more useless degrees than a thermometer. I mean, a doctorate in archaeology? What use is that, unless one works in a museum? It was old man Elster's dying wish that Maddie look after his only son, though, and he made certain that a provision for an allowance for Edmund was written into the will, with specific instructions that should it run out, Maddie was to pick up the slack. From what I understand, he blew through his original inheritance years ago."

"So basically he goes to school and lives off his sister."

Peter tapped his beer bottle against his chin. "And does whatever she tells him to do. He's a good lapdog, that one."

Peter took another sip of his beer, and I took a swig of my Coke. Out of the corner of my eye I saw the waitress go past with a large tray on which rested two shepherd's pies. The aroma was intoxicating, and I heard my stomach give a low growl. Peter grinned. "Their shepherd's pie is amazing," he commented.

"It is, and I think that's my lunch that just went past." I

started to push my glass away, then stopped. I looked Peter right in the eyes. "What do you know about Maddie's staff?"

"Her staff? Well, she pays them extremely well, and in return they give her their undying loyalty. Why do you ask?"

"Just curious," I said. "You hear stories all the time about rich people getting ripped off by members of their staff stealing from them."

He barked out a laugh. "I doubt that would apply to Maddie. Just like her family, she has put the fear of God into all of them so no one would dare double cross her."

I took another swig of Coke and this time I did push the mug away. "Well, I've got to get going. Nice talking to you, Peter."

"Charley." Peter's hand shot out and covered mine. "If you ever hear that Maddie is putting that book up for sale, or if you should come across a copy somewhere, I'd appreciate it if you'd notify me." He reached into his pocket, pulled out a card, and slid it over to me. "My cell number is on the back."

I picked up the card and shoved it into my pocket. "Sure thing, Peter. Have a good day."

I left Peter nursing his beer and hurried over to the table where Phyllis sat. She looked up as I slid onto the bench opposite her. "I was wondering if you'd show up in time to eat," she said, pointing at the two shepherd's pies sitting on the table. "Find out anything?"

"He admitted to going there to ask Maddie about selling that book, and he also mentioned that he briefly considered stealing it. He reconsidered, though, mainly because of the type of lock Maddie has on the case. It's considered practically foolproof."

"Did you believe him?"

I paused, then nodded. "I did. He went into a good deal of detail about Maddie's family. Basically he reiterated what you told me—that they're all odd. He said her staff is very loyal. He didn't think that anyone would dare cross her." I picked up my fork and dug into my pie. "I think a closer look at the family members is in order. Staff too, starting with Janice Rutger."

"I know she's always used the Irene Saunders Employment Agency," ventured Phyllis. "You could give them a call. I don't know how much Irene would tell you, though. She respects her employees' and clients' confidentiality."

"I could still give it a try. I should also talk to Howard Ellis about the handyman he sent over there. Maddie seemed to think he was pretty interested in the book."

"Sounds like you've got a plan." Phyllis shot me a sly look. "You wouldn't by any chance be trying to impress Ian Grant with your sleuthing skills, would you?"

"Bite your tongue," I said. "I just feel responsible, since Janice hid that book in my store and I'm the one who found her body. I feel I should see this through. Of course if I should turn up any leads, I'd turn them over to Detective Grant immediately."

"Of course," said Phyllis as she scooped up the last morsel of pie.

Our waitress returned just then to take our empty plates. "In the mood for dessert?" she asked. "We have an excellent bread pudding special today, and our Irish coffee is half price till six."

"Thanks, but I'm stuffed," I said, rubbing my stomach.

"I am too, but there's always room for a good Irish coffee," said Phyllis. "Come on, Charley. Your store is only five minutes from here. You'll make it back before closing time."

"Oh, all right." I held up two fingers. "Make it two."

Once the waitress had departed, Phyllis waggled her finger at me. "You didn't answer my question. You danced around it."

I shot her an innocent look. "Sorry. What was the question again?"

Phyllis let out an exaggerated sigh. "You wouldn't be trying to impress the good detective with your sleuthing skills, would you, dear?"

I didn't reply, because my attention was suddenly drawn to the bar area, or more accurately, to the man who'd just walked in and sat down at the stool I'd occupied just a short time ago. Even at this distance I couldn't mistake that strong jaw, or that mass of curly brown hair. He was still dressed the same too: Dockers, loafers, and a V-necked sweater.

It was none other than my errant book dealer . . . Jeffrey Thomas, in the flesh.

FOURTEEN

I tore my gaze away from Jeffrey Thomas and looked at Phyllis. "Don't look now," I whispered, "But another person of interest is here. The book dealer himself, Jeffrey Thomas."

"Really! Where?" Phyllis turned toward the bar area and craned her neck to and fro.

"I told you not to look," I chided as I reached out and gave her hand a quick squeeze. "Just casually glance at the far end of the bar. He's on the stool directly opposite the restrooms."

Phyllis glanced casually in that direction then turned back to me. "Oh my! He is good-looking, isn't he? I've got to admit, I'd never take him for a con man."

"We don't know that . . . yet," I said. "I would like to have a word with him about that business card he gave me—why there was no contact info on it."

Phyllis sat up straight. "Well, you just might get that chance. He's headed in this direction."

I glanced up quickly. Jeffrey Thomas was indeed headed straight for our booth. He came to a stop beside us and his lips parted in a dazzling smile as he looked down at us. "Charley James, right? I thought I recognized you. Fancy running into you here."

"Yes, imagine that," I murmured. I felt something jab at my ankle and added, "This is Phyllis Wooster. She owns the coffee shop in town."

"The Jumpin' Beans?" Thomas inclined his head at Phyllis. "I got an iced mocha latte there earlier today. It's definitely a pleasure to meet you. The latte was one of the best I've had in a long time."

"Thanks," Phyllis said. "All the credit goes to Ida, my barista. She was trained in New York."

I looked at Phyllis. "Mr. Thomas is a rare book dealer," I said. I looked back at Thomas. "Phyllis has a collection of first edition Nancy Drew books."

His eyes lit up. "You do? How is the condition? Pristine?"

"Yes, and they all have glossy internals and frontispiece, and the light blue cover. And before you ask, no, I'm not in the market to sell them—at least not yet."

"Well, if you change your mind, I hope you'll think of me," Thomas said with a smile. "I don't have a business card on me right now, but I'm sure Ms. James can share my information with you."

"Oh, I'm sure," Phyllis murmured. She raised her wrist, looked at her watch, and let out a moan. "Oh dear, I'm late for an appointment. I'm so sorry, but I really must dash off." She slid out of the booth and slung her purse over her shoulder. "Nice meeting you, Mr. Thomas. I'll catch up with you later, Charley," she added and tossed me a meaningful look over her shoulder as she hurried out of the tavern.

The waitress returned with the two Irish coffees. "Where did your friend go?" she asked as she set the two mugs down.

"She had to leave." I looked at Thomas. "Are you in the mood for an Irish coffee? It's on me," I added as he hesitated.

His lips twisted into a lopsided grin. "I'm always in the mood for a good Irish coffee, and it's even better when it's free," he said. He reached out and grasped the mug handle. "Thanks."

The waitress left, and we both took a sip of the drink, which I had to admit was delicious. It had just the right balance of Irish whiskey and Kahlua. Thomas appeared to enjoy the drink too. "Man that is good," he said, smacking his lips. "They sure don't skimp on the liquor here."

I savored the flavor on my tongue for a moment before I set my mug down and said, "I'm glad I ran into you, Mr. Thomas. Shortly after you left the shop, I found out some information on a Poe book that could be the one you're looking for. It's called *A Compendium of Poe—Complete Works, plus Stories Adapted for the Screen.*"

Thomas's eyes widened over the rim of his mug. "Why, I do believe that is the name of the book! Don't tell me you managed to locate a copy?" he asked, his tone eager.

"Not exactly," I hedged. "I just happened to hear of someone who owns one. I wanted to tell you about it, but . . ." I reached into my tote and pulled out the business card he'd given me. I laid it down in front of him. "It's a little difficult when there is no contact information."

"No contact information? What do you mean . . .?" His voice trailed off as he looked at the card before him. Two bright spots of color appeared on his cheeks, and he shook his head. "Oh, goodness, is this what I gave you? How embarrassing." He picked up the card and tapped it with his forefinger. "I probably should have mentioned that I'm fairly new to this business. The card I gave you was an early one I had made up—a prototype. I was trying out different typefaces, trying to hone in on the perfect one. Honest, I thought I'd gotten rid of all these."

He ripped the card in half in one swift motion, then dove into his pocket and extracted his wallet. He pulled out a cream-colored card and passed it across the table to me. "Here. I only have this one on me right now, but it's the one I thought I gave you earlier."

I picked up the card. It had images of books, closed and open, across the border. Printed in boldface type were the words:

JEFFREY THOMAS
RARE BOOK DEALER
I BUY ENTIRE COLLECTIONS

Underneath that was a phone number and an email address. But what claimed my attention was the street address in the lower left-hand corner: 12 Princeton Court—Austin Heights, Pennsylvania.

I looked up sharply. "Your office is in Austin Heights?"

"Well, it's not an office per se. I rent a studio apartment in a large house. It's only temporary, until my business takes off.

That's why I only had a limited number of cards made up." He looked at me curiously. "Does the fact I live there bother you for some reason?"

I laid the card back down on the table. "That depends. Do you know a woman named Maddie Elster?"

"Maddie Elster?" Thomas leaned back in his seat. "I don't know her personally, but I have heard about her. She's sort of a legend in that town, and she's supposed to have a rather . . . forceful, shall we say, personality?"

He'd looked me right in the eyes when he answered, so I had the sense he was telling the truth. "No argument there. Princeton Court. I'm not familiar with that street. Is it anywhere near Manor Lane?"

His brow crinkled as he thought. "Manor Lane—I'm not sure. I think I might have passed it once or twice. Why?"

I shrugged. "No reason."

He leaned forward a bit. "Somehow I get the impression you're the type of girl who doesn't just make off-the-cuff remarks."

"It's just that I happened to be in Austin Heights earlier, on Manor Lane, visiting Maddie Elster."

"OK. So?"

"You remember I mentioned I'd heard about someone who owned a copy of the Poe Compendium book?"

Puzzlement shifted to understanding and then to excitement. Jeffrey Thomas leaned across the table and said, "Maddie Elster is the person who owns that book?"

"She has a copy of that book," I said carefully. "It's autographed by both Vincent Price and Boris Karloff. The signatures are legit—she had them authenticated."

Thomas let out a low whistle, and his hand reached up to touch his slightly parted lips. He gave a small shudder then collapsed back in the booth. "Wow! I did not know that. Those autographs would certainly drive up the price of the book."

"Really? How much do you think it would go for?"

Thomas pursed his lips. "A pristine copy with Price and Karloff's signatures? An eager fan could offer as much as two, three thousand. One might even get a bidding war going, all the way up to five, six thousand, maybe."

I drummed my fingers against the tabletop. "That hardly seems like enough to kill over," I murmured.

Thomas's eyes narrowed. "Pardon?"

I waved my hand and smiled. "Oh, nothing. I was just thinking out loud."

Some emotion flickered in Thomas's eyes, but it was gone in an instant, too quickly for me to discern exactly what it might have been. When he spoke, his tone was cool. "I imagine she's not in the market to sell her copy, right?" At my nod he went on, "Well, now that I know about it, maybe I'll pay her a visit, give her one of my cards. I'll tell her to look me up if she is ever in the market to sell." He picked up his Irish coffee, took another long sip, then set the mug back on the table. "Heck, maybe I'll just take a ride over there now. It can't hurt to put the word out, and who knows? Maybe I can convince her to sell her copy. My buyer will pay almost anything, and once they find out it's signed to boot . . ."

I gave my head a decisive shake. "I don't think that would be a very good idea."

He frowned. "Why not?"

"Well, ah . . . she had the beginnings of a terrific headache when we left her. I don't think she'd be in too receptive a state of mind right now."

Thomas frowned. "I wouldn't have to see her today. I could just leave a note and my card," he began, but paused as a jangling tone emanated from his pocket. His hand dipped in and emerged clutching an expensive-looking iPhone. He looked at the screen, then at me. "Excuse me a moment. I've got to take this."

He got up and moved away. The waitress returned and laid the leather holder containing the bill in the middle of the table. I pulled the leather holder in front of me, but I didn't open it. Instead I folded my hands on top of it, pondering what had just transpired. Jeffrey Thomas's explanations seemed plausible enough, and yet there was something about him that just didn't hit me right. Something was definitely off, but just what that something was, I couldn't yet discern. A shadow across the table jarred me back to reality, and Thomas tossed me an apologetic smile as he slid back into his seat.

"Sorry," he said. "I had to take that." He inclined his head toward the leather holder. "I insist you allow me to pay. Consider it my treat."

"That really isn't necessary," I demurred.

"No, I insist." He reached out and pulled the leather holder in front of him. He opened it, looked at the bill, and then reached into his pocket again for his wallet. He took out two twenties and slid them inside the holder, then pushed it back across to me. "It's the least I can do for the tip you gave me on the book."

I started to protest when yet another shadow fell across the table—I looked up and almost groaned aloud when I met Barbie's frosty gaze.

"Charley." Her gaze flicked briefly over Jeffrey Thomas, then back to me. "I've been texting you. Don't you ever look at your phone?"

I shot her what I hoped was a contrite expression. "I am sorry, Detective Donaldson. I—ah—had an important meeting this afternoon, and I shut my phone off."

"Well, will you be home tonight? I managed to get in touch with Zane and she said she'd be there."

I folded my hands in front of me on the table. "I have no plans. I just need to stop by the store, see how the cleanup is coming along."

"Good. I'll be there around seven thirty with my fingerprint guy." She glanced over at the bar area. "Excuse me, I see my order is ready."

Barbie turned on her heel and walked over to the bar. "Swell," I muttered at her retreating back. "Just how I wanted to spend my evening."

Thomas was looking at me with renewed interest. "I'm sorry—did I hear wrong, or did she say she'd be at your home later with her fingerprint guy?"

"Nothing wrong with your hearing. Yep, that's what she said."

Thomas scratched his temple. "If you don't mind my asking, why does that detective want your fingerprints?"

"There was a break-in at my store. They need our prints to eliminate them from any they find. It's routine, really."

Thomas's eyes widened. "A break-in, huh? That's a shame. I hope there wasn't much damage."

"There was enough."

"I'm truly sorry to hear that. I liked your store." He glanced at his watch and slid out of the booth. "I'm sorry, but I really have to get going. Keep me posted if you hear about another copy of that book." He gave me a slow grin. "You have my contact info now."

He strode over to the bar and paused to speak to the bartender. On an impulse, I pulled my phone out, switched to camera mode, and snapped a quick photo of him. As Thomas left the bar I sank back in my seat. What had I learned from this meeting? That Jeffrey Thomas was apparently careless where business cards were concerned, and that he apparently operated his business out of his residence—which just happened to be in the same vicinity as the Elster residence.

Coincidence?

I was reminded of a quote by Emma Bull, something about levers and pulleys. It certainly seemed as if there was some unseen force at work here, but what?

I pulled the check holder over to me and looked inside. Apparently Thomas wasn't a big tipper. I added a ten to the two twenties and then slid out of the booth. I'd barely taken two steps toward the front door when a voice suddenly called out, "Charley James! Wait up!" I turned around and saw Riley May Connor balancing a paper bag in one hand, striding purposefully toward me from the bar. I stifled a groan. Could this day get any better?

"What luck," she crowed. "Running into you."

"Yeah, it's incredible. What can I do for you, Riley?"

"I heard that you and Phyllis Wooster took a little field trip out to Maddie Elster's house today."

I stared at her. "Riley May Connor, are you following me?"

She put her hand to her heart and gave me a look of mock

terror. "Goodness no! I'd never do that. I just happened to be in Austin Heights visiting my aunt. She lives a few blocks from Maddie Elster's house, and I saw the two of you leave." She paused and looked at me expectantly.

I said the first thing that popped into my head. "Maddie is a book collector. She had some questions about a book."

"O-K," Riley said after a moment. "And Phyllis Wooster was there because—?"

"I'd never met Maddie before, and Phyllis knows her," I said. I couldn't help but feel a little thrill of satisfaction at the disappointed look that crossed Riley's face. "Sorry to disappoint you, Riley, but that's all there was to it."

I started to move away, but Riley fell into step beside me. "Any news about the break-in? Have the police honed in on any suspects?"

Would I never be rid of this woman? "Not that I know of."

She leaned closer to me. "I couldn't help but overhear your conversation with Detective Donaldson," she said. "Why does she need your fingerprints? Don't tell me the police suspect you of trashing your own store?"

I gritted my teeth and said slowly, "No, they just need mine and Zane's to eliminate them from any other prints they turn up."

Riley nodded. "That makes sense." She started to turn away and then paused. "Say, that guy you were sitting in the booth with—how well do you know him?"

"Not that well. He came into the shop yesterday inquiring about rare books. He's a book dealer."

"Oh." She tapped her chin with her forefinger. "I'm not absolutely sure, but I thought I saw him standing across the street from your bookstore the night it was trashed. I could be wrong—I mean, it was dark, and I only got a glimpse before he took off but . . ." She shrugged. "He just seems familiar to me." She glanced at her watch and let out a yelp. "Sorry, I've got to go." She held up the paper bag. "The troops are getting hungry."

Riley hurried away, and I paused for a moment, thinking. If Riley had seen Thomas lurking around my store that night, then maybe he could have been the one who'd trashed it? His sympathetic reaction could have been an act, and if so, it might be possible he'd been Janice's partner—and very possibly her killer.

FIFTEEN

It was after five when I reached my shop, and the first thing I did was pause to take a look at the picture window. It was evident that Mandy and Jake had spent a good deal of time on the display. A large shower curtain hung down from a rod on one side of the window, a hand holding a large knife protruding from a tear in the center. A few feet away, two mannequins hunched in fear as black birds, suspended by a wire on the ceiling, swarmed around their heads. And on the far side, a mannequin in a wheelchair with a camera slung around its neck faced a large cut-out picture window overlooking what appeared to be a tall building with many windows. The silhouette of a man holding a carving knife was outlined in one of them. All the Hitchcock books were arranged between the exhibits, as well as DVDs of the movies. I chuckled as I caught sight of the sign in the corner of the window: ***DVDs display only. NOT FOR SALE!***

I moved over to the door where another sign greeted me. *Closed. Will re-open soon.* I twisted my key in the lock and pushed open the door. Braedon had been looking at something on the computer behind the counter, but his head jerked up the moment the door opened. The look of annoyance on his face quickly morphed into a smile. "Hey, Charley. We didn't think you'd make it back here today."

I walked over and set my purse on the counter. "I wasn't sure about that either," I admitted. "My errand took longer than I expected."

Braedon waved a hand in the air. "Hey, no need to apologize. You're the boss. Anyway, everything's under control. All the shelves are restocked, and the entire store has been vacuumed and dusted."

I glanced around and pointed to the orange and black streamers hanging from the ceiling. "And decorated too, I see."

"Oh yeah. There are some plastic bats hanging from the ceiling in the back, and a skeleton and a witch near the children's section. I set up the Halloween tree on the table and arranged the Poe books around it. I found some orange and black balls and hung them on the tree, but I still think it needs something more."

"Betty mentioned she had a spare raven," I said. "I'll see if I can get it from her tomorrow."

Braedon smiled. "A raven would be perfect," he said. He nodded toward the window. "That's the pièce de résistance, though. Doesn't it look great?"

"It does," I agreed. "Mandy and Jake certainly did an excellent job."

"Mandy did the lion's share," Braedon said. "Jake got a call and had to take off. Anna and I helped out a bit in between cleaning and restocking, but that window is all hers." He grinned. "Except for the sign about the DVDs. That was my contribution."

"She certainly put in a lot of work. Where on earth did she get that wheelchair?"

"A customer from the diner who volunteers at the hospital got it for her," said Braedon. "One of the wheels is broken and they were going to scrap it. And she got that drawing of the apartment house from another customer of hers at the diner. He's an art major at the university."

"Her customers certainly are good to her," I remarked.

Braedon winked. "Of course they are. They're both good-looking guys who go to the university. The one who volunteers at the hospital is pre-med. And if you ask me, they both have crushes on her too." He hesitated and then said, "I hope things are all right between Mandy and Jake."

I looked at him. "What makes you say that?"

"Well, I overheard him on a call the other day. He was mumbling into the phone, but I'm sure I heard him call whoever he was talking to 'Ree-Ree.' From the tone of his voice it sounded as if he might be calling someone by a pet name."

I frowned. "You probably just didn't hear right," I said.

Braedon drew himself up straight. "I have ears like a bat,"

he said. "Anyway, from the tone of Jake's voice—I don't know—"

"It was probably a family member, a cousin or something. He seems crazy about Mandy." I glanced around the store. "Say, where is everyone, anyway?"

"Well, you just missed Anna. She left five minutes ago, and I had to practically push her out the door. And Mandy left shortly before that."

"Well, we're going to open tomorrow for a half day, one to five. Then Friday we're back to regular hours. Anna's off tomorrow, and I'll let Mandy know, so you go on home now, Braedon, and thank you for all your help."

Braedon left and I went back behind the counter. I perched on the stool and shot off a quick text to Mandy, informing her that we'd be open for business tomorrow and telling her the reduced hours. I'd no sooner sent the text than my phone buzzed with an incoming call—from Mandy. I hit the accept button and said, "The window looks fabulous."

"You like it? Oh, I'm so glad," Mandy said. "We worked on it all day."

I didn't bother to tell her that I knew she'd done most of the work. "I'm glad you called," I said. "Did you get my text about opening at one tomorrow?"

"Yep. I just wanted to know how you liked the window. Anyway, I've got to go. Jake is taking me to that new Italian place in Scotswood tonight. Aperitivo."

"Ooh, fancy," I said. "Are you going to wear your gown with the long train? And a diamond tiara?"

Mandy giggled. "No, I'll just settle for that new black dress I bought and the new earrings Jake gave me." She made a smacking sound with her lips. "I can't wait to try their house specialty, roasted chicken with gnocchi ala Romana. Irene Saunders had it and she says it's to die for."

My ears perked up. "Irene Saunders? Not the same Irene Saunders who owns the Saunders Employment Agency?"

"Yes, she's one of my good customers at the diner. She's a real foodie. We always have such good conversations—before Lenny shouts at me to get back to work." Lowering her lashes she added, “Irene even offered me a job working in her office, but I told her that I was happy working at the diner and your bookstore.”

“I’m happy to hear that,” I said. “But if you think I’m holding you back . . .”

“Oh, no, not at all,” Mandy said. “I’m not sure a nine-to-five desk job is for me. I like interacting with people. Anyway, I better get going. Jake will be here any minute and I’ve got to finish my makeup. I’ll see you tomorrow.”

Mandy hung up and I just sat a moment, tapping my phone against my chin. I turned to the computer and called up the Saunders Employment Agency website. It was a few minutes after six, too late for regular office hours, but there was a number for after-hours inquiries. I dialed it, and after three rings a sweet voice said, “Saunders Employment Agency. Irene Saunders speaking. How may I help you?”

“Ms. Saunders, my name is Charlotte James. I own a bookstore here in Austin, Mainely Mysteries, and my clerk Mandy Thatcher has spoken very highly of you. She thought perhaps you might be able to help me with some . . . information.”

“Oh yes, I’ve heard about your store,” Irene said. “I know Mandy works there. She’s such a sweetheart! I tried to steal her away from you, but she didn’t want to leave.” She paused for a breath and then said, “So just what is it Mandy thought I could help you with? You said something about information?”

“I’ve been trying to get in touch with a woman who worked for Maddie Elster, and I understand Ms. Elster hires most of her staff from your agency. Mandy thought that if she did come from your agency, you might be willing to give me her contact information.”

“Oh.” There was a moment of silence and then Irene said, “Wouldn’t Ms. Elster be able to help you with that?”

“I asked, but Ms. Elster has a new secretary who unfortunately erased all the files on non-employees,” I said quickly.

“That’s too bad,” said Irene.

I could hear the hesitation in her voice, so I said quickly, “I’m anxious to locate her because she ordered a rather expensive book from me which just came in. I need to know if she still wants it. My distributor only gives me a certain window to return the book for credit."

My appeal to her sense of business paid off. "I can certainly understand that," said Irene. Another pause and then, "What is this woman's name?"

"Janice Rutger."

Irene repeated it. "It doesn't sound familiar," she said. "Then again, Maddie has hired so many people over the years. I'll have to go through my records and get back to you. Do you have a number I can text you on?"

I gave her my cell number, thanked her, and hung up. Then I wrote myself a note to get Mandy a gift card to her favorite restaurant, Bangkok Wok—although after her dinner tonight with Jake, that might well change!

Poe greeted me as I let myself in the back door. He let out a plaintive meow, making me painfully aware his dinner was late. "Sorry," I said to the cat. "I had a very interesting afternoon, but that's no excuse." I bent and gave him a pat on the head. "Don't worry, I'll rustle up something good for you to eat."

Poe cocked his head, and then followed me over to the refrigerator, as if to ensure I kept my word. I'd prepared some meals for him in plastic containers on the bottom shelf. I removed one containing smoked salmon and held it up. "How's this?"

Poe let out a loud purr.

I spooned the salmon into his bowl. Poe hunkered down with another contented purr. After that shepherd's pie I wasn't a bit hungry, but I could use some iced tea. I'd just pulled the pitcher out of the fridge when the doorbell rang. I glanced at the clock. It was only a little after seven. I frowned as I remembered Barbie mentioning she'd be dropping by with her fingerprint guy. "Swell," I muttered. "Although it's best to get it over with." I went to the front door and peeped out the side window. My breath caught in my throat when I saw who was standing there—definitely not Barbie. I swung the door open and stood, hands on hips. "Wh–what are *you* doing here?" I cried.

Ian Grant tipped his head. "And a good evening to you, too, Charlotte."

My frown deepened. "I thought you were away today and coming by tomorrow."

"I got done early, so I thought I'd swing by," Grant said. "I really think that the sooner I take possession of that book, the better."

I swallowed. "Zane isn't home yet," I said.

"I passed by the bakery on my way here. It looked as if she were locking up, so I'm sure she'll be here any moment now." He angled his head at the door. "Might I come in?"

I leaned against the door. "I actually thought you were Bar—Detective Donaldson," I blurted. "She said she'd be coming by tonight with a fingerprint guy," I said.

He looked amused. "So you're disappointed I'm not Detective Donaldson? No worries, I'm sure she'll be along later. In the meantime, may I come in?"

I moved aside to let him enter. As he passed, his body brushed for a fleeting instant against mine, and I felt an electric shock go through me. I pushed a hand through my tumble of russet curls and waved my other hand in the air.

"We can wait in the living room for Zane," I said.

Grant followed me into the living room. I motioned for him to take a seat. He settled himself comfortably on the loveseat, and I perched myself on the arm of a chair opposite. There were a few moments of strained silence and then I cleared my throat. "So—any progress on the case?"

He shot me a look. "You know I can't share that information," he said.

"I know the rules. I just thought maybe you could make an exception for the person who discovered the body."

"Once again, I can't share information with a civilian, even one as observant as you."

"I take it that's your way of paying me a compliment?"

"Perhaps. I will say this, though." Grant pinned me with his stormy gaze. "According to the confirmed time of death, you arrived on the scene minutes after it occurred."

"Really?" I frowned. "That must mean . . ."

"That you didn't miss the murderer by much," he finished. He moved a bit closer to me. "You know, it really would have upset me if I'd been standing over your dead body as well."

I swallowed, aware of his closeness, and the aroma of his aftershave. "Would it have really upset you?" I whispered.

"Yes," he said softly. For a moment we gazed intently into each other's eyes, our lips only inches away. We stood like that for what seemed to me an eternity, and then Ian coughed lightly and took a step back. "So I'd appreciate it if you could just go back over that evening's events. Did you happen to notice anyone hurrying away from that floor? Or anything else suspicious?"

That was my cue to come clean and tell Grant everything I knew about Janice and the book, the jewelry I'd found hidden, and the second driver's license in the name of Jane Radcliffe. Maybe even broach my theory that she might have been killed by her partner, but probably not over Maddie Elster's jewelry.

So, of course, I said nothing.

I looked him right in the eyes and said, "I'm sorry. I didn't notice anything unusual, or anyone hurrying away from the scene of the crime."

He looked at me searchingly for a few moments, and then nodded. "OK."

I breathed an inward sigh of relief. "I'm sorry," I said. "I wish I could be of more help."

That searching look again. "Do you?" he asked softly.

I swayed toward him, just a tad. "You know I do," I said. "Do you want me to prove it?"

Once again I was mesmerized by his gaze. "Not necessary . . . unless you want to." His voice was husky. "What do you want to help me with, Charlotte?"

He lowered his head until his lips hovered right above mine. "What I want," I whispered, and then we both heard a door slam and then Zane popped into the living room. We quickly broke apart before she saw us and let out a sigh.

She pointed a finger at Grant. "Oh, good, you're here. I can't wait to get rid of that book."

I bit down on my lip in frustration. The moment had passed.

Would there be another? I stole a quick glance at Ian and, from the expression on his face, wondered if he was thinking the same thing. Rats! It seemed as if our timing was always off.

Zane walked over to the painting and moved it to reveal the wall safe. She spun the dial and, a few moments later, pulled out the book, which she immediately held out to Grant. "Here," she said. "It's all yours."

Grant took the book and looked at it. He frowned. "So this is what all the fuss is about? A book about Edgar Allan Poe? And a cheesy-looking one at that."

I leaned across him and flipped to the title page. "It's autographed by Vincent Price," I said. "And one of Boris Karloff's photos has his autograph too."

"Nice," said Grant. "So our thief is a Poe and horror movie fan?"

"Possibly." I retrieved Jeffrey Thomas's card and handed it to him. "I happened to run into that book dealer today. He gave me a new card with contact info. You might want to have a chat with him."

Grant looked at the card, then stuck it in his pocket. "I'll do that, thanks." He tucked the book under his arm. "I've got to be going. I want this under lock and key as soon as possible. Ladies. Have a good evening."

"Oh, I will now," sang out Zane as she hurried up the stairs to her room.

I walked him to the front door, where he paused and laid a hand on my shoulder. That weird electric sensation coursed through me again as I looked up at him. "I mean it, Charlotte. If you should remember anything about that evening, anything at all, I'd appreciate it if you'd get in touch with me."

"You'll be the first person I'll call."

"I certainly hope so," he said. "You're a brave woman, Charlotte James, but you're also stubborn. Too stubborn for your own good, I think."

"Aw gee, and those are my good qualities," I said.

His gaze bored into mine, and I felt my knees start to weaken. "I just wouldn't want to see you get yourself into a . . . situation. One you couldn't handle."

"Thanks for your concern, but I'm a big girl. I've been on my own for quite a while. I'm pretty good at handling difficult situations."

"I have no doubt of that. Just . . . be careful. There's a killer out there, somewhere, and like I said, I'd hate to be standing over your dead body next."

I tried to suppress a shudder but failed. "I'll be careful."

He held up the book. "Just to be on the safe side, I'm still going to have a squad car go by here every hour for the next few days. No sense in taking unnecessary chances."

"Thank you. Zane will be relieved to hear that."

He tucked the book back under his arm. "And you? Are you relieved too?"

I ducked my head. "Of course. Thank you for your concern. You have a good evening now, Detective."

He shot me a devilish grin. "I know how I could have a better one. How *we* could."

Once again, he dipped his head to mine. I raised my chin, closed my eyes in delicious anticipation, and then . . . a knock on the door!

"This is incredible," muttered Ian. He flung open the door, and we saw Barbie standing there. There was a short stocky guy with her, and I recognized him as one of the fingerprint techs who'd been at the store.

"Detective Grant," she said. She angled her gaze at me. "Charley."

The corners of Grant's lips twitched upward. "Detective. Ms. James was rather disappointed to see me earlier instead of you."

"Yeah?" Barbie raised an eyebrow and looked at me, taking in my flushed cheeks. "Somehow I doubt that."

Grant chuckled. "I'll leave you to your business. Good night again." He shot me a longing look, and then he was gone.

Once the door closed behind Ian, Barbie looked at me. "Zane is here, I hope?"

"Yes, she's upstairs."

"Good. Get her and let's get this over with, shall we?"

Thankfully the procedure didn't take long—less than ten

minutes. As the tech packed up his equipment, Barbie looked at both Zane and me. "Thank you for your cooperation, Zane, Charley," she said. "We'll be in touch when we have some news to report."

I bet you will, I thought, but I just smiled sweetly and said, "Thank you. As usual, it's been a pleasure doing business with you, Detective."

"Yeah? I wish I could say the same," Barbie muttered. She gave me a black look as she swept out, followed by the tech. Once they were outside, I shut the door—hard.

Zane chuckled. "Well, that was an experience. Did she seem to be acting odder than usual?"

"I don't think Detective Donaldson is entirely convinced that I had nothing to do with trashing my own store," I remarked. "And as much as I hate to admit it, she's partially right."

Zane looked at me, wide-eyed. "What do you mean, Charley? How could you be responsible for that?"

"Because whoever did it was, no doubt, searching for the book Janice Rutger left in my store. They obviously assumed that I wouldn't find it."

Zane shuddered. "Well, no one made an attempt to trash the house, so maybe they don't know you found it."

"Either that, or they didn't know where I lived," I said.

Zane's jaw dropped. "Oh gosh, you're right, Charley! And if they don't know you turned it over to the police, why . . . they could still come here looking for it."

"Don't worry, Grant thought of that. He's still going to have a squad car go by every hour for a few more days, just in case."

Zane blew out a sigh of relief. "Thank goodness. OK, I'm going to heat up that leftover mac and cheese for dinner. Should I make a salad too?"

"I had a late lunch with Phyllis, so I'm not hungry. Just make something for yourself."

As Zane busied herself in the kitchen, I went back into the living room, kicked off my shoes, and hunkered down on the sofa, Poe beside me. My phone buzzed with an incoming text. I looked at the screen and my heart leapt when I saw it was from Irene Saunders: Sorry to report no one named Janice

Rutger was employed by Maddie Elster through our agency. We have no record of anyone by that name.

I nibbled my lower lip. "Well, she had to have come from somewhere," I said to Poe. "And Maddie was such a stickler for references, she wouldn't have hired just anyone." I sighed. "I guess I'm going to have to bite the bullet and ask her."

But before I could dial her number, my phone rang, and the caller ID showed the name of Madeleine Elster. I hit the accept icon eagerly. "Maddie, I was just about to call you," I said.

"Yeah? Well, I just wanted to let you know that my jewels have been recovered. An officer stopped by earlier to let me know."

Ah, so they had found them. "That's great, Maddie."

"The officer said someone would let me know when I could have them." She paused and then added, "You said you were about to call me? What about? News on my missing book, I hope. I've got to tell you; it took all my willpower not to tell that police officer about it. I still think . . ."

I cut her off. "I forgot to ask you something. How did you happen to hire Janice Rutger?"

"I deviated from my normal routine for that one." Maddie sighed. "I usually use a reputable agency and do multiple checks. But Janice had such good references—plus her former employer was unimpeachable. Hah! It just goes to show, you can't be too careful these days. I wonder what she stole from *him*."

I was starting to get a funny feeling deep in my gut. "Just who was Janice's former employer, Maddie? Do you remember?"

"Well, of course I do." Maddie sounded insulted. "It was Gordon Knight."

SIXTEEN

"Gordon Knight?" I cried out. "The same Gordon Knight who originally owned the Poe Compendium?"

"Of course that Gordon Knight," Maddie said, her tone somewhat impatient. "Obviously the man was taken in by the little con artist. I'm starting to wonder if he even wrote that glowing letter of recommendation she showed me."

"Wasn't he already dead when she came to work for you?"

"Yes, but she said that he knew he was ill, so he wrote her this letter before he died, so that she'd be certain of getting gainful employment. I know he did it for some of his other staff, so . . . I never even bothered to have her checked out. Well, I'll *never* make that mistake again, let me tell you!" She let out a long, deep sigh. "Well, no sense crying over spilled milk. At least I know I'll get my precious gems back, although it will probably be later than sooner. I imagine they have to find out who murdered the little witch first." She coughed lightly. "I'm sorry, Charley, but I really think it's a mistake not to tell the authorities about my missing book."

"It's not a mistake, I promise you," I said quickly. I could tell Maddie was on the verge of changing her mind. "Please, please don't notify anyone yet that your book is missing. You promised to give me time to look into it."

"I don't know. You investigating on your own could be dangerous. I would hate to feel responsible if anything should happen to you."

"I'll be very careful, I promise."

Maddie hung up, and I leaned back on the sofa. I shook my head to clear it, and then proceeded to make some sense out of my jumbled thoughts. What had I learned so far?

That Janice Rutger had also worked for Gordon Knight, which meant she could have known about the Poe book. She might have intended to steal it sooner, but Knight locked it away in that chest. Janice must have found out that Maddie bought that chest, and I had no doubt she'd faked that letter so she could get into her employ. I ran my hand through my hair. "Maybe the place I should start with is Gordon Knight."

I pulled the laptop back in front of me and googled Gordon Knight. A ton of hits appeared on the screen—ninety-five pages, to be exact—so I did another search to narrow it down—Gordon Knight, Scientist, Austin, Pennsylvania. This time I got thirty pages of hits. I started scrolling through them. I saw that Knight had a website, so I went there first. Someone had put a brief disclaimer on the title page, listing Knight's dates of birth and death. There was a notation that the scientist had passed "quietly, following a brief illness." I clicked on the "About Me" page. At the top was a photograph of a good-looking man in his late fifties, military haircut, and close-cropped moustache. Below was a short biography: Gordon S. Knight had been educated at Cornell University, graduating with a degree in advanced chemistry. From there he'd gotten a Master's at Johns Hopkins and then crossed the pond to England to obtain a Doctorate of Biochemistry at the University of Oxford. He'd started his career as an analytical chemist at a large company in England and worked his way up to senior chemist. He then accepted a position with Axitrom Chemicals, heading up their Chemistry-Research Department. Everything in the biography was strictly about work. He was unmarried, no children. He'd had a sister, deceased, who'd had one daughter. No names were given. The bio did mention that Knight visited the Axitrom Chemicals lab in Los Angeles frequently. I wondered if he'd met Price and Karloff on one of those trips and gotten the actors to sign his book.

Below the biography was a list of articles that Knight had published in various scientific journals.

There was another page on the website called "Photographs." I clicked on that. A collage of photos came up, mostly showing Gordon Knight receiving one award or another. Near the bottom of the page were a few photographs depicting Knight in casual dress. In one he was surrounded by some other men.

The caption read, *The Gang and I at our Weekly Hangout—The Down and Out, Old Saybrook.*

Old Saybrook was about twenty minutes from here. I continued reading the caption. *From left to right, Arnold Mintzer, Harold Phleb, Gordon Knight, Douglas Winchell . . .*

I paused. Douglas Winchell was the name of Maddie's brother-in-law. I squinted at the photograph. It was slightly grainy, but I could make out enough to tell Douglas Winchell had ruddy cheeks, wore thick tortoise-framed glasses and, judging from the bottle in his hand, was a Heineken man.

"I wonder," I murmured, tapping my chin. "Could this be the same Douglas Winchell?" I hated to call Maddie again, but I didn't know of anyone else who might know. I grabbed my iPhone and was just about to punch in Maddie's number when a sudden thought occurred to me. I got out my jacket and pulled out the card Peter Bridges had given me earlier.

I dialed the cell number on the back, and a few minutes later a male voice barked, "Bridges here."

"Hello, Peter, it's Charley James."

Peter laughed. "Either you miss my company or you've found another copy of that Poe book for sale," he said, a hopeful note in his voice.

"I'm sorry, I haven't found another copy of the book. I just wanted to pick your brain about something."

"You're in luck. I'm only watching *Jeopardy*, and I swear it's a re-run. Pick away, my dear."

"It's about Douglas Winchell. You said you used to be friends with him. Would you happen to know if he was also friendly with Gordon Knight?"

There was a long moment of silence and then Peter replied, "Well, they were friendly at one point. Douglas had been laid off, and Gordon took him on as an accountant." Peter paused and then continued, "He'd only had the job a few months when Gordon abruptly fired him. That started him drinking again."

"Oh my goodness," I cried. "Do you know why he was fired?"

"Douglas never said, and I never asked. With Gordon it

could have been anything." Peter coughed lightly. "Gordon had a temper—that I know. Doug said he threw a fit once when he caught him looking at some of the rare books in his collection. Threw him out of the library and told him to mind his own business."

"Really? Did Doug mention what books?"

"No. I didn't press him for details. He was quite upset over it, and Gordon fired him shortly after. I thought maybe he'd hire him back one day, but then Gordon apparently took ill and died soon after." Peter paused. "Why are you so interested in Douglas, might I ask?"

"Oh, I was just curious. I was surfing through the Internet, and I happened upon a photograph of him and Gordon Knight in a bar."

"The Down and Out." Peter gave a curt nod. "Used to be their little gang's gathering place. I think Doug might still go there on a Wednesday. Beers are half price."

I thanked Peter and hung up, then curled up in my chair. I was betting that one of the books Gordon had gotten upset over Doug looking at was the Poe Compendium. Janice Rutger and Winchell had both worked for Knight. Odds were good they might have known each other—the question was, how well? Well enough to join forces to steal the Poe book? Doug might have enjoyed sticking it to his former sister-in-law, as well as acquiring one of his former employer's valuable possessions—particularly one that might have cost him his job.

But, if Janice had attempted to double cross him and sell the book on her own, was Douglas Winchell capable of murder?

That was what I had to find out. And tonight was Wednesday. I pushed back my chair and stood up.

I was in the mood for a half-price beer. And I knew just where to get one.

A half hour later I pulled into the parking lot of the Down and Out. The bar, with its white frame, gray trim, and dark wooden shutters might have received an accolade or two as one of the top ten bars in Pennsylvania, but it still didn't look like much—which was probably part of its charm. The bar owners had gone for the kind of simple décor that could only be improved with peanut shells on the floor and the promise of half-price beer two nights a week.

I pushed through the front door and stood for a moment, letting my eyes adjust to the dark interior. The bar was packed, in sharp contrast to the seating area, which was only half-full. There was an empty stool way over on the far end, near the kitchen door. I made my way over to it and slid onto the stool next to a frowzy blonde-haired woman in too-tight NYDJ jeans and a blouse that was low-cut enough to show a generous glimpse of her "girls." I waved a hand at the bartender, a large, bearded man who looked like he'd be more at home refereeing a wrestling match. He made his way over to me, slung his towel over one shoulder, and placed both hands flat on the bar counter. The smile he shot me was somewhere between a leer and a grin. "Well, pretty lady. What can I get you?"

I tugged a bit self-consciously at the gold chain around my neck and glanced at the nametag pinned to his shirt. "What's on tap, Dale?"

Dale cocked a shaggy brow at me. "We've got over one hundred different varieties of beer here, Miss. What are you in the mood for?"

I leaned across the counter. "Tell you what. Surprise me."

The corners of his thick lips twitched upward, and his gaze flicked briefly over my breasts before he replied. "OK, then."

A few minutes later he set a frosty mug in front of me, along with a small bowl of salted peanuts. I looked at the mug. The beer was a rich amber color. I lifted the mug to my lips and took a tentative sip. "Wow," I said. "That's really good. What is that?"

"Boulevard Pale Ale. It's a smooth, fruity, well-balanced beer. I figured you'd like it."

I raised my mug. "You figured right. Thanks, Dale."

"No problem. You need anything else, just yell." He closed one eye in a broad wink and shot another quick glance at my chest before shuffling off to the other end of the bar.

The blonde turned and gave me the once-over. "Man, you sure have Dale wrapped around your little finger," she remarked.

Her tone was gravelly, like she'd inhaled years of cigarette smoke. "He's usually not that nice to newbies." She looked me up and down. "You're definitely a newbie. Never seen you in here before."

I let my shoulders lift in a casual shrug. "I heard about Half-Price Beer Night. Thought I'd try it."

She made a guttural sound in her throat that might have been a snort and turned back to her companion, a large, beefy-looking guy in a white t-shirt wearing a Pittsburgh Pirates ball cap. Someone had put money in the jukebox in the corner, and Billy Joel belting out "Uptown Girl" filled the already noisy room.

I glanced casually around the bar as I drank my beer. A couple of women, attired in tight dresses, were shimmying in front of the jukebox, bottles of Bud in hand. Far off to the right, four guys in well-worn t-shirts and jackets were arguing over who'd end up in the Super Bowl this year. My gaze traveled up and down the length of the bar, but I didn't see anyone who resembled the photograph of Douglas Winchell. It would be my luck he'd skip Half-Price Beer Night this week.

Dale reappeared and nodded toward my almost empty mug. "Need a refill?"

"Please."

I handed him the mug. He returned a minute later with a fresh one, which he put in front of me, along with another bowl of peanuts. I grabbed a fistful of nuts and popped one into my mouth. "You worked here long?" I asked.

"Ten years. Put myself through college and then decided the tips here were too good to go into teaching. So I do CPA work at tax time, and the rest of the time I work here."

I gave a casual glance around. "I imagine most of these folks have been coming here for years?"

"Some of 'em were here before me," he said with a laugh. "Most are pretty good tippers, too."

I reached into my quilted crossbody bag and pulled out the photograph I'd printed out before I left my house. I slid it across the counter. "Ever see any of those guys in here?"

He squinted at the photo. "It's a little grainy, but . . . oh yeah. I remember him." He pointed a stubby finger at Gordon Knight. "The scientist. He used to come in a lot. Except toward the end, when he got sick. He was a good tipper." He rubbed his chin with his hand. "I remember one night he got really soused and started mumbling something about the seventies. 'Seventy-seven's my baby,' he said. 'And eleven's my key. Got to keep it safe.'" He shrugged. "That guy loved to talk in riddles. It used to aggravate the hell out of his buddies."

Riddles indeed. Seventy-seven was the number of the page that had been torn out of Maddie's book. As for eleven, I had no clue—and I couldn't get to either book to see if page eleven were still intact. Aloud I said, "I bet. So the other guys in this photo—they still come in here?"

"One by one they stopped coming in—except for him." He tapped his finger against Doug Winchell's face. "He still comes in here quite a bit. Most nights I have to call a cab for him. He doesn't live far, but I still don't want to risk him driving that beat-up heap of his half-crocked. It's a shame."

I picked up the photo and slid it back into my purse. "Has Mr. Winchell been in here recently?"

"He practically owns that stool you're sitting on," Dale said with a smirk.

"Has he been here tonight?"

Now his eyes narrowed. "Why do you want to know? Are you a bill collector or something?"

I waved my hand. "Oh, no, nothing like that. I'm . . . friendly with his late wife's family. They haven't seen him in a while, and they're concerned about him."

"Concerned, huh? From the way Doug talked about them, I didn't think they wanted anything to do with him. His sister-in-law for sure." Dale shook his head. "I heard she's a real piece of work. And as far as his kids go, he hadn't spoken with his daughter in months. And the son's practically non-existent."

"That's all true," I admitted. "But his sister-in-law and daughter have recently come to regret the way they've acted toward him. They, ah, needed someone to test the waters. See how the reception would be."

He slung his towel across his shoulder and angled his chin toward the rear of the bar. "Well, you can find out for yourself. He usually sits here at the bar, but he's in one of the back booths tonight. Had to meet someone, he said."

Meet someone? Who? I wondered. Two men at the other end of the bar waved and Dale ambled off toward them. I put a tenner on the counter, then picked up my mug and casually started to stroll toward the restrooms. There were two booths in that area. One had a man and a woman, who were engaged in a deep conversation, a platter of fajitas untouched on the table in front of them. Judging from the sappy look on both their faces, it was a romantic interlude.

Sitting alone in the second booth was a man. He was slumped over, his head bent, a Yankees baseball cap pulled down low over his face. I walked past slowly, but I couldn't tell from the angle the man was sitting at if he could be Douglas Winchell or not.

A pretty raven-haired waitress in a short skirt paused before the booth. She wrapped her knuckles on the table. "Hey, hon. Another usual?"

The man's head jerked up. He pushed back the cap on his forehead. "Please."

The waitress grabbed the mug and hurried off toward the bar. The man pulled the cap back over his eyes and slumped back in his seat, but not before I'd gotten a good look at his face.

He was slimmer than in the photograph I'd seen, but the features were the same. It was Douglas Winchell.

I decided bold was best and I walked right up to the booth, set my mug down on the table, and slid onto the bench opposite him. "Mr. Douglas Winchell?" I asked.

Winchell raised his head. His eyes gleamed. "Who in blazes are you?" he asked.

"My name is Charley James, Mr. Winchell," I said. "I'm acquainted with your sister-in-law, Maddie Elster."

"Ah, dear old Maddie. That witch." Winchell spat out the words. "She's one of the reasons my life is in ruins. She kept me from the love of my life and poisoned my daughter against me."

"I know, and I'm sorry, Mr. Winchell," I said.

"Yeah, yeah." He waved his hand and slumped further down in his seat. "You can't stay here," he said abruptly. "I'm expecting someone. State your business and leave."

"Your sister-in-law recently suffered a loss," I said. "Someone in her employ stole a large amount of jewelry from her."

Winchell's head snapped up, and his eyes gleamed. "Yeah? A thief snuck in her employ, in spite of all the background and credit checks she runs?" His laugh was bitter. "Who was it? They deserve a medal."

"Apparently it was one of her maids—a Janice Rutger."

His spine stiffened, and his hand flew to his throat. His long fingers rubbed against it for a second and then he shrugged. "Yeah, well, good for her. She got away with it, I hope."

I ignored his comment and went on, "I thought perhaps you might have known her. She worked for Gordon Knight at the same time you did."

Winchell's lips thinned. "Oh yes. Gordon. The man I worked for, the man I thought was my friend."

"I've heard from Peter Bridges about your misfortune," I said. "I'm sorry."

The waitress returned with a large mug of beer. She set it in front of Winchell and looked inquiringly at me. I held up my half-full mug and shook my head. She shrugged and walked away. Out of the corner of my eye I saw a tall, gray-haired, well-dressed man wearing a tan Brooks Brothers raincoat enter through the side door. He started to head in our direction, and then stopped abruptly. He turned and made his way back over to the bar. Was this the person Winchell was supposed to meet? I wondered. I considered saying something, and then changed my mind. After all, I'd gotten here first.

If Winchell had noticed the man, he gave no indication. He took a long sip of beer, set the mug down, and then looked me straight in the eyes. "Good old Peter. Still likes to gossip, I see. Don't feel sorry for me, little lady," he said. "Save your pity for someone who deserves it—like my sister-in-law."

I stole a quick look back to the bar. The man I assumed was here to see Winchell was staring in our direction, sipping beer and tapping his fingers impatiently against the bar counter.

I figured it wouldn't be long before he came over and interrupted us, so I leaned forward, thinking now might be a good time to play my trump card. "Jewelry wasn't the only thing Janice Rutger stole from your ex-sister-in-law," I said. "She also stole one of her books."

"She did, eh?" He picked up his beer and took a long sip. "Well, she certainly had plenty to choose from. Maddie has quite the collection. Inherited it from her father." He twirled his beer. "Had my wife lived, she'd have gotten the whole damned bunch."

"Your sister-in-law didn't inherit this one," I said. "I understand she got it at an auction. Janice stole it and substituted another."

He frowned at me. "And just how do you know that?"

"Because she hid the book in my store."

Now his eyes popped. He leaned forward, and his tongue darted out and licked his lips. "What? She hid the book, you say?"

"I own Mainely Mysteries, a bookshop in Austin. Janice hid the book there, but I—or rather, my cat—found it."

He was silent for a long moment, just staring at me. Then he said in a whisper, "It's Maddie's book you found? You're certain?"

"I went to Maddie's house myself, Mr. Winchell. She verified that the book in the case definitely isn't hers." When he remained silent I went on, "You knew Janice Rutger when the two of you worked for Gordon Knight. Have you any idea why she would have taken that book?"

Winchell stared at me, then abruptly released my wrist and scrubbed his hands across his face. "That book was Gordon Knight's pride and joy," he muttered. "It was his baby. He spent more time with that book than anything else, except his precious experiments. He loved that actor—Vincent Price, loved all his old movies. He'd watch 'em endlessly sometimes when he couldn't sleep. Loved that Ligeia one in particular."

Winchell paused in his ranting, and I leaned forward. "Is that why that page was taken out of the book? Did Mr. Knight do that?"

Winchell's head snapped up, and he stared at me. "What did you say? A page was taken out of the book?"

"Yes, page seventy-seven. It's a drawing of Ligeia lying in her tomb. A still of Vincent Price from that movie is on the reverse side."

"Seventy-seven," Doug repeated. "Yes, that's right. Seventy-seven." His hands gripped the table. "I don't understand. Jan couldn't have—she promised—something's off." He half rose from his seat. "Excuse me. I've got to find Jan, talk to her."

"I'm afraid that's not possible, Mr. Winchell. Janice is dead."

"Dead!" His eyes popped again, and he slumped in his seat and put his head in his hands. "Dead," he repeated. "Good Lord, this changes everything."

I leaned forward. "What does it change, Mr. Winchell? Did you know Janice planned to take your sister-in-law's book? Were you her partner?"

He lifted his head and looked at me with a puzzled expression. "Her . . . partner? No, no, not me—at least not the way you think. I would never sell that book for profit! It's far too valuable for that."

Winchell slid out of the booth. He stood uncertainly there for a minute, his eyes wild. He pulled his baseball cap off and ran his hand through his already disheveled hair. "Something's off," he muttered again. Out of the corner of my eye I saw the well-dressed man slide off his stool. He stood off to one side, taking in the scene with great interest. Several other people seated at the bar swiveled their heads in our direction as well.

I reached up to tug at Winchell's arm. "Sit down, Mr. Winchell," I said. "We haven't finished our discussion."

He whirled on me and jerked his arm free. "How do I know you're telling me the truth? How do you know she's dead?"

"I know she's dead because I am the one who found her body," I said calmly. "I went to her hotel room to ask her about the book she'd left—that was before I knew it belonged to your sister-in-law—and found her body."

His face blanched. "Oh no. Poor Jane."

I stared at him. "Jane. You called her Jane," I said.

His brows drew together. "No, I didn't."

"You did," I said. "You knew she also went under the name of Jane Radcliffe. How do you know that? Did she tell you?"

He paused. "She told me when she talked about the girl being a bad influence." His eyes narrowed. "And it's not you?"

"Of course not. I didn't know Janice," I said.

"Then it's someone else," he muttered. "But the joke's on them. Without seventy-seven it's useless." He threw his head back. "Yes, siree. Seventy-seven eleven. It all goes together."

Apparently Doug Winchell had also adapted a knack for talking in riddles. "I don't have the book, Mr. Winchell. What does that mean, seventy-seven eleven goes together?"

He waggled his finger in front of my face. "Oh no," he said shrilly. "You're not getting any more out of me." He gripped the edge of the table with a shaky hand. "Jane wanted to do the right thing. I know she did," he muttered. He curled his fingers into a fist and pounded it on the table. "The invisible man—he got to her. Gee, he wanted that book."

I stared at him. "The invisible man? Who is the invisible man?"

"No time to explain." Winchell looked wildly around the bar. "I've got to get out of here. Can't trust anyone."

I cast a wary glance toward the bar area. The gray-haired man I'd figured was Winchell's appointment had vanished. I reached for his arm again. "Please, Mr. Winchell, I promise that you can trust me. If you'll just sit down . . ."

He jerked sideways out of my grasp. "No, no, no. I–I've got to go." He started to move away, then stopped. He whirled and pointed a finger at me. "Take some advice, Miss," he said loudly. "Get rid of that Poe book. Get rid of it, or you might die too!"

Then he turned on his heel and wove drunkenly out of the bar.

SEVENTEEN

By the time Braedon and Mandy reported for work the next day, I'd wiped down the counters, unpacked part of a shipment of new children's books that had arrived that morning, and set up a witch and a pumpkin on the counter near the register. "Looking good, Charley," said Braedon. "No one could ever tell the store was a shambles less than forty-eight hours ago."

"All thanks to you guys," I said. "And I got quite a few compliments on the window when I was in the bakery this morning," I said to Mandy. "Maybe you should take some courses in interior design."

Mandy wrinkled her nose. "I've thought about it," she admitted, "but I don't know if I'd enjoy doing it so much if it were my actual job. It's more fun to just do it for a lark."

"Hey, jobs can be fun," I said. "The trick is to do something you love. Then it doesn't seem like work."

Mandy cocked her head at me. "In other words, you love selling books?"

"Sure. I love reading them too."

"I think we must all share a love for books, otherwise why would we be here?" said Braedon. He rubbed his hands together. "Is there anything you need us to do before we officially open?"

"You could put out the rest of the children's books that were delivered," I said. "We've got all of the *Little House on the Prairie* books back in now, and I noticed there were more Halloween-themed books in the second box that I didn't get to. I saw *The Halloween Tree* and *Dragon's Halloween* in there along with some others. Maybe you could set them out on that little table by the children's reading nook?"

"That's a great idea," said Braedon. "I saw some fabric pumpkins in a box in the back. I can intersperse some of them with the books, maybe add a few leaves from that tree outside."

I grinned. "That sounds perfect."

Mandy turned to Braedon. "C'mon, Brae, I'll help you unpack those Halloween books."

They headed for the rear of the store, and I finished setting up my laptop next to the register. I hadn't gotten much sleep since my encounter with Doug Winchell the night before. After his exit from the bar, I'd attempted to follow him, but by the time I'd paid the bill and gotten outside, he'd vanished. I'd gone back inside, intending to ask Dale if he might know where Winchell lived, but he'd gone off shift.

The fact that Winchell had known Janice Rutger had also gone under the name of Jane Radcliffe intrigued me. He said that Jane had told him when she was complaining about some girl being a bad influence. On who? Her? Or Gordon Knight perhaps? Once I got home I did a search on Jane Radcliffe, but the ones that popped up were either too young or too old, and several of them were deceased. I'd gone to bed, hoping that maybe a good night's sleep would clear my tired brain cells and things would look better in the morning.

No on both counts.

I called up Google and was all set to do another search on Gordon Knight when the bell above the shop door tinkled, and I remembered I'd forgotten to lock the door behind Braedon and Mandy. "Sorry, we're not open till one," I called out, and then paused as I saw who stood on the threshold. It was a man, dressed in a dark gray business suit—Armani?—and a silk tie with blue and gold stripes. His shirt was a light blue, which matched the color of his eyes behind wire-framed glasses. He looked to be somewhere in the late fifties or early sixties, and he was expensively groomed, with a dapper haircut and manicured hands. Wealthy was the first thought that popped into my head, followed closely by: *What the heck is a guy like that doing in here?* Somehow he didn't seem like the literary type to me. More like the type that had stuff read to him.

"The door was open," he said. One corner of his lips curled up in disapproval as he crossed the space from door to counter with quick, confident steps. As he drew closer I had the notion I'd seen him somewhere before but couldn't place him. He inclined his gray head at me and spoke in an even, cultured tone. "Are you Charlotte James?"

"Yes, I am."

"Good. I'm Edmund Elster. Maddie Elster's brother."

"Ah." So this was the fabled brother. That explained the moneyed look. I extended my hand. "Nice to meet you, Edmund. What can I do for you?"

"Maddie sent me," he said. "The police called earlier, said they were ready to release her jewelry—the pieces that horrible maid stole. She sent me to fetch them, and she told me to specifically stop by your shop and make sure you knew that and also . . ." He pulled a slip of paper out of his pocket, unfolded it, and read, "And also that there isn't much time left on the agreement. Whatever that means." He slid the paper back into his pocket and gave me an affable smile. "I'm assuming that makes sense to you? I do so hate it when my sister talks in riddles."

"Like Gordon Knight," I murmured.

Elster heard me and frowned. "Not that bad, but close," he said. "Did you know Gordon Knight?"

I shook my head. "No. Someone just mentioned that he liked to talk that way."

"Well, it's very annoying. Our brother-in-law did it sometimes too. I think he picked it up from Knight. He used to work for him."

Recalling my conversation with Doug Winchell from the evening before, I thought that a vast understatement. "I appreciate you stopping by to let me know about the jewelry," I said. "Would you mind giving your sister a message from me? Tell her that our agreement is no longer in effect. She can do what she wants."

He sighed deeply and threw up both hands. "My memory isn't what it used to be. I'll have to write that down. I don't dare get anything wrong." He felt in his pocket, frowned, then shot me a sheepish look. "Might I borrow a pen? And a scrap of paper?"

I led Edmund over to the counter and got him some paper and a pen. No sooner had I done that than the bell tinkled again, and this time Jake stood framed in the doorway. He touched two fingers to his forehead. “Good morning, Charley. I know you’re not open yet, but is Mandy here?”

“She’s unpacking some Halloween books with Braedon,” I said.

“I won’t keep her long,” he said. “I’ve just got to tell her something.”

“This seems to be the day for people delivering messages,” I said.

Jake looked puzzled, and then his gaze strayed over to the counter and Edmund scribbling there. Looking at his phone next, he abruptly said, “On second thought, there’s no need to bother her. I can call her later.”

With a quick wave he was out the door. I hurried over and twisted the lock so there would be no more surprise guests entering the store before one.

Mandy’s head peeped around the corner of the book stacks. “I thought I heard Jake,” she said.

“You did,” I said. “He dropped by to tell you something, but then he changed his mind and said he’ll call you later.”

Mandy frowned. “I hope everything’s all right. I know he was waiting for an important call about a new assignment.”

“I’m sure everything’s fine,” I said, making a shooing motion with my hand. Mandy turned and went into the back of the store just as Edmund finished writing his note. He set the pen back on the counter, folded the paper, and slid it inside his breast pocket. “I’ll be on my way, then,” he said. “I’m supposed to see a Detective Donaldson.” He made a face. “I hope she’s more pleasant in person than she sounded on the phone. She said to come by anytime, so I may as well get it over with.” He patted his stomach. “I’ll probably need a drink when I’m done. Can you recommend someplace where I could get a good beer around here?”

Just like that, his remark jogged my memory, and I remembered where I’d seen Edmund before. “You were at the Down and Out last night,” I cried. “I saw you at the bar.”

Edmund stared at me. The puzzled expression morphed into one of understanding. “Oh yes. I thought you looked familiar. I saw you with my brother-in-law last night.”

"I'm sorry if my speaking with him disrupted your plans," I said.

The understanding look changed into one of puzzlement. "Plans?"

"You were meeting him there, were you not?"

He held up both hands. "Oh, no, not me," he said. "I admit when I saw him there I thought I might have a word with him, if he weren't too drunk. But we hadn't made plans to meet up, not at all. Maddie would kill me if she thought I did."

"What did you want to speak to him about?"

"If you must know, I wanted to give him a heads up on his daughter. Jewell's a rather spoiled girl. Maddie spoiled her after Amanda died. The girl has no mother, virtually no father, and a brother that's as good as dead—no one's heard from him in years. Jewell has been more difficult than usual lately. Not only has she started drinking, but she put that awful streak in her hair because she knew it would annoy my sister. Her animosity toward Maddie is starting to get more and more evident. She's resentful because Maddie won't release enough money from her trust for her to go to culinary school. Maddie thinks she'd be better off with a business degree from a fancy college instead. I thought maybe if I told Douglas what was going on, I might be able to persuade him to visit with the girl. I thought it might do her some good."

"I thought Jewell didn't want anything to do with her father," I said. "At least, that's what I've heard."

"That's what she says, but I think deep down, if she could have a real sit down with her father, it would do her a world of good. Of course, if Maddie ever got wind of me interfering, she'd cut off my allowance for a month, at least." Edmund's eyes narrowed into little slits. "Just what did you say to him that got him so upset?"

"I was asking him about Janice Rutger."

Edmund's eyes got narrower. "The maid who stole Maddie's jewelry? Why?"

"They were both employed by Gordon Knight. I was curious as to just how well they knew each other."

Edmund pulled on the lapel of his suit. "I doubt all that

well. Doug was never very social, not like Amanda. I can't think why asking about Janice Rutger would upset him so, but—it's really none of my concern, I guess." He raised his arm and glanced at the gold watch on his wrist. "I guess I'd better get going. I wouldn't want to delay meeting Detective Donaldson any further."

I nodded. "Mr. Elster, could I ask you a favor? If you should hear from your brother-in-law, could you let me know? We, ah, didn't get to finish our conversation last night and there are a few points I'd like to clear up."

Edmund paused. "That could be a while," he said. "When Doug takes off on one of his benders, sometimes it's days before anyone hears anything from him. To tell you the truth, I've been calling his cell all morning and nothing. No answer."

"You have his cell number?"

"Yes. It's the same one he had when he was married to my sister. Never gave it up. Maddie wanted me to delete it from mine, and I told her I did, but . . . I didn't. I thought that maybe someday I'd have to get in touch with him about his daughter."

"Could you give it to me?" I asked. "I promise never to tell Maddie, and after I talk to him I'll delete it from my phone."

"I suppose it would be all right." He rattled off a number and I quickly wrote it down. "Like I said, I've been calling it with no luck. Maybe you'll fare better."

He started for the door. I put out my hand. "One last thing, Mr. Elster. Do you happen to know a man named Jeffrey Thomas?"

Edmund cocked his head to one side. "The name isn't familiar. Why?"

"He's a rare book dealer. He heard about your sister's collection, and he was going to contact her to see if she had anything she wanted to sell."

"Rare books, huh? Well, Maddie does have some first editions in excellent condition. *Little Women*, *Huckleberry Finn*, *To Kill a Mockingbird*." His eyes flashed as he added, "By rights that collection should have been left to me, not Maddie. She likes books, sure, but she doesn't appreciate them the same way I do. I mean, look at the monstrosity she's got singled out in a glass case." He let out a giant sigh. "Oh, what's the use? No sense crying over spilled milk, right?"

And with that, Edmund Elster turned on his heel and strode out of the store. I watched him hurry down the street in the direction of the police station before I closed and re-locked the door again. Elster certainly seemed resentful of his sister's inheritance of their father's rare book collection. Could he be resentful enough to have done something about it?

There was actually a small line waiting outside the store when I opened at one. The first person to step inside was Betty Stubing. She gave a quick glance around and said, "Wow, the store looks terrific—especially your window display."

"You can thank Mandy for that," I said. "While you're here you should check out the Poe display."

One of Betty's eyebrows lifted. "Oh? Did you take my advice about the tree?"

"I did. I got one of those orange and black trees and Braedon decorated it with some matching ball ornaments—although it could use a little extra something." I leaned in closer to her and wiggled my eyebrows. "A talking raven, perhaps?"

"Aha," said Betty. "I'll bring it by tomorrow—or else I'll send my brother in with it. And speaking of my brother, that's why I'm here. I told him what you said about Clive Cussler putting out a new book and he wants me to order it for him."

"No problem. As a matter of fact, I think I ordered five copies of that one. I'll just tuck one away for him."

Betty clapped her hands. "Great, thanks so much, Charley. When will that order be in?"

"It should be here before Halloween."

"If it's not too busy, I'll stop by then," said Betty. "I'll be in costume, though. Last year I was an ice cream cone. This year I'm not sure what I'll be. Oreo cookie is one possibility. Chocolate shake is another."

"They both sound yummy. Maybe we should all dress in costume too," I said. "I can make up bags of candy to give out to the kids."

"Hah! The adults want the treats more than the children—at least that's how it is at my store. If you get a chance, you should stop by that day. I'm whipping up some special treats."

I leaned in closer to her. "No hints?"

She winked at me. "Let's just say one can do marvelous things with some vanilla ice cream, chocolate chips, and gingersnap cookies. Oh, by the way, guess who dropped in my shop yesterday? That know-it-all book dealer. Came in for a root beer float or, as he called it, a 'black cow.' Hm, maybe that would make a good costume too." She paused and tapped her finger against her chin. "You know I have that sign above my counter that says please shut your cell phones off when in line? Well, he paid absolutely no attention to it whatsoever. He was on his phone the whole time. It sounded like he was arguing with someone. I didn't mean to eavesdrop—you know me—but it was hard not to when he was there right in front of me. He said something like, 'consequences will be serious if it doesn't turn up' and then I motioned to him that he was next, so he shut his phone off." She glanced at her watch. "Oops, I've got to get back. Thanks for putting aside that book, and don't worry—I won't forget the raven."

EIGHTEEN

I tried to reach Douglas Winchell several times during the day, but each time my call went to voicemail. I left him several messages asking him to call me, but I wasn't too hopeful of getting a reply. Edmund Elster had said when Doug went on a bender, he was sometimes unavailable for several days, and it had certainly looked to me like he was well on his way to a bender last night.

I arrived home a few minutes before six and let myself in the back door. Poe wound himself around my ankles, then stole a meaningful glance toward his food bowl. I dropped my jacket across the back of one of the kitchen chairs and set my tote bag on the floor before going to the pantry and getting out a can of salmon for Poe's dinner. While he slurped contentedly from his bowl, I spied a note propped up on the kitchen island. It was from Zane: *You're on your own for dinner tonight. Billy Blanchard asked me to go to Steak and Brew. Probably C U tomorrow. Z.*

I set down the note. Zane had had a crush on Billy Blanchard ever since high school. He'd gone into business at his father's hardware store after college and, from what I understood, had helped to make the business even more successful. At least he was taking Zane to a decent restaurant for dinner. Most of her dates ended up being dinner at McDonald's and bowling.

I opened the refrigerator and surveyed the contents. Nothing seemed especially appealing to me, and to be honest, I didn't feel like cooking. I rummaged around in the junk drawer and found the take-out menu from Antonio's Pizzeria. I called and placed an order for eggplant parm. The man who answered the phone—not Antonio—said there would be a forty-minute wait if I wanted it delivered. Since I had no desire to go back out, I said that would be fine.

That done, I flopped down at the kitchen table and leaned

back, my eyes closed. My thoughts traveled immediately to the Poe book, and the mystery surrounding it. Someone desperately wanted that book—but why? Somehow I wasn't buying the idea that it was a fanatical Poe fan or even a Vincent Price fan. There had to be more to it—but what?

A year ago my inner thriller writer would have come up with a plot that would have put every James Bond novel ever written to shame. Now, the old brain cells were drawing a blank.

I thought about Jeffrey Thomas and the strange conversation that Betty had overheard. Was the "it" he referred to the Poe book?

Then there was Douglas Winchell. From our odd conversation it was apparent Winchell knew something about that Poe book. Peter Bridges had mentioned Knight got upset when he'd caught Doug looking at some of his books. Was it the Poe book? He'd also called Janice Rutger Jane, which indicated to me they might have a closer relationship than just two of Knight's employees. Could Doug have been the mysterious partner?

I dismissed that thought quickly. He hadn't seemed very surprised when I mentioned Janice had taken the book, but he'd gotten upset when I mentioned Janice had left it in my store. His agitation had increased when I'd mentioned the missing page. "What did he say? Oh, right. Without seventy-seven it's useless. I imagine he meant the book. But then he said seventy-seven eleven all went together. What does that mean? And he said the invisible man got to her. Who is he, and how does he figure in this?"

Poe had finished his dinner and now hopped up on the chair next to mine. I reached out and gave him a pat on the head. "I guess Edmund Elster was right. Doug certainly was talking in riddles. It means something, I know it does, but what?"

Poe let out a loud meow. Apparently my cat was as puzzled as I was.

I got up and went over to the hall closet. I dragged out a whiteboard and propped it up on the kitchen island. Then I got a Magic Marker out of the junk drawer and drew a large rectangle in the center of the board. In the center of the rectangle I wrote *JANICE RUTGER*. Underneath her name I wrote, *Maddie Elster's maid. Stole jewelry and Poe book. Why? Had to have partner. Who? Also went under name of Jane Radcliffe.*

Off to the right of the rectangle I drew three more squares, each beneath the other. In the top one I wrote Doug's name. Below that: *Became upset to learn page missing from Poe book. Knew Janice Rutger also went under the name of Jane Radcliffe. Seemed anxious to speak with her.*

After a minute I added: *Said invisible man got to her. Who is he?*

In the next square I wrote Jewell's name. Below that: *Niece who resents Maddie. Did she partner with Janice to steal book for revenge?* In the other square I wrote Edmund's name. Under that I put: *Resents Maddie getting book collection. Revenge?*

I stepped back to study them. I couldn't shake the feeling that Janice's partner could have been one of the family members. Revenge seemed the most likely motive for both Jewell and Edmund, but would either of them entertain murder?

I didn't know.

On the left side of the rectangle I put another square, and in this one I put Jeffrey Thomas's name. Below his name I wrote: *Book dealer interested in Poe book—for himself or client? Betty heard him argue with someone about consequences if "it" didn't turn up. Did he mean the Poe book?*

I stepped back again to study what I'd written. I remembered Riley May Connor saying that she thought she'd seen Thomas lurking around my store the night it was trashed. Could he have been the one responsible for the damage?

I felt something brush against my ankles and I looked down at Poe. "You're right, Poe. I forgot to put down that mysterious handyman Maddie thought was interested in the book. What say we give Howard Ellis a call and take care of that little detail right now?"

Poe meowed his assent, but as I picked up my cell, it suddenly buzzed, indicating an incoming text. I clicked on the Message icon and sucked in a breath when I saw who the text was from:

Chastity McAllister at Living the Dream Books. Received your inquiry and would be happy to talk about our process and service. Please call the below number at your earliest convenience.

"Excellent," I crowed. "How does now sound?"

I pulled out a chair and sat down, then dialed the number. It was picked up on the third ring. A very soft voice with a lilt of a southern accent said, "Chastity McAllister speaking."

"Ms. McAllister, this is Charlotte James. I'm calling in response to a text I received from you a few minutes ago."

"Charlotte James? Oh, yes. My, that was quick." I heard a rustle of paper and then, "You mentioned in your inquiry that you are interested in self-publishing a book?"

"I'm considering it," I said carefully. "I have long admired the works of Edgar Allan Poe, and I would love to publish an in-depth look into his life and works. However, I fear that my book might be too similar to another one previously published on the same subject."

"Oh? What book might that be?"

I gave the full title of the book. "It was previously self-published by Trilby Press. I understand that they revamped and re-opened as your company."

Her tone took on a suspicious note. "Did they? I'm sorry, I wasn't aware of that. I've only worked here a few months."

I wasn't buying that, but I wasn't about to challenge her right now. "Be that as it may, I have tried to acquire a copy of that Poe book so I could compare it to my own without much luck. I can't find a copy anywhere, nor can I get any information on the author either. I was hoping that you might be able to help me along those lines."

There followed a few moments of silence, and when Chastity McAllister finally spoke, her tone was less than cordial. "All I can tell you is that we have no copies for sale of any books that were previously published under the Trilby banner," she said. "Since the book has been out of print for years, I greatly doubt any similarities between your manuscript and that volume would matter."

She made a good point, but I wasn't about to let her know.

"Surely you can understand my concern for a fellow author," I said, in as pleading a tone as I could muster. "Even though his book has been out of print for a while, I would still feel rather . . . guilty if he thought I were copying his work."

I heard her suck in a sharp breath. "You're worried about plagiarism," she cried.

"Not plagiarism exactly. Just the books being too similar in content. That was why I originally contacted Living the Dream Books. If I can't secure a copy of the actual book to compare, then I wanted to do the next best thing. Speak to the author himself."

"I see." I heard tapping sounds emanating from the phone. "So in other words, you're not about to self-pub your book until you either compare yours with that other one or speak with the author."

"That's correct."

"Well, then, I guess we're at a standoff, Ms. James."

"Understand this, Ms. McAllister. If I do decide to self-publish, I'm going to purchase a lot of copies. A lot. I want this valuable compendium to be readily available to the general public."

Now the tone changed from bordering on hostile to interested. "And by a lot you're talking . . ."

"Several thousand, to start."

A long pause and then, "The largest print run we do at one time is ten thousand books."

I did a quick calculation in my head. That would come to almost one hundred and twenty-five thousand dollars. "A little less than what I planned, but that's fine," I said. "However, if you won't help me, well, then I'll be forced to go another route." I held my breath, hoping I was right and that she wasn't about to let that much money slip away.

"Let me see what I can do," she said. "I promise to get back to you as quickly as I can."

I thanked her, hung up, and looked at Poe. "Well, the ball's in her court," I said. "Let's see if she comes up with anything."

Poe yawned as the doorbell rang, signaling the arrival of my eggplant parm.

* * *

The storm started a little after eight. Rain fell hard and moisture dripped steadily from the trees as thunder crashed overhead. I'd always hated thunderstorms, and the one tonight seemed especially loud. It even seemed to upset Poe. Instead of curling up in his cat bed in the kitchen, he dashed upstairs and took refuge under my bed. I'd retired early, hoping to get a good night's sleep, but I gave up that dream around nine thirty. Leaving Poe ensconced under my bed, I went down to the living room where I curled up in the easy chair. I tucked my legs under me, covered myself with a fluffy throw, and opened the latest John Grisham thriller I'd picked up last week. What with all the lightning and thunder, though, I found it hard to concentrate on the printed words. I found myself getting up to check outside every time I heard a creak or a moan. *It's only the wind*, I told myself, and yet . . . I couldn't shake the feeling that I was being watched. I peered out into the darkness several times, but the street was deserted. I heard nothing and saw nothing but falling rain and branches swaying in the wind. Around eleven o'clock I gave up, shut off the lights, and climbed the stairs to my room.

I awoke around one a.m. to a sharp meow in my ear. I opened one eye and saw Poe on my chest. His golden eyes were wide. "Meow," he said again.

I glanced at the clock on the bedside table and groaned. "One a.m.? Go back to sleep, Poe. We don't have to get up until seven."

The cat shot me an injured look and leapt down from the bed.

I rolled onto my back and listened. The rain had stopped, and all was quiet, except for the sound of water dripping from the trees—and Poe's sharp meows, increasing in intensity.

Something had that cat upset. I threw off the covers and eased myself slowly out of bed. I looked at the cat, crouched beside the bedroom door. He raised a paw and scratched at the wood, meowing all the while.

"What's gotten into you, Poe?" I whispered. I slid my feet into my leopard-print bedroom slippers and padded over to my dresser. I retrieved my cell phone and called up the flashlight app. Once that was done, I moved silently over to the door, opened it a crack, and peered out. I saw only darkness beyond. When Poe meowed again, I bent down and gave him a pat on the head. "OK, OK, you win. I'll check it out."

I opened the door and stepped out into the hallway. Moonlight streamed in from the hall window, so I had no need of the flashlight as I crept silently down the hall. I passed Zane's room and paused. I pressed my ear to the door and listened. Nothing. I opened the door a crack and peered in. Zane's bed was unmade. I shut the door and continued on down the hall. The door to the bathroom was wide open, and the room was empty. The final door on this floor was to what Zane always called her "office." It had her computer, printer, and an old file cabinet that she kept recipes in. As I approached the door I paused. It was open, just a crack, but I was certain the door had been closed earlier. My heart started to hammer in my chest, and I pushed the door all the way open, turning on the flashlight app as I did so. My eyes widened and I gasped as I took in the scene before me.

All the drawers in the filing cabinet and desk were open, and papers were scattered about. The shelves on the wall that had held reference books had been practically torn off the wall, the reference books that had been on them flung all around the floor. A few of them looked as if their spines might be cracked. Two of the books had had dust jackets that now lay beside the books and appeared to have been ripped in half. It didn't take a genius to figure out that someone—most likely the same person who'd trashed my store—had come in search of the Poe book. "So much for squad car patrol," I muttered.

A banging noise made my head jerk up. It had come from downstairs. Still clutching my phone I raced back into the hall and over to the stairway. A dark shadow seemed to move and shift at the bottom of the stairs. I shone the light in that direction and gasped as I caught sight of an arm, clad in what appeared to be a dark-colored jacket.

"Stop, thief," I cried, and then I ran down the stairs. Halfway down I heard the sound of a door banging. It had come from the direction of the kitchen, so I turned and ran in there. I shone my light at the back door and saw Poe, raised on both hind legs, scratching and sniffing at the door. I had a quick look outside, but I could see nothing save the light from the garage.

A car came down the road and went on past. Close to the house, a branch cracked, a bit louder than if caused by the wind. Off to my left, the neighbor's Doberman started barking.

Poe let out a low, guttural growl, unlike any sound I'd heard him make before. I went into the kitchen and grabbed a knife from the butcher block on the island. I surely wasn't going to search outside without a weapon. I went back to the door, opened it cautiously, and then stepped outside.

I called up my flashlight app again and swung the light in an arc. It took me a few minutes, but I saw it—muddy footprints leading down the flagstone path and over to the base of the elm beside the house. I stepped closer to examine the prints. They were huge—a size-twelve or -thirteen foot. The intruder was either a basketball player or they'd worn a bigger shoe to disguise their real print. I returned to the side door and examined it quickly. There were some dents and scuff marks around the lock that I was fairly certain hadn't been there earlier.

I sighed and switched the flashlight app off. No sense putting it off. I had to do what needed to be done. I dialed 911, and when the operator answered I said, "This is Charley James. I need to report a break-in."

The officers who answered my summons weren't Ian Grant, nor Barbie, nor even Randy Zucker; rather it was a guy and a girl, both of whom looked as if they'd just graduated high school. They took down the information, looked through the house, and then put yellow tape up around Zane's office, explaining that some techs would be by in the morning to dust for prints. "It's been bad out there all night," said the female officer. "It's winding down now, but lots of the roads are flooded, and there are a ton of accidents. As a result we're pretty shorthanded, so I'm afraid tomorrow morning is as good as it's gonna get."

"Yep," said the other police officer. "We've put a wood plank over that print in your yard. Hopefully that will keep it intact."

They left and I went back into the kitchen. Poe wound his furry body around my ankles, and I leaned down and picked him up. He nuzzled against my chest, and his pink tongue darted out to swipe at my chin.

"Thanks, Poe," I said into his soft fur. "If you hadn't woken me up, I'm sure whoever it was would have trashed the whole house, just like they did the store."

I figured I should probably let Zane know what happened. I set Poe down and picked up my cell phone. I saw I had two texts from Zane. The first was sent a few minutes before midnight: Storm pretty bad. I'm going to wait it out at Billy's. The second was sent just a few minutes ago: Storm stopped. Be home soon.

I hesitated, wondering if I should text or call her to let her know what happened. In the end I decided to wait. It would probably be a rough drive home, and I didn't want her driving upset.

I set my phone on the table and flopped into one of the kitchen chairs. Whoever it was had undoubtedly been after the book. I wondered if the intruder, whom I assumed to be Janice's partner, knew about the missing page. I remembered Douglas's words—without seventy-seven it's useless—and figured probably not. I picked the phone back up and started to open my contacts page for Douglas Winchell's phone number when my phone rang again. I gasped when I saw the number on the screen and hit the accept icon eagerly. "Mr. Winchell! I've been trying to reach you."

His voice, just a shade over a whisper, came over the line. "I saw your messages. But I had to be careful. Gee is probably watching me, and I didn't want anyone to know I contacted you."

"Who's watching you, Mr. Winchell?"

"I just told you," he said. Then he added, "They'll soon realize it's useless. Without seventy-seven and the key, positively useless." He paused. "Eleven is the key."

"The key to what?"

"Jane thought that book was her key to a better life," he went on. "The invisible man talked her into taking it. Gee. I told her it was a bad idea and that she shouldn't trust him. I told her who to contact."

Oy, not this again! "Who is this invisible man you keep mentioning?" I asked. "Did he and Janice plan to steal the book and Maddie's jewels together? And who did you tell her to contact?"

"Dunno anything about jewels," muttered Winchell. "Gee, the invisible man, wants the book, or more to the point, he wants what's hidden there." He giggled. "It's ironic, really. Anyway, I told Jane who she should contact to set things right. She kept worrying about him, though. Said she was a bad influence."

I bit down hard on my lower lip. I could tell from the way Winchell was slurring his words that he was drunk, but I also figured in that condition he might be more willing to part with information, if I could only get him on track. "Mr. Winchell," I said, "I know you're trying to help, but there are some things I need to know. Who is this invisible man, and who did you tell Janice to contact?"

He giggled again. "Vincent Price was the invisible man," he said.

"You're talking about the movie? The invisible man was Claude Rains. I know because I've seen it."

"Price was the invisible man in *The Invisible Man Returns*, smarty," Winchell shot back. "Look it up. Price was the invisible man. So is he. Sometimes you can't hide who you are."

If Doug Winchell had been in front of me, I swear I would have smacked him. "You're not making any sense, Mr. Winchell."

"Oh yes I am. You need to look up that movie."

"There's no time for that," I said sharply. "Can't you just tell me who this other invisible man you're talking about is?"

He was silent for so long I thought either he'd fallen asleep or we'd been disconnected, and then he coughed. "Can't tell over the phone," he rasped. "Walls have ears. Could be listening.

Meet me . . . meet me at my rooming house. I'll wait for you at the back entrance. Twelve forty, Clifford Street." He paused. "And come alone."

Then the line went dead.

NINETEEN

For a few minutes after the call ended I sat in stunned silence, and then Poe put his paw on my leg. I looked at the cat. "Elster wasn't kidding about Winchell talking in riddles," I said. "And this one sounds like a doozy. The invisible man wants the book? Seventy-seven eleven? And who did he tell Janice to contact?" I stood up so suddenly that Poe did a backward flip. "I guess there's only one way to find out, huh? I'm going to have to go meet him."

Truth be told, I wasn't exactly thrilled with the idea of going to Clifford Street. Located on the north end of Austin, it was what people referred to as the "seedy side of town." It consisted of mostly abandoned warehouses, a pet crematorium, a small park, and what was referred to as the "low-rent" district: ancient nearly dilapidated buildings that served as rooming houses for those with little income. "Some night for Zane to be away, huh?" I said to the cat. "Even though Winchell specifically said to come alone, I'd feel better with Zane to watch my back, even if she waited in the car. Unfortunately, I have no idea just when she'll be home, and I want to talk to Winchell as soon as possible."

Poe blinked then let out an injured meow. Then he rubbed against my legs.

"What's that? You want to come with me?" I leaned down and picked up the cat. "Well, OK. You can be my backup in place of Zane. Just watch your tail, OK?"

"Meow."

I grabbed a pad and scribbled a short note to Zane: *Had to go out. Be back soon.* I started to pull on my jacket when the doorbell rang. "Great," I said. "That must be Zane. Who else could it be at this hour? She must have forgotten her key." I chucked Poe under his chin. "Sorry, boy. Looks like you get to stay home after all."

I hurried out into the foyer. "I'm coming, Zane," I called. "Forgot your key, huh?" I flung the door open then stopped as I saw who was standing there. It definitely wasn't Zane. I let out a groan. "Oh no. Not you!"

"Sorry to disappoint you once again, Charlotte." Ian Grant's voice held a touch of reproach. "I heard about the break-in when I got back to the station and I thought I'd come here, make sure you were all right."

"That's very nice of you," I said. "Two officers were already here. They secured the crime scene and said techs would be here tomorrow. They explained all about the storm."

"It was a bad one," Grant agreed. "Fortunately things are starting to calm down now, so I thought I'd come here and see for myself." He gave me a once-over. "I'm sorry, were you going out? So late?"

I had to think fast. "I ran out of Poe's favorite salmon dinner," I said. "The Quick Chek is open till three a.m. So, yeah, I was on my way out."

Grant's gaze skittered to Poe, who had followed me and now sat hunched beside me. "Far be it from me to deny a cat a late-night snack," he said. "Or you either. But surely you can spare a few minutes for me to have a quick look around?"

"This really isn't a good time," I began, but Grant had already pushed past me into the house. "There really isn't much to see," I said. "He got into Zane's office, but I scared him off before he could search the first floor."

Grant frowned. "The intruder was upstairs? You're lucky he didn't pay a visit to your bedroom."

"Maybe he was afraid of waking us up. I'm sure he didn't know Zane was out on a date."

"Oh?" Grant raised an eyebrow. "So she's not home? You're here alone?"

Poe let out a meow and I couldn't help but chuckle. "I'm not alone. I've got Poe here with me. Anyway, Zane's on her way home now. She should be here soon."

"Smart girl," Grant said. He looked me square in the eye. "So, tell me. Are you ready to come clean and tell me everything? Because I know you've been keeping something from me."

I widened my eyes. "Moi? Keep something from you? You flatter me, Detective Grant."

"I believe we've had this conversation before," he said, his tone stern. "It's not a good idea to conduct your own investigations and leave the police out of it, particularly when a killer is on the loose and especially when both your store and your place of residence have been visited by someone who is most likely the killer."

"Well, we both know what this person is looking for," I said. "And I no longer have it. You do."

"But this person doesn't know that."

"True. OK, fine. I may as well tell you, because you'll probably be hearing it from Maddie Elster soon anyway. That book is hers."

Grant arched a brow. "The Poe Compendium belongs to Madeleine Elster?"

"Yes. She acquired it when she bought a trunk at an estate auction that previously belonged to Gordon Knight."

"I see. But when you found the book in your store, you didn't know it was Ms. Elster's. You thought it belonged to Janice Rutger."

"To be honest—I didn't know what to make of it. That Jeffrey Thomas had been in the shop earlier and told me about a Poe book that someone was selling around here. When I saw that book, well . . . I told you the truth. I wanted to talk to Janice about where she'd gotten it."

"And you thought she'd tell you the truth?"

"I thought maybe I could get a bead on her, figure out if she was lying or not. I had no intention of returning the book until after I'd done a little . . . research."

"By research you mean snooping," Grant said.

"Investigating," I corrected. "Janice was acting very furtive when she was in my store. She kept looking out the picture window. I figured either she was waiting for someone who she was going to sell the book to, or maybe her partner."

"You figured she had a partner? You didn't think she acted alone?"

"She didn't seem the type. She struck me as too nervous. I

thought perhaps she might have been in league with that book dealer, or possibly Douglas Winchell, Maddie's brother-in-law. But after seeing Winchell's reaction to the news that Janice was dead, I dismissed that theory."

Grant stared at me. "Wait—what? You tracked down Douglas Winchell? You thought he was this partner?"

"Yes. Both he and Janice worked for Gordon Knight, so I thought maybe they might be in cahoots."

A tiny vein started to bulge on the side of Grant's neck. "Charlotte," he said roughly, "do you realize the danger you put yourself in, playing detective like you did?"

"I don't think I was in any real danger. I think whoever broke in must have been at the tavern and heard Winchell screaming at me about the book being cursed. Maybe it was the person he was supposed to meet there. He told me he was waiting for someone."

"Let's say you caught up with this intruder. Do you think he'd just say sorry for the mess and leave? You don't think he'd have tried to get you to tell him where the book is? He might have had a weapon."

"But I didn't catch up with him, so that's a moot point," I said. As Grant lapsed into a stony silence I added, "So . . . what happens now? Are you going to charge me with obstruction of justice and cart me off to jail?"

"Don't tempt me," ground out Grant. "It's becoming very apparent to me that you are not going to give up on this, and you are probably going to continue with your little Nancy Drew investigation." He ran his hand through his hair. "Which leaves me no choice."

I looked at him. "What do you mean, no choice?"

A beep sounded from Grant's jacket pocket. He pulled his phone out, looked at the screen, then slid it back into his pocket. "I can't go into detail right now. I want you to stay put here until you hear from me. Have you got that?"

"I'm sorry, I can't do that," I said. "I need to get Poe his snack, remember?"

Grant looked down at the cat. "Can you wait a few hours,

buddy?" he asked. "I'll bring you some cans of salmon when I come back."

Poe blinked, then rolled over on his side.

"I'll take that as a yes," said Grant. "And just to make sure . . ." He held out his hand. "Give me your car keys."

My jaw dropped. "What, you don't trust me?"

"Frankly, no, I don't." He wiggled his fingers. "Hand them over."

"You know, this is totally unnecessary," I sputtered as I handed over the keys. "It's like you don't trust me, and after all we've been through together."

"Which is exactly why I don't trust you," Grant said as he pocketed my keys. He stalked off toward the door and I trailed after him. "Lock up after I leave," he said. "Watch TV. Your friend should be back soon, and I promise I won't be long."

"I'll await your return with bated breath," I said in the best saccharine tone I could muster.

"Trust me, Charlotte. It will be well worth your wait."

He left and I slammed the door—loudly—behind him. Then I leaned against it. "Ooh, that man is so infuriating," I said. "The nerve of him, taking my car keys." I looked at Poe. "As if that's going to stop me from meeting Doug Winchell."

Poe cocked his head. "Meow?"

"Yep, you heard me. I know Phyllis always parks the Jumpin' Beans van behind her store, and she leaves a spare set of keys under the floormat. So, get ready, Poe. We're going places."

After I changed into black jeans, a black turtleneck, and a black jacket, Poe and I snuck out the back door and hurried the short distance to Jumpin' Beans. The spare set of keys were under the seat cushion—Phyllis had moved them. I started up the van and turned it in the direction of Clifford Street.

Twenty minutes later I parked the Jumpin' Beans van on a side street two blocks down from our destination. Poe hopped out and did a kitty stretch while I locked the van and made sure the alarm was on—couldn't take any chances in this area. Then the two of us headed over to Clifford Street.

The address Doug had given me belonged to a run-down

four-story brick building that definitely looked as if it had seen better days. The building sat next to a large expanse of woods that had one time been the proposed site of a shopping mall that had never materialized. A light wind kicked up, the last remnant of tonight's storm most likely, as Poe and I made our way to the building. A sign on the front door read: *VENDORS AND GUESTS PLEASE RING FOR ADMITTANCE.* That might have been why Doug had said he'd meet me at the rear of the building.

The rear proved to be even less inviting than the front. Broken bottles and cans were strewn about, obviously not having made it into the giant dumpster that sat over in a dark corner. I looked around. The area appeared to be deserted. No sign of Doug, or any other person either.

"Mr. Winchell," I said in my best stage whisper. "Mr. Winchell, it's Charley James. I'm here like you asked. Where are you?"

No answer, just a stony silence, and then . . . I did hear something. A very faint sound, not too close, like the rustling of leaves. I spun around and stared into the darkened woods, but I saw nothing. I waited a few moments, but the sound was not repeated.

"Come on," I said to Poe. Poe's tail swished as he walked beside me down a short walkway. A few feet away I saw a door with a shade pulled all the way down. A small sign beside it read: *DELIVERIES ONLY.*

I tried the door. It wasn't locked, but it seemed to be stuck. I raised one leg and gave it a swift, hard kick. It groaned open, and Poe and I stepped inside what looked to be an office. A large metal desk sat square in the center of the floor, a battered file cabinet off to one side. "Mr. Winchell," I called out softly. "Are you here? It's Charley James."

I looked around. There was another door at the far end of the room that was partway open. Suddenly Poe let out a low growl and sprang forward. He shot through the door, leaving me no choice but to follow.

This room was larger than the other. Another, bigger desk took up most of the floor space, and there were two filing cabinets, in not much better shape, off to the left. To the right was an enormous stack of boxes. Poe walked over to them, then paused. His tail bristled and shot straight up. "MEOW!"

I moved forward and Poe shifted his position so I could see what had gotten his attention. Douglas Winchell lay there, his sightless eyes staring out, his jaw slack. A thin ribbon of blood dribbled out of the hole in the middle of his forehead. I put a hand to my mouth, bit down, then backed up a step—and collided with something hard. Then I felt fingers dig into my elbow.

"Well, well," said a familiar voice. "Fancy running into you here. I thought I told you to stay put."

I swung around and met Ian Grant's piercing gaze. His grip on my elbow tightened. "Charlotte James—it looks like you've got some explaining to do."

TWENTY

"Well?" Grant asked as I remained silent. "What are you doing here, Charlotte, when I specifically asked you to stay put till I got back? And how did you manage to get here?"

I clamped my lips together and returned his stony stare with one of my own. "I am not a child," I said. "You can't order me around."

"Oh, I beg your pardon. I think I can when you act like a disobedient child."

I pouted, thinking I'd enjoyed our encounter the other evening much better than now, when Grant was acting like a pompous know-it-all.

I started to say something when another figure entered the room. "Grant? Is everything all right?"

"It depends on how you look at it," Grant said.

The figure moved forward, and I got a better look. It was a man, slightly over six feet, wearing a beige trench coat over gray Dockers and a gray striped V-necked shirt. He had chiseled features, probing gray eyes that I thought were actually more silver, and curly hair with just a hint of salt and pepper at the temple. He approached us and looked down at Doug Winchell's body. "Swell," he muttered. "It's Winchell. Now I guess we'll never know."

"Never know what?" I cried. I looked at Grant. "Who is this guy? How does he know Doug Winchell?"

"Oh, I'm sorry," said Grant. "Am I forgetting my crime scene manners?" Grant fisted a hand on his hip. "You know, Charlotte, if you'd done as I told you and stayed put, you would have spared yourself this."

The man looked at me, frowned, then looked at Grant. "Who is she?" he asked. "I take it she's not a detective?"

"Only an amateur one," Grant returned. He jerked his thumb at me. "This is Charlotte James."

"Ah," the man said. His gaze raked me up and down. "So she's the one who found the book?"

"The book? Wait, what? Are you talking about the Poe book?" Now I grabbed Grant's arm. "Who is this guy?"

"This guy happens to be Special Agent David Trent with the FBI," said Grant.

My jaw dropped. "FBI?" I squeaked. Trent opened his trench coat, and I saw a shiny badge clipped to his belt. "What does the FBI have to do with all this?"

"A great deal, I'm afraid." Trent gave me a long, steady look before he said, "I think that you and I need to talk, Ms. James, but not here. I know you have a lot of questions . . ."

"That's putting it mildly," I mumbled.

"And I imagine you were hoping to meet with Mr. Winchell to get some answers," Trent went on as if I hadn't interrupted. "I was looking for the same thing myself."

"So Winchell was involved with the FBI? What was he, one of your informants?"

"I'm afraid it's a bit more complicated than that—and nothing I care to explain right here, right now."

Grant put his hand on my shoulder. "Can I trust you to go home, Charlotte? And wait there until Trent and I secure this crime scene?"

I looked at both of them. "Do I have a choice?"

"Actually, no," said Trent. "Please, Ms. James, return to your home. I promise you my visit will be well worth the time—for both of us."

I parked the Jumpin' Beans van back in its spot and then Poe and I returned home. The first thing I noticed when I opened the front door was the aroma of fresh coffee, and a moment later Zane appeared, holding a steaming mug. "Where have you been?" she cried. "And what is that yellow tape around my office door? Please don't tell me . . ."

"No one was murdered tonight . . . at least not here."

Zane's hand flew to her throat. "But someone was?"

"Doug Winchell."

I flopped onto the couch and propped my feet up on the coffee table. "I've had a rather interesting evening, to say the least." I pointed to her mug. "Got more of that delicious-smelling coffee?"

She handed the mug to me. "Here, take mine. I want to hear what happened to Doug Winchell."

In between sips I related the events of the evening, ending with, "So this FBI guy, Trent, and Grant are supposed to come here to fill me in—at least, I'm assuming that's why they're coming here."

Zane let out a low whistle. "This sounds like it could be serious, Charley. I think the smartest thing you did was turn that book over to Grant. Maybe now that the FBI is involved, they'll catch whoever is responsible and our lives can go back to normal—or a semblance of normal, anyway."

The doorbell pealed, and Zane hopped up. "That's probably them. I'm going to go upstairs, give you guys some privacy. You can fill me in on the details in the morning."

Zane hurried upstairs and I went and opened the door. Grant strode in, followed by Trent. Trent carried a familiar-looking white plastic bag under his arm. I took their coats and hung them in the hall closet, then led them into the living room, and they both sat down on the couch. Trent placed the plastic bag on the coffee table. I eyed it as I asked, "Can I get you anything? There's fresh coffee."

"Coffee would be nice," said Trent. "Black, please—and thank you."

"Me too," said Grant. After a moment he added, "Thank you, Charlotte."

"Don't mention it."

I went into the kitchen. I poured coffee into three mugs, added cream to mine, and put the mugs on a tray, which I carried into the living room. I set the tray down, picked up my mug, and sat down in the recliner opposite the couch. I waited until both men had taken sips of the beverage before I said, "OK, Special Agent Trent. You said this visit would be worth my time, so . . ."

Trent set his mug down on the coffee table and leaned back. He steepled his fingers beneath his chin. "How much do you know about Gordon Knight?" he asked.

"Only what I found out on the Internet," I said. "That the man was a very gifted scientist."

"That he was," said Trent. "Detective Grant told me that you informed him Winchell was supposed to be meeting someone at the Down and Out when you spoke with him." He turned his finger inward and pointed at his chest. "Winchell was supposed to meet with me."

I stared at Trent. "You? Winchell was meeting with the FBI?"

Trent nodded. "Yes. Mr. Winchell contacted us a few weeks ago. He said that he had some information regarding his former employer, Gordon Knight. The call went to me, because I have been working on Knight's case."

"Wait, wait," I cried, waving my hand in the air. "Did you say Knight's case?"

"Yes. The man was a very gifted scientist. Shortly before he retired from Axitrom Chemicals, Knight contacted our offices. He told us that he'd perfected a formula for an advanced rocket propellant that could revolutionize and revive the space program."

Trent paused to take another sip of coffee.

"Why would he contact the FBI about that?" I asked. "I would think he'd have tried someone at NASA."

"Under normal circumstances, yes, but Knight was a very paranoid person," Trent said. "It might have been due to the onset of his illness, but the man had gotten to the point where he didn't trust anyone, save for certain members of his staff. He refused to divulge details of his formula because he was convinced that he was being watched by enemy agents who were going to take his formula and adapt it to make their nuclear weapons more powerful. He wanted protection. Then, a few weeks later, he called back and said that his experiments had been failures, and he'd destroyed the formula. He refused to return our calls or see any of our agents, and he died two months later, so his case was put in the cold file.

"Last week Doug Winchell called our office. His call was

put through to me, because I'd been the lead agent on the Knight case. He told me that he had proof Knight hadn't destroyed his formula, that he had indeed perfected it and hidden it where he thought no one would ever find it. Winchell said that Knight had been right, that someone was indeed after it, but he thought he'd convinced one of the parties involved to turn it over to us. He wanted to meet with the FBI to make arrangements for us to meet with this party and take possession of it. I was supposed to meet with him last night, but I got delayed. When I finally arrived at the Down and Out, Winchell was gone." Trent fixed me with a piercing stare. "The bartender told me he'd left after having an upsetting conversation with a good-looking red-haired woman, who, I assume, was you?"

I tugged at an auburn curl as I nodded. "Yes. I went there to speak with Mr. Winchell. He did tell me he was waiting for someone, and I'd assumed he meant his brother-in-law, who I saw enter the bar."

Trent laced his hands in front of him. "I'm interested in this conversation you had with Winchell. Just what did you say that upset him so much he ran out on our meeting?"

I inclined my head toward the plastic bag. "I believe you've got it right there in front of you. He got upset when I told him that Janice Rutger had left that book in my shop."

Trent reached over, picked up the bag, and opened it. He tipped the bag forward, and the book spilled out onto the coffee table. "Ah yes. The Poe Compendium. During my last conversation with Mr. Winchell, which was earlier today, he mentioned the book was important. He also said that without seventy-seven eleven the formula was useless."

"He said pretty much the same thing to me," I admitted. I pointed to the book. "Page seventy-seven is missing from that copy. When I told Winchell that, he got extremely agitated. He said that seventy-seven and eleven went together, but eleven was the key."

Trent and Grant exchanged a look and then Grant said, "What the heck does that mean?"

"If I knew, I'd tell you," I said. "I thought he was drunk

when he called me. He said a lot of things that didn't make sense."

"Such as?" Trent prompted.

"Such as the invisible man was after the book," I said. "When I asked him what he meant, he said that Vincent Price had played him in a movie, and it had been Knight's favorite. He said that Price was the invisible man, and so was the man after the book."

"Crazy talk," said Grant. "The guy must have been really loaded."

"He was drunk, but I'm not so sure about the crazy," I said. "Edmund Elster said that Doug liked to talk in riddles, just like his former employer. This all means something, but just what it means I have no idea."

Trent frowned. "I can't go back to my office and tell my agents we've got to start searching for an invisible man. They'll think I've gone off my rocker."

I pulled my cell phone out of my pocket. "Winchell told me I needed to look up that old movie, *The Invisible Man Returns*. I bet he was trying to give me a clue."

Both Trent and Grant rose from the couch and crowded around me as I called up the movie on my phone. The synopsis read:

> *Wrongly accused of murdering his brother, Geoffrey Radcliffe (Vincent Price) is found guilty and sentenced to die. But when sympathetic Dr. Griffin (John Sutton) injects him with a serum that renders him invisible, Radcliffe is able to escape and search for the real culprit. With Inspector Sampson (Cecil Kellaway) of Scotland Yard hot on his trail, Radcliffe begins to suspect that a recent hire in his family's mining company might have the answers he seeks.*

"Sounds like a typical 1940s B horror movie," observed Grant. "But what sort of clue could he have been trying to leave you?"

"What about this line about a recent hire having the answers

Price's character seeks," I suggested. "Janice Rutger, the woman who left that book in my store, used to work for Knight."

"She was one of his more recent hires," admitted Trent. "She and Winchell were hired within a few months of each other. According to the staff we interviewed, though, Knight thought very highly of Ms. Rutger, which miffed quite a few of the older hires."

"Peter Bridges mentioned Gordon threw a fit because he caught Winchell looking at some of his books," I said. "I thought maybe it had been the Poe book." I looked at Trent. "If Knight thought so much of Janice Rutger, I wonder if he might have confided the location of this formula to her?"

"According to the agent who interviewed Ms. Rutger, she didn't consider herself particularly close to Mr. Knight at all."

"She could have been lying," I said. "And now we'll never know."

"True." Trent sighed. "Everyone who might have a clue as to where Knight put this formula is dead—Knight, Janice Rutger, and Winchell."

"No, there's one other person," I said. "This 'invisible man,' whoever he is."

Trent rose. "Ms. James, you have been very helpful," he said. "I agree with Detective Grant that for your own safety, you should halt this investigation of yours and leave it to us to find the killer." He bent, picked up the Poe book, and slid it back into the plastic bag. "I'm sorry to cut this short, but I've got an early flight today. I want to get this book over to our lab, see if they can come up with anything."

I walked both men to the door. Before he followed Trent out, Grant looked at me. "I'd certainly feel a lot better if I knew that you'd take our advice, Charlotte. But knowing you, I'm not holding out much hope."

"Nice seeing you again too, Detective," I said sweetly as I shut the door. Poe appeared and wound himself around my legs. "Yes, I know. They mean well, but I have too much invested in this investigation to just drop it and move on—and when has Charley James ever been a quitter?"

Poe cocked his head and meowed softly.

"OK, OK, I may have quit on the Steve Sheppard series—but that's only temporary, until I get my groove back." I tapped my forefinger against my chin. "I just thought of something. The main character in that movie, Geoffrey Radcliffe, has the same last name as Janice's New York alias—Jane Radcliffe. Some coincidence, huh?

"And this seventy-seven eleven stuff—Doug said that they went together, but eleven was the key." I looked at the cat. "Maybe it's steganography. That's the practice of concealing information within another message or physical object to avoid detection."

I went back into the living room and sat down on the couch, and Poe jumped into my lap. He looked up at me as I continued, "What about this? Gordon could have hidden his formula in the pages of the book by printing in code. Letters could be underlined or done in bolder face type to stand out on sequential pages, with the letters spelling out a message or a code. Or possibly the data is scrambled, and one would need a separate key to interpret the code. But Maddie would have noticed if the pages had writing or marks on them other than that one liquid paper mark." I leaned back and laced my hands behind my head. "The word 'invisible' keeps popping up. *The Invisible Man Returns* was Knight's favorite movie, right? What if . . . what if the formula is written in the book in invisible ink!"

Poe let out a loud meow.

I nibbled my lower lip. "Maybe he wrote it on page seventy-seven, the one with that drawing of Ligeia." My eyes narrowed as I thought. "OK, let's say he wrote the formula in invisible ink on page seventy-seven. He was paranoid, right, so he most likely scrambled the data, and one needs a key to interpret it. That's where eleven comes in. Eleven is the key to figuring out his formula—but eleven what? Unless . . . he could have written the key in invisible ink on page eleven of the book," I said excitedly. "If I were writing this, that's what I'd do!"

I looked at the time. "Too late for a call tonight. But first thing in the morning, we're getting some answers."

Before I went to bed, though, I checked all the doors and

windows to make sure everything was locked up tight. I hadn't mentioned anything to Grant, but I owned a gun. I kept it in a locked box in my drawer, and I sincerely hoped the occasion didn't arise when I had to prove to Grant that I was a crack shot.

Somehow I managed to snag a few hours' sleep before my alarm went off at seven a.m. I checked my phone for messages. There was one from Zane: Had an early order to fill. I still want to know what happened! Maybe we can have lunch?

I texted her back I'd be by around noon. I showered, dressed, and had a light breakfast of toast and coffee. Then I decided to do what I'd not gotten a chance to—follow up on what Howard Ellis could tell me about the handyman he'd sent to Maddie's house. I googled BuildPro and found that while they didn't open until nine, there was an emergency number one could call. I dialed the number and, after a few prompts, was directed to leave a voicemail message. "Mr. Ellis, this is Charley James. I need to speak to you regarding a rather urgent matter. Please call me as soon as you get this." I left my number and hung up. I'd just finished washing my plate and mug when my cell buzzed with an incoming call. I snatched my phone up, saw the BuildPro number, and hit the accept icon. "Mr. Ellis. Thank you for calling back so quickly."

"No problem, Ms. James," Howard Ellis drawled into the phone. "Whenever I hear the word urgent I always try to get back to the caller as soon as I can. So, how can I be of help?"

"I'm trying to track down one of your employees—specifically, the young man you sent over to repair Maddie Elster's shelves."

"Maddie Elster?" Ellis sounded perplexed.

"Yes. You sent a young man over to repair her shelving. Early twenties, slender, dark-haired? Maddie couldn't recall his name."

"That's a rather sparse description, Ms. James. It could fit any number of young men in this town. However, in this case, I suppose it doesn't matter."

"Why do you say that?"

"Well, Maddie Elster did call to request we send someone over," said Ellis slowly. "But then a few hours later one of her staff called and canceled the request."

"What!" I cried. "Are you sure?"

"Of course I'm sure," Ellis huffed. "My secretary took the call, and she might be seventy, but she's sharp as a tack. She said it was a man who called, and he said that Ms. Elster was sorry, but our services weren't required."

I frowned into the phone. "Maddie was certain the guy was from your company."

"Well, then she's mistaken," Ellis said. "As far as that description goes, it's a pretty flimsy one. I only have two younger guys working for me that fit it, and neither of them went there. As a matter of fact, they were both together at a job over at the high school that day. I remember it specifically because the principal called me personally to thank me for the speedy service. Now, if there's nothing else, I really must be going."

I thanked Mr. Ellis for his time, and after he hung up, I placed my call to Maddie Elster. Fortunately she herself answered the phone. "Maddie, it's Charley. I was just speaking to Howard Ellis," I began.

"Who?" she interrupted me. "Who's Howard Ellis?"

"BuildPro," I said patiently. "The company you called to repair your shelving in your den. The handyman you said you found staring at the Poe book."

"Oh, right. Him. What about it?"

"Howard said that man didn't come from his company. He said that one of your staff called and canceled the request."

"What! Was he sure?"

"Yes. How did you know that handyman came from BuildPro? Did his overalls have the company logo on them?"

"Now that you mention it—no, I don't think they did. I was looking for his name, but it wasn't on there. And now I don't think there was any logo on them either. He was just wearing a pair of overalls."

"What about his truck? Did it have the BuildPro name on it?"

"I–I'm not sure. Oh my gosh." She let out a gasp. "No

wonder he did such a lousy job. Do you think that he could have been Janice's partner?"

"I think there might be a very good chance he was," I said. "If I were you, Maddie, I'd call Detective Grant and alert him. Give him a description of the man."

"I'll do just that," said Maddie. "I'm going to grill my staff, too, and find out just who canceled that order."

"Wait, Maddie, before you hang up, can you do me a favor? Can you take a look at your Poe book and tell me what's on page eleven?"

"Right now?"

"Please, Maddie. I wouldn't ask, but . . . it's important."

"Fine. Hold on." I heard her put down the phone and clomp off. A few minutes later she came back on the line. "Page eleven, right? It's just a chapter breakdown, and a listing of photo credits. Do you want me to take a picture of it and send it to you?"

"That would be helpful, thanks."

She hung up and a few minutes later my phone pinged with an incoming email. I opened the attachment and stared at a chapter listing, plus the beginning of some very lengthy photo credits.

I supposed it was possible the key to the formula might be hidden here, but I was inclined to think not. But if it wasn't page eleven, then what could it be?

I arrived at the store, and I'd just finished setting up the register when the door opened and Mandy came in. I was shocked at the sight of her—her eyes were red, her clothes were rumpled, and her hair stuck out at odd angles. "Mandy," I said. "What's wrong?"

Her voice was barely audible. "Charley, I–I'm not sure I can work today. As a matter of fact, I probably shouldn't have come in at all."

I walked around the register and slipped my arm around her shoulders. "What's wrong, honey? Are you sick?"

"Yeah," she mumbled. "Heartsick. Just when you think you know someone, it turns out you never knew 'em at all."

I arched a brow. Trouble in paradise? "You had a fight with Jake?"

"I don't know," she wailed. "He's ghosting me. I've sent him oodles of texts and he hasn't answered. He doesn't return any of my calls either." She looked at me woefully. "I think—maybe he's got another girlfriend."

"What?" I said. "Calm down, Mandy. Maybe something happened to his phone?"

She shook her head. "That phone is brand new. I doubt that. He's avoiding me and the only reason I can think of is . . . oh, I don't even want to think about it."

"Take it easy. There might be a very simple explanation."

"Yeah, and I know what it is. He's found someone else. Oh, Charley, I really loved Jake, and not just because he took me to fancy restaurants and gave me jewelry. I cared about him."

I pulled some tissues out of my sweater pocket and passed them to her. "Go in the bathroom and splash some cold water on your face," I advised. "You can take an extra half hour for lunch today. Amberson's is having a sale. Why don't you go and buy yourself a pretty new outfit? I know when I'm down, shopping always makes me feel better."

Mandy dabbed her eyes with the tissues. "New outfit for what? It's not like I've got someone to take me to dinner now."

"No, but you're young and pretty. You'll go out with your friends, and sooner or later you'll meet someone else. Get a nice dress, something that will attract a man."

"There was a red dress in the Amberson's window the other day," Mandy said, her tone hopeful. "Maybe I will just go try it on."

"That's the spirit." I paused. "Now go splash that cold water on your face."

Mandy hurried off toward the restroom, and I leaned an elbow against the counter. I remembered what Braedon had said—was it possible Jake did have another girlfriend?

I started to move toward the door when my phone buzzed with an incoming text. It was from Chastity McAllister: Sorry to report that I was unsuccessful in locating any info on Mr. Gil

Sullivan. I did, however, find out that the Poe Compendium had an extremely small print run—less than a hundred copies—which is probably why none are available. We are still open to discussion, however, on your book! I look forward to hearing from you.

"Wow, that is small," I said. I hit the delete button. "Sorry, Chastity. Looks like we won't be doing business together—not that I ever intended to."

I slid my phone back into my pocket and went to the door to flip the sign from Closed to Open, then paused as I heard a bloodcurdling scream. "AAAAA, Charley!"

"Mandy!"

I hurried into the back area. The back door that led to the alley was open and Mandy was leaning against it. Her face was pale, and her eyes were wide. She reached out and grabbed my arm as I approached.

"Oh, Charley! I just opened the door to get some fresh air and I . . . I saw it!"

"Saw what?"

She burst into tears and ran from the storeroom. I went over to the door and looked out. There, on the door, was a square piece of paper, held in place by a knife with a jagged edge. I went over and looked at the words printed on the paper. They were in deep red, with little drops of red dripping down the sides, like blood:

HAND IT OVER OR ELSE

TWENTY-ONE

I made the call to 911, and less than ten minutes later a squad car parked in front of my shop, lights blaring. I glanced out the window and tried to suppress a frown as I saw Barbie emerge. I opened the door just as she reached for the handle, and she squinted at me. "You called about a threatening note?" she asked.

"Yes. Mandy found it when she went to go outside earlier."

I led Barbie into the storeroom and opened the door. "She stepped out and saw it pinned to the back of the door," I explained.

Barbie looked at the note, then at me. "You do attract them, don't you, Charley," she said. "This is getting to be a regular thing with you."

"Not by choice, I assure you."

Barbie shrugged. She took out her phone and snapped a few pictures, then she pulled a pair of Latex gloves out of her pocket and a baggie. She removed the note and put it into the baggie along with the knife. "We'll see if we can get any prints, but I'm thinking whoever did this was probably smart enough to wear gloves—especially if it's the same person who trashed your store."

Barbie's beeper went off. She pulled it out, looked at it, then shoved it back in her pocket. "I've got to go," she said. She held up the baggie. "I'll let you know if the lab guys come up with any prints—but don't hold your breath."

I shot her a wide smile. "I wouldn't dream of it. Have a nice day, Detective."

I shut the door behind her and leaned against it. My fingers went up to massage my temple. I was missing something, I knew it, but I just couldn't figure out what that was. I went to the door, flipped the sign from Open to Closed, and sought out Mandy. She was dusting the shelves in the back. "Go on home," I said. "You need to rest today and so do I. I'll text Braedon and tell him he doesn't have to come in till tomorrow morning."

Mandy threw me a grateful glance. "I'm glad for the extra day of rest, Charley, but I hope you're not closing the store just on account of me."

"No, that note didn't do anything for my nerves either. Now scoot before I change my mind and decide to stay open after all." I made a shooing motion with my hand, and Mandy immediately dropped the duster, grabbed her purse, and practically ran out the door. I locked it behind her, then shot Braedon a quick text: Closing store today. Come in regular time tomorrow. Then I called the ice cream shop. When Betty answered she sounded rather harried. "Betty, you sound out of breath," I said.

"I just had a whole flock of kids from the high school here who would rather have ice cream for lunch than the cafeteria special," she replied. "It's bad for their diets and their teeth but great for my business. What's up?"

"Phyllis mentioned that Gordon Knight used to stop by your store when he was in the area," I said.

"Gordon Knight? Oh yes, the scientist. He was very fond of ice cream, especially chocolate chip mint. He'd buy a whole half-gallon and sit at a table and eat most of it before he left."

"Phyllis said he liked to talk to you. I was just wondering if he ever mentioned his niece?"

"Gordon never talked about his family," Betty said. "Our conversations usually centered around ice cream—different flavors, what ones were his favorites, which flavors fared better in winter or summer. Sometimes he'd find a way to work Poe or Vincent Price into the conversation, but that didn't happen too often. When he was in my store, it was all about the ice cream."

"Oh." I gulped, trying to hide my disappointment.

"But . . . he did bring his niece in and introduce us one time," Betty went on. "She was a pretty girl. I remember she was in college, majoring in library science. She wanted to be a librarian. I think she did get a job close by after she graduated. Now what was her name again? I remember thinking it was an unusual one. Clarissa? Clarinda? Something like that." A pause and then, "Oh, oh, more teenagers. Sorry, Charley. Got to run."

I disconnected and got out my laptop. It wasn't much, but it was something. I figured I'd start with libraries. Maybe I'd luck out and Clarissa or Clarinda had gotten a job near here. I started small, a twenty-mile radius. Twenty-nine popped up. I sighed and looked at Poe, who'd flopped up on the counter beside me. He swiveled his head at the list and made a growling noise deep in his throat.

"I know," I said. "But it could have been worse."

Two hours later I'd gone through the entire list with no luck. I was going to do another search when my phone buzzed. I saw the ice cream parlor's number on the screen and hit the accept icon. "I'm so sorry I had to cut you off before," Betty said. "I think my teen invasion is done for today—at least I hope so. Anyway the reason I'm calling is because I gave you the wrong name. Honey Dobbs came in right after that last bunch of kids. She showed me her engagement ring. She said she and her fiancé David are getting married next spring, and the formal announcement is going to be in the paper next Tuesday . . ."

"That's very nice," I interrupted. "I'll be sure to congratulate Honey when I see her. But you mentioned something about a wrong name?"

"I was getting to that," Betty said. "Honey talking about her engagement announcement made me remember that I'd seen the notice of Gordon's niece's engagement. She married a nice guy, Artie Kroger from Peoria . . . anyway, even though she got married four years ago, I remembered the name because I thought it was so pretty."

"And it is . . ." I prompted as Betty paused for a breath.

"Larissa Kroger. I'm glad I remembered it," said Betty. "Sometimes it takes a while for the old brain cells to fire up, if you get my meaning."

I thanked her again and hung up. I called up Google, typed

in "Larissa Kroger engagement notice," and thank the Lord, the notice popped up. It was from three years ago. The photograph of Larissa and her fiancé Arthur was pretty grainy, but I wasn't concentrating on that. I quickly read through the announcement, and sure enough, there it was: Larissa was employed as a librarian at the Westmore Public Library.

I called up the Westmore Public Library website and, under staff, found a photo of a striking blonde with the caption below: *Larissa Kroger, Head Librarian.*

I turned and gave Poe a triumphant look. "Bingo," I said. "Good thing I closed the shop today, because I'm going on a little field trip. According to this, Larissa is on duty today between noon and six."

Poe sat back on his haunches and let out a loud warble. I reached out and stroked his head. "You're starting to sound like Ian Grant. Yes, I'll be careful."

I deposited Poe at the store and then set out for Westmore. I'd timed my arrival so that it was just a few minutes after twelve when I entered the building. I immediately went over to the reception desk. A girl was seated behind the computer there, but one glance assured me that she was far too young to be Larissa Kroger. This girl looked to be fresh out of high school, perhaps a freshman or a sophomore in college. She looked up with a smile as I approached, and I saw the nametag pinned to her blouse read *Judy*.

"Good mor—sorry, afternoon," she corrected herself with a smile. "How can I help you?"

I returned her smile with one of my own. "I'm looking for Larissa Kroger. I was told she was working today?"

"Yes, she is," responded Judy. "I think she's helping Mary in the archives at the moment, but she should be out here soon."

"Thanks."

I moved over to study a display of Halloween books. The books had been arranged in a circle around a large jack-o'-lantern that had a stuffed raven perched on top of it. Right behind the stack of books stood a witch hunched over a cauldron. A beautifully printed sign positioned behind the witch read, *Scare Up A Good Story this Halloween!* I was leafing through a copy of *Halloween Pie* when a soft voice at my elbow said, "Interesting book, right?"

I turned and locked eyes with a woman about an inch taller than me. Unlike the sleek blonde bob in the photograph on the library website, her hair was done up in a messy knot on top of her head, and her wire-rimmed glasses were perched on the edge of her nose. Her bright blue eyes twinkled as she added, "I've always been a sucker for that book. I mean, a witch who bakes pumpkin pie? C'mon."

I looked at the nametag pinned to the very expensive-looking brown tweed blazer she had on. "You're Larissa Kroger," I blurted.

She smiled, revealing a set of perfect white teeth. "Yes, I am. Judy said you wanted to speak with me?"

"Yes, I do." I held out my hand. "Charlotte James. I own a bookstore, Mainely Mysteries, over in Austin."

She took my proffered hand and peered at me over the rims of her glasses. "I've heard of your store," she said. "You specialize in mysteries, right? My favorite kind of book—although I do admit I tend to gravitate more toward the thriller genre lately. I've been reading a lot of James Patterson and C.J. Barrett." She released my hand. "Did you want to speak to me about a particular book?"

"Actually I wanted to speak with you about your uncle—Gordon Knight."

Her pleasant expression morphed into a frown. "Uncle Gordon? Why? Did you know him?"

"Only by reputation," I said. "I know the woman who bought your uncle's trunk at the auction—Madeleine Elster."

Her frowny expression cleared somewhat. "Oh, yes, Ms. Elster. I remember her. She was quite thrilled to get that trunk."

"Yes, she was," I said. "I need to ask you, though, about the trunk's contents."

"Its contents?" The frown returned, deeper this time. "There was so much jammed in there, and I didn't see anything valuable." She laughed. "Then again, I really didn't look all that hard."

"So you didn't know about the book inside? *A Compendium of Poe—Complete Works, plus Stories Adapted for the Screen.*"

"So that's where it was." Her lips twisted into a rueful grin. "I guess the joke's on me. That'll teach me to not be in such a hurry. Sure, I knew about that book—it was my uncle's pride and joy." Her voice trailed off and she was silent for several seconds before turning back to me. "I don't suppose Ms. Elster would consider selling the book back to me?"

I shook my head. "I doubt it. She prizes that book and keeps it in a glass case. She was particularly impressed by the signatures of Vincent Price and Boris Karloff."

Larissa clapped her hands. "Oh, I remember that," she said. "Uncle Gordon was so thrilled when he got Price's signature. It was a few years before the actor passed. He'd gone on a business trip to Los Angeles and a colleague of his knew someone who worked for Universal Studios. Long story short, it was arranged for him to meet with both Price and Karloff. He gave them copies of the book, and they autographed his. He was so proud. I remember him telling me that it was fitting that he got the 'invisible man' to sign his copy. He had quite a laugh over that."

"I've heard that your uncle was a bit . . . obsessed with both Poe and Vincent Price."

"Oh gosh yes. Aside from his scientific research, they were the most important things in the world to him. It was always his intention to pay tribute to the two most influential men in his life, as he put it. That was why he wrote it."

"Why he . . ." I stared at her as something clicked in my brain. "Your uncle's middle initial is an S. Do you know his middle name?"

"Of course. It was his mother's maiden name—Sullivan."

And just like that, everything started to fall into place. "Your uncle wrote that book. He was Gil Sullivan!"

She nodded. "Yes. He'd worked on it for years, actually, accumulating information on both Poe's works and those movies, acquiring movie stills and photographs. He used to say that doing it relaxed him when his job got too stressful. It was a hobby that turned into more of a grand obsession. Once he'd completed the book, he felt that it should be shared. He tried to find a traditional publisher, but none seemed to be interested. My gosh, he could have papered his den with the rejection letters he received. He was determined to see his baby in print, though, and self-publishing seemed like his only option."

"Why the pseudonym?"

"He was afraid people in the scientific community might lose respect for him, maybe even ridicule him. He tended to get a bit . . . paranoid about things," she added. "He really got a kick out of using that pseudonym."

"I can imagine," I said. "He must have really wanted that book to see the light of day to spend all that money."

"He didn't spend all that much," Larissa admitted. "Once he did the research and found out everything involved in publishing and promoting a book, he decided that he'd just put in a minimal order. The smallest they did was one hundred, but he convinced them somehow to only make twenty-five."

Wow, that certainly was a small print run! "What happened to the other twenty-four copies?" I asked.

"Well, one went to Vincent Price and one to Boris Karloff. He offered some to his staff, but none of them were interested. He was going to give me one, but then there was a flood in his basement and all the remaining copies were ruined except his. Bummer, right? He thought about doing another print run, but he never got around to it."

I blew out a breath. "Are you sure all the copies were ruined?"

"Yes—oh, wait. I think that there was one staff member who did take a copy, one of the maids. But as for the rest—they were all ruined beyond repair."

There was no doubt in my mind that Janice Rutger had the only other surviving copy—minus Price's and Karloff's, and who knows where they were? "It seems to me that you and your uncle were pretty close?"

She shrugged. "As close as he'd allow anyone to get. Uncle Gordon never married, so he never had children. My father used to say he was married to his work. My parents were killed in a car accident shortly after I graduated college, and Uncle

Gordon took me under his wing. Helped me out with finding an apartment and the rent till I got a full-time job. He even paid for my wedding and gave us a great honeymoon in Hawaii. He always told me that I was more than just his niece—I was the daughter he never had."

Larissa reached up to brush a tear from her eye. "Sorry," she murmured. "It's been awhile since his death, but talking about him still chokes me up."

"I'm sorry to dredge up memories," I said, "but there's something I have to ask you. Did your uncle ever mention anything to you about seventy-seven? Or eleven?"

"I know he always considered seven a lucky number," she said. "And he was born on November eleventh. So those numbers held significance for him." She smiled. "You didn't know my uncle, but he loved to talk in riddles—cyphers. He was a very methodical man. He had quite a few notebooks—journals. Some were scientific in nature, and others had the information he'd gathered for his book. He numbered all of them."

"Quite a few, you say?"

"Oh yes. At least a dozen, possibly more. I really don't remember. They were all there, though. My husband helped me pack them up."

"I see. And where are these journals now? Do you have them?"

"I sold them," she said, "to a bookstore that specializes in that sort of thing." She chuckled. "Left for Dead Books, can you believe it?"

I pursed my lips. "Believe it or not, Larissa, I can."

TWENTY-TWO

I thanked Larissa for her time and returned to my car. I drove directly to my store, parked in the back alley, and let myself in the rear entrance. Poe, who'd been lounging in the corner, immediately got up and came over to me. He rubbed up against my ankles and let out a loud meow. I picked him up and cuddled him against my chest.

"See, I told you I'd be back in one piece. Safe and sound."

He let out a loud purr and I carried him into the store and set him on the counter. I took off my jacket and put it on the back of my chair, then dug out my laptop and fired it up. I went into the lounge area and made myself a cup of coffee from the Keurig machine, then returned to the counter. I sat down and, in between sips, typed "Left for Dead Books" into the search engine. A few seconds later I was on their website. It was nothing fancy. There was a picture of the outside of the store, which was located in Evanston, about a twenty-minute drive from Austin in light traffic. There were a lot of photos of the store's interior, which was crammed floor to ceiling with books. A sweet-faced elderly woman in a turtleneck sweater sat behind the counter in one of them. The caption read: *Left for Dead Books—where even the most useless volumes come alive*. Below that was a short paragraph:

> *Treat your used books to a second life at Left for Dead Books. We specialize in old and antique journals by academia. We are open Monday through Friday nine to six, Thursday nights till ten. Saturday we are open noon to five. We are closed Sundays. Any questions, please call the number below.*
>
> *Violette Faye, Proprietor.*

I picked up my cell and dialed the number. After six rings a pleasant, well-modulated voice came on the line. "Left for

Dead Books. This is Violette speaking. How can we help you?"

"I'm looking for some old journals," I said. "I was told your store might carry them."

"Do we ever," she crowed. "What sort are ya looking for? We got academic, scholarly, scientific . . ."

"I'm actually looking for specific journals. Some are scientific in nature, some aren't. They belonged to Gordon Knight. You purchased them a while ago from his niece, Larissa Kroger."

"Oh, those." I caught a note of irritation in Violette Faye's voice. "I've had a few people in looking at them, but to be quite honest, the handwriting turns them off. They're not very legible."

"I'd still love to see them," I said, trying to keep the excitement out of my voice. "Your website says you're open till six tonight?"

"Yes, but not tonight. My sister is coming in from Boston and I have to pick her up at the airport at six, so I'm closing at four today. I'm hoping to get a jump on the airport traffic. It can be brutal."

I looked at my watch. It was a few minutes after two. "I should be able to get there before that," I said. "Could I ask you to put them aside for me?"

Violette Faye chuckled. "I don't think you have to worry about anyone buying them out from under you, but . . . sure."

After assuring Violette Faye again that I would be there well before four, I was just about to close my laptop when I heard an insistent tapping at the front door. I looked up and let out a groan as I saw who was there—Riley May Connor. I wondered just what I'd done in a past life to deserve this woman haunting me.

I pointed to the sign. "We're closed," I mouthed.

The tapping morphed into a loud banging.

I sighed, got up, and opened the door a crack. "Can't you read? The store's closed until tomorrow."

"I need to talk to you, Charley. A little birdie told me you found a threatening note tacked to your back door this morning."

I raised an eyebrow. "There really isn't much to tell. It was most likely a pre-Halloween prank."

"A prank, or could it be connected to the death of the woman you found at the Austin Inn?"

I set my lips. "I have no idea, and even if I did, I wouldn't discuss it with you. Now if you don't mind . . ."

I went to close the door, but Riley wedged her foot in between the door and the jamb. "Believe it or not, I'm here to help you."

"Help me? How?"

"I know you've been poking around about the Elster family, and I've got something interesting to say on that subject. But I'd rather say it inside," she replied. She cast a meaningful look up and down the street. "The walls have ears, and all that."

I hesitated. "You've got five minutes," I said. "I've got an appointment, and I have to leave soon."

"Fair enough."

Riley stepped inside and went over to the counter. She eased a hip against it and said, "I saw you with Douglas Winchell the other night. He's Maddie Elster's brother-in-law, although no one in that family recognizes him as more than an annoyance. I've heard rumors that he was involved with some pretty shady characters."

"And that's the interesting tidbit you wanted to tell me?"

"You've been getting pretty tight with that family," said Riley. "Winchell had a rocky relationship with his kids—Maddie saw to that. He's been acting very erratically of late. There's been speculation that said behavior might bring Efram out of exile."

I widened my eyes and tried to look innocent. "Efram? That's the son who was sent to boarding school, right?"

Riley opened her purse and started to rummage in it. "That's what Maddie would like everyone to believe. Truth of the matter is, Maddie had that boy sent away."

I'd been straightening a few odds and ends on the counter, and now I paused. "What?"

"Oh, yes. The great Madeleine Elster always maintained that

Efram was a troubled child, that she tried to get him the best shrinks available, but they didn't seem to do any good. If you ask me, she wanted to get him out of the house before something bad happened. She didn't send him to any boarding school—that would have been too good for him. No, Maddie gave him twenty thousand dollars and a train ticket to New York and told him to hit the road and never come back. She said that was all he'd ever get out of his mother's estate, and he wasn't going to hang around here and ruin any chances his sister had of pursuing a normal existence. Hah!" Riley smiled triumphantly. "That girl did just the opposite. Partied and did drugs, did everything to disgrace the Elster name, far more than poor Efram ever could. Did it as a rebellion. Maddie wanted her to go to an Ivy League college, while all Jewell ever wanted was to go to culinary school. From what I understand she'd have made a great chef."

I looked at Riley. "You do seem to know a lot of detail about the Elsters. Why are you so interested in them?"

Riley shrugged. "They make an excellent subject for a human-interest story—or possibly an exposé."

"OK, I can see how they might appeal to your journalistic sense, but you mentioned you were here to help me, and I really don't see how this is accomplishing that objective."

Riley's lips pressed into a white slash. "I'm giving you a heads up and some good advice. If Efram Winchell is indeed coming out of hiding, you should be on your guard. If he thinks you're in league with his father or his aunt, he might not take too kindly to that fact."

I raised an eyebrow. "What are you suggesting, Riley? That Efram Winchell might have trashed my store and left a threatening note because he thinks I'm friendly with them?"

"All I'm saying is, it's a possibility."

"That's very nice of you," I said. "But I can't help but wonder—what's in it for you? Are you hoping I might lead you to Efram so you can interview him?"

"Not at all. I just felt it was my civic duty, since you seem to be so involved in this investigation, to give you a friendly warning."

"Warning noted," I said briskly. "If that's all you came to say, you can leave now."

Riley waggled her finger in front of me. "You should be nicer to me, Charley. It never pays to make an enemy of a member of the fifth estate, silly. You should know that. After all, you spent a lot of time in the Big Apple before you moved here. What was it you did there again? Research work for a magazine?"

I swallowed. "I don't see how that's any of your concern. You're not doing a human-interest story on me, after all."

"Well, maybe not right now. But who knows what the future holds? I think you're a pretty fascinating character, Charley James. And I think you'd make a fascinating article too."

"Fascinating is a pretty strong word. I don't think of myself that way. Now, if you'll excuse me, I've really got to get going."

"Of course." Riley walked to the door, opened it, then paused. "Remember what I said, Charley, and keep your eyes and ears open. I'd really hate to see anything happen to you—unnecessarily."

She left, and I locked the door and leaned against it. As much as I hated to admit it, she did seem to have very good sources of information. If she decided to concentrate her efforts on me, would she find out that I was C.J. Barrett?

I couldn't worry about that now.

I returned to the laptop, called up Google and, under "images," punched in Efram Winchell's name. A lot of Winchell images appeared, mostly of Walter Winchell, a famous gossip columnist. I scrolled through the list and finally came across a few that could be the Efram I was searching for. They weren't very clear shots, most of them taken when he was thirteen, probably right before he'd either been sent to boarding school or exiled to New York. All I could tell from them was that he was slight of build and his hair color was a light brown. Not much to go on.

Next I typed in "Efram Winchell—New York City" and hit enter. Once again, a few pages of Winchells but nothing on

Efram Winchell. I frowned. Maybe Riley's source on Efram being exiled to New York was wrong. I closed the laptop, slid it back underneath the counter, then shut out the lights and shrugged into my jacket.

Poe let out a plaintive meow as I headed for the back door. "Don't worry, boy," I said. "I'll be back for you—I promise."

Traffic was unusually heavy, and thanks to Riley's unscheduled visit, it was after three thirty when I pulled up in front of Left for Dead Books. I got out of my car and hurried up the short walkway and into the store.

The secondhand bookstore smell hit me the instant I walked through the door. Similar to the musty-grandma's-attic-y smell of a thrift shop, the used bookstore smell was punctuated by the hot, dry, desert smell of print. Ink on paper. Old glue. Who would ever have thought that the slow rotting of books would be like catnip to some people? I didn't find the smell unpleasant; rather, it was quite the opposite.

The store was small with wall-to-wall shelves crammed with books. There was a counter off to the far right, also covered with books—and an enormous, buff-colored cat. As I approached the counter, the cat lifted his head, slitted his green eyes, and let out a loud meow.

"Hello," I said. "Are you the bookstore cat?"

"Every bookstore has one."

I jumped as a brown and gray head popped up from underneath the counter. I recognized Violette Faye at once from the photograph on the website. She smoothed down the pink and gray striped smock she wore and looked at me. "Sorry. I didn't mean to scare you." She nodded toward the cat. "That's Jasper. Don't let his largesse fool you. He really runs the place."

I laughed. "I can believe it. We have a shop cat too, a black one. His name's Poe."

"Good name for a black cat." Violette's smile widened. "I'm thinking you're the woman who called about those journals?"

"Yes, I am."

"They're over here. I tucked 'em away, just in case someone

who wanted to try their hand at deciphering illegible handwriting came in." She chuckled at her own joke and crooked her finger. "Right this way."

I followed Violette down a tiny stretch of hall to a table tucked in between two large bookcases overflowing with children's books. There was a cardboard box on top of the table. Violette walked over, opened the box, and tipped it to the side. "Here you go."

I peered inside the box. There were a dozen notebooks crammed inside. I picked one up and, seeing no number on the cover, flipped to the first page. Written there in a bold, strong hand was: *PROPERTY OF SILAS GREENE.*

I shut the book with a cry and looked at Violette. "These aren't the ones I was looking for," I said. "The journals I want belonged to Gordon Knight."

Violette waved her hand. "Sorry. I bought two bunches on the same day, and I guess I got 'em mixed up. The Knight ones went a few days after they were brought in. The handwriting in those was very legible," she added pointedly.

"Really? I don't suppose you remember who purchased them?"

Violette chuckled. "I always remember the cash customers. It was a woman."

"Do you remember her name? Or what she looked like?"

"She didn't give her name—it was a cash transaction, remember? What did she look like?" Violette's brow furrowed as she thought. "I'm not usually much on details, but I think she was thin, blonde. Had on a nice pair of jeans. I'm pretty sure they were designer."

I pulled a card out of my purse and handed it to her. "If you should remember anything else, I'd appreciate it if you'd give me a call."

"Sure." Violette took the card and shoved it in her pocket. "I hate to rush you, but the traffic going out to the airport will be miserable and I'd like to get a jump on it."

She shut the lights off and we walked out together. I headed for my car, but I'd only opened the door when I heard a shout. I looked up to see Violette Faye hurrying toward me.

"I just remembered something." She gasped as she drew near. "That girl had a purple streak in her hair. Does that help you any?"

I gave Violette Faye a thoughtful look as I slid behind the wheel. "You know, I think it might."

TWENTY-THREE

My thoughts were in a whirl on the drive back to Austin. Blonde, thin, designer jeans—and a purple streak in her hair. I could think of one person who fit that description. But why would Jewell Winchell buy those journals? She'd have no interest in them, unless, perhaps, she was purchasing them for someone else?

I remembered what Riley had said just a few hours ago—that Efram Winchell might be returning to his old hometown. Perhaps he had, and he'd contacted his sister. He might have convinced her to go to the bookstore to get those journals.

I frowned. OK, maybe that was possible, but . . . how would Efram have known about Knight's journals? He'd left long before Knight passed. For that matter, how would Jewell? Something was off, but I couldn't figure out what.

Well, there was only one way to find out. I had to ask Jewell myself.

A half hour later I was admitted through the gate and parking my car in Maddie Elster's driveway. I got out, walked to the front door, and rang the bell. A few minutes later the sour-faced maid answered the door. Her expression turned even more sour when she saw me. "Ms. Elster isn't available at the moment," she began, but I held up my hand.

"I'm not here to see Ms. Elster," I said. "I'd like to speak with Jewell Winchell."

Her eyes widened slightly at that request. She motioned for me to follow her and led me into the parlor. "I'll get Ms. Jewell," she said. "Wait here."

I didn't have long to wait. Less than ten minutes had elapsed before Jewell burst through the parlor door. In the dim light of the parlor, the girl looked even paler than ever. She had on a pair of tight jeans and a purple silk blouse. She tossed her head, and I got a good look at her light purple streak. "Ms. James? You wanted to talk to me?"

"Yes, Jewell," I said. "I have a few questions for you."

The girl looked puzzled. "Questions? For me? About what?"

I looked her right in the eyes. "Why did you buy Gordon Knight's journals?"

Her mouth dropped open. "What are you talking about? I didn't buy any journals. And who is Gordon Knight?"

"OK, I'll try it a different way. Did your brother Efram talk you into buying those journals for him?"

She stood ramrod straight and lifted her chin in the air. She averted her gaze as she answered, "I have no idea what you're talking about. I haven't talked to my brother in years."

I took a step closer to her. "Are you sure about that?"

She lifted her chin. "Of course I am."

"Well, I think you're lying. I think that you have spoken with your brother. I think he talked you into helping him and Janice Rutger steal your aunt's book."

She stared at me, her lips white. "Steal my aunt's book! Golly, I–I would never do something like that. For one thing, if I did, my aunt would have me shipped away like she did Efram." Her gaze skittered away from me again. "I couldn't have plotted anything with my brother because I haven't heard from him in years."

"I know you're lying, Jewell," I said. "You've got two options. You can either come clean with me, or with Detective Grant. Your choice."

For a few moments she just stood there, lips clamped together, eyes flashing. Then she threw up her hands. "All right, OK, you win," she said. "But I haven't heard *from* my brother—I've heard *of* him. Efram has been in prison."

"Prison!" I gasped. "How do you know that?"

She raised her chin as she answered. "Janice Rutger told me."

"Janice Rutger?" I found it hard to contain my surprise. "And how did she know that? Did she know your brother?"

"Not exactly." Jewell put a finger to her lips, then went over to the door. She peered out, looked up and down the hallway, and then closed the parlor door. She leaned against it and looked at me. “You can never repeat a single word of what I am about to tell you to my aunt,” she said. “She doesn’t approve of the family hobnobbing with the staff, and she definitely would not approve of me knowing anything about Efram. Swear you won’t tell her.”

I made a crossing motion over my heart. “I swear. I won’t repeat a word of what you tell me to your aunt.”

“OK.” Jewell let out a breath. “Well, Janice and I got to be pretty friendly. She was always nice to me. She encouraged my aspiration to become a chef. Sometimes after the cook left for the evening, we’d go to the kitchen and try out some recipes.” Jewell smiled reminiscently. “While we were cooking, we’d talk about different things. I complained a lot about Aunt Maddie, how restrictive she could be. Janice talked about her other job with Gordon Knight. She liked working for him, until near the end. She said he got delusional at times and would babble on and on about different things.”

“What sort of things?”

Jewell shrugged. “Just stuff. She said a lot of it didn’t make much sense. Apparently when he got like that he would confuse Janice with his late sister. He thought he was spilling secrets to her. But I’m getting off track. The reason she knew Efram was in prison was because her brother and Efram were cellmates.”

“Janice had a brother in prison?”

“Yes. You see, Janice Rutger wasn’t her real name. It was Jane Radcliffe. They’d lived in a small town, and after he went to prison, she felt she should make a clean break, get a fresh start. So she changed her name and moved to Austin. That’s when she started working for Gordon Knight.” Jewell tapped her chin. “She was close to her brother, though. Called him once, sometimes twice a month. When she came here to work, and we got to be friends, she told me that Efram and her brother were cellmates.”

“I see,” I said. “So she never actually met Efram?”

“No. But her brother would talk about him, and then she’d tell me about it. According to her, the brother and Efram were pretty tight. She worried about her brother too. It was over some woman who worked in the café at the prison that her brother was involved with. She thought this chick was a bad influence on him. She said that where women were concerned, he'd never had much sense. That was how he landed in prison."

"What was he in for?"

"Forgery. Apparently he was quite good at it. He forged a huge check at the accounting firm he was working at. He was going to use the money to run away with a woman who also worked there, but then she denied knowing anything about it." She paused. "I don't know what Efram was in for. Janice never told me. I do know that before he took off, he swiped some of Aunt Maddie's jewelry. He told me that it would be his secret stash, and she had so much she'd never miss it. I thought maybe he'd gotten caught robbing a store, or something."

"Maybe," I said. "Getting back to this brother of Janice's—do you happen to know his first name?"

"She used to call him Jay," Jewell said. "I don't know if that was his name or a nickname. He was supposed to be coming up for parole soon—Efram too, I think." She made a crossing motion over her heart. "I never talked to him, I swear. If I did, and Aunt Maddie found out—" She shut her eyes and shuddered. Then she opened them and looked at me. "You believe me, don't you?"

I expelled a breath. "Yes, Jewell. I believe you."

"Oh, good." She clasped her hands in front of her. "And you won't say a word to my aunt?"

"No, I won't, but—do you happen to know what prison Jay and Efram were in?"

"I know it's somewhere here in Pennsylvania. She called it a correctional institute. Are we done now?"

I laid my hand on her shoulder. "Yes, Jewell. We are."

I said goodbye to Jewell and left without waiting to be escorted out. I hurried back to the shop, where this time Poe was fast asleep on his bed in the back room and didn't even wake up when I hurried inside. I went over to the counter, pulled out the laptop, and immediately did a Google search on Jay Radcliffe—prison sentence—Pennsylvania. I had to weed through several pages of articles before I finally found the one I wanted, dated four years prior:

Local Man Sentenced to Prison Term

A 27-year-old man who admitted that he forged a check drawn on a local business earlier this year has been sentenced to five years in state prison.

Thomas Geoffrey Radcliffe was arrested and pleaded guilty to forging the check in the amount of $20,900. Radcliffe has been arrested before on suspicion of forgery at Atlas Flooring in Philadelphia. No charges were filed, however.

Radcliffe, who was represented by Doris Sharp of the County Public Defender's Office, declined to comment at his arraignment. His term at Orleans Correctional Facility will begin on Monday. Ms. Sharp also declined to comment.

I read the article through once, then went back and read it again. I scrolled through a few more pages before I found a follow-up article. This one was very brief, to the effect that Thomas Geoffrey Radcliffe, arrested four years prior for forgery, had been granted parole. A photograph of a tall, thin man exiting the prison alongside his attorney Doris Sharp accompanied the article. The photo wasn't a very good one, but it was clear enough for me to recognize Jane's brother as the man I knew as Jeffrey Thomas. I noticed something else too: Thomas's middle name was spelled exactly the same as Vincent Price's character in *The Invisible Man Returns*. This led me to think that Thomas Geoffrey Radcliffe must have been the man that both Doug Winchell and Gordon Knight referred to as "the invisible man."

Jewell said that Thomas had told his sister he'd met Efram in prison. I hadn't seen any articles on Efram being incarcerated during my previous search. I did another quick search on Efram, this time putting in "Orleans Correctional." I scrolled through four pages before one article caught my eye, from the Police Blotter, just a few weeks after Thomas's notice appeared: *Police arrested Remy Winshell on Saturday for passing forged checks from Woodward Accounting firm. Winshell pleaded guilty and will serve his sentence at Orleans Correctional Facility.*

I noted Winchell was misspelled and wondered if that had been deliberate on Efram's part. That and the fact his first name was abbreviated could be the reason I hadn't been successful in my prior search. I noted he'd been arrested for forgery—so he and Jane's brother had something in common.

I got up and started to pace as I sorted through everything I'd just learned. Thomas G. Radcliffe, aka Jeffrey Thomas, was Jane Radcliffe's brother. Jane had worked for Gordon Knight and, according to Jewell, during the last few weeks of his life had been delirious and confided things to her, thinking she was his late sister. There was no doubt in my mind one of those things had been about his secret formula and its location. Jane had undoubtedly told her brother, who had immediately honed in on a gold mine and had most likely talked his sister into getting her hands on the book. Jane had no doubt tracked the book to Maddie, and shortly afterward showed up at Maddie's door along with her letter of recommendation, which may or may not have been forged. Jane had the only other available copy of the Poe book, so they must have waited to make the switch until after Thomas was out on parole, no doubt so he could forge the signatures.

I rubbed my forehead. Efram fit in here somehow, but how? As Thomas's cellmate, he'd no doubt have been able to find out what was going down. Efram was also up for parole—for forgery as well. It was possible that Thomas could have enlisted Efram's aid. The two of them could have planned to steal the book together. Or, maybe Thomas hadn't confided in his cellmate. Maybe Efram had overheard enough to put two and two together and possibly decided to try and claim the book first. They were scheduled to get out on parole within weeks of each other—it wasn't beyond the realm of possibility the two might be in a race to see who could acquire Gordon's formula first. Could Efram have killed Doug, believing he stood in his way? And had Thomas killed his sister when she decided she wanted out of their plan as well?

I shuddered. Poor Jane and Doug had become collateral damage in a game that had big stakes at risk.

There was still a big part of the puzzle missing, though. Who was the woman who'd purchased Knight's journals? It wasn't Jewell . . . so then who? Jewell said that Jane had been concerned about a woman that Thomas had met in prison—that she'd thought this woman was a bad influence on her brother. She'd also warned her brother not to trust her. Was it possible this woman could have been involved with both Thomas and Efram and was playing one off against the other, intending to hitch her star with whichever one of the men found the book and formula first?

If this were the plot of a thriller, that's how I'd write it.

My back was starting to ache, so I got up, stretched, then walked over to the picture window and looked out at the street beyond. It was dusk now, and the other shops on the street that were also open late tonight were ablaze with lights. There was a large smattering of clouds overhead, signaling another approaching storm. I wrapped my arms around myself and peered out into the night.

A movement off to my left made me tense. Outside, I thought I saw a bush move. I waited a few minutes, but the motion wasn't repeated. I returned to the counter and fired up my laptop again, then jumped as Poe hopped up on the counter and stretched full length beside me. I rubbed his head. "I see you're awake now," I said.

Poe gave my arm an impatient nudge with his head. I bit down on my lower lip in frustration. "I really hate to do this," I said, "but maybe there's an easier way. Maybe good old Riley May Connor can utilize one of her contacts to get some information on our jailbirds."

I dialed the newspaper office and got the night receptionist. "Is Riley May Connor working tonight?" I asked.

"Who?" I repeated the name. "I'm sorry," the night receptionist said. "There is no Riley May Connor employed here."

"Are you sure? Maybe her name isn't on your register. She's fairly new. She replaced Derek Proust."

"Michael McBride replaced Derek Proust," said the

receptionist in a tone worthy of the North Pole. "He doesn't start until next week. And my register is up to date. There's no Riley May Connor working here."

"I must be mistaken. Sorry to bother you," I murmured and hung up. I tapped my phone against my chin. So Riley May Connor wasn't Derek Proust's replacement—was she even a reporter? I thought about it. She certainly seemed to pop up at very opportune times—after my store was trashed, after that note had been found at my back door. She'd been visiting her aunt and had seen me at Maddie's . . . and she'd been in the Down and Out when Doug Winchell had his meltdown. My eyes widened as I remembered something else about her, too.

Riley had a purple streak in her hair.

My thoughts were coming thick and fast now. Braedon had said he'd overheard Jake talking to someone he called "Ree-Ree." Could "Ree-Ree" be a nickname for Riley?

I called up the search engine and typed in "Riley—Nicknames." When the website came up, I ran my finger down the list of names. "Ree is indeed a nickname for Riley," I said to Poe.

Poe sat up on his haunches, pawed at the air, and meowed loudly.

"What about this?" I said. "Thomas and Efram were cellmates, and Riley was Thomas's girlfriend. What if Efram and Riley became involved, and they decided to somehow double cross Thomas and get the formula for themselves? Either way, the plan depended on Jane switching the books and giving them Knight's, but thanks to Doug, Jane developed a conscience and was going to turn it over to the FBI instead. When she didn't meet her brother, he went to her hotel room where she probably told him that she wasn't going through with it. He demanded the book, but she said that she didn't have it anymore, and in a fit of anger, her brother strangled her. As for Doug Winchell, it's possible that Efram figured out his father was behind Jane's change of heart. Maybe he thought Jane had given Doug the book, but when Doug refused to divulge anything, Efram killed him. The three of them have been hunting for that book ever since. They trashed my store, broke into Zane's house, and left that threatening note."

Poe blinked. A guttural sound escaped his throat.

"You're right," I told the cat. "We're forgetting the missing page." I started to pace back and forth. "Jane must have known her brother wouldn't take kindly to her decision, but she wanted to make sure that if he did find the book, it would be useless. So she took that page out of the book and hid it . . . where?"

I looked up and my gaze fell on the door marked "Restroom." I remembered Jane's face, so thin and pinched, looking around fearfully and then asking where the restroom was . . .

I slid off the stool and hurried over to the restroom, which was small and cramped to say the least. I frowned as I looked around. There was barely room enough for the small sink and toilet. My thoughts flew to the *Godfather* movies, the first one specifically. Michael Corleone had hidden a gun in the bathroom to use to shoot the men who'd attempted to kill his father. Specifically, he'd hidden the gun in the toilet. I knelt down on the floor and ran my hands around the toilet's bottom. Nothing. Then I lifted the tank lid and held it up. A plastic bag was taped there, one with a zipper. Inside was a manila envelope. I set down the lid, ripped the bag off it, and took out the envelope. I slit the top with the edge of my nail and pulled out a single sheet of paper. One side had a drawing of Ligeia in her tomb, the other a still of Price in the same movie.

I stood there for a few moments, just staring at the page. Then I replaced it in the envelope, shoved it into the zipper bag, and went back outside. I fished in my bag and found the card David Trent had given me. I dialed the number and swore softly under my breath when the call went to voicemail. I left a message for Trent to call me, that I'd discovered something important about the missing page. I disconnected and paused. I really didn't want to wait on this. I tried Grant's number and swore when that went to voicemail, too. "Detective Grant," I said, "This is important. I'm at the bookshop, but I'm leaving in a few minutes for the police station, and I'd appreciate it if you could meet me there ASAP."

I debated putting the page in my tote; in the end, I carefully shoved it down my pants, then I grabbed my tote, switched out the light, and made sure the door was locked. Poe followed me and meowed loudly when I paused at the back door.

"Don't worry, Poe," I said. "I promise that the next time I leave this store, you're coming with me."

I stepped through the shop's back door into the cool night air. It was eerily quiet—there was no wind to stir the tree branches, and there were no sounds, save for the chirping of a lone cricket. I turned the key in the lock and dropped the key into my tote. I was just about to turn toward my car when I felt all the hairs at the back of my neck start to tingle. A feeling washed over me—a feeling that eyes, unfriendly ones at that, were watching my every move. Off to my right a branch cracked, breaking the stillness of the night. I was aware of another presence—someone standing far too close to me. I started to turn. "Who's th—"

I never got the rest of my sentence out. A shot of intense pain streaked through my head, and all went dark.

TWENTY-FOUR

An airplane droned overhead. Suddenly it dipped and started to plummet, straight toward me. I tried to raise my arms to shield myself, but I couldn't move. Something held me down. I eased one eye open. I was lying on hardwood floor, my hands bound in front of me. I raised my head a bit and saw my ankles were also bound. I let my head fall back with a groan, and off to my right a shadow moved.

"Ah, I see Sleeping Beauty has awakened."

The shadow stepped into the light, and I recognized Jeffrey Thomas, aka Thomas Geoffrey Radcliffe, his handsome features warped into a scowl. I twisted my head a bit and blinked my eyes a few times. After a few seconds I recognized my surroundings. I was in the basement storeroom of Mainely Mysteries.

Thomas knelt down beside me. "Thank goodness the lock on the outside basement door was easy to pick," he said. "It would have been a chore to lug you down those basement steps. Now that you're awake, we can talk," he said. "I really don't want to hurt you if I don't have to. Just give me the book and nothing will happen to you."

Oh, yeah, right. I really believed that. I twisted my head slightly so that I could look him right in the eye. "It was you who broke into the store, wasn't it? And my friend Zane's house?"

He looked at me for a long moment. "My sister double crossed me. She was supposed to switch that book, and then we were going to have ourselves a nice little bidding war for that formula. The money we'd have gotten would have ensured we'd be living like kings for the rest of our lives. But . . . no. She had to listen to Efram's father. He's the one who convinced her to turn on me."

"You and Efram were cellmates and friends," I said. "Did the two of you plan this together?"

Thomas sighed. "We did, at first, but then . . . Riley told me that Efram planned to double cross me, take the book for himself. I wasn't about to let that happen. Thank goodness Riley kept an eye on him. She kept me apprised of his every move—one of which was to strike up a relationship with some girl who works in your store. He thought she might be a good source for gossip, and he was right. She couldn't wait to tell him that you found a Poe book tucked away behind one of the shelves, and she was hoping to talk you into letting her buy it."

"A relationship . . ." I gasped. "Jake? Mandy's boyfriend Jake is Efram Winchell?"

Thomas laughed. "Amazing what hair dye and a pair of contact lenses will do, isn't it? He thought for sure someone would recognize him when he posed as the guy from Build Pro, but he passed with flying colors. Apparently, absence didn't make the heart grow fonder in his case."

I licked my lips. "You went to your sister's hotel room that night, and when she told you she'd changed her mind and didn't have the book, the two of you argued, didn't you? And in a fit of anger, you strangled her."

He stared at me, then held up both hands. "Hey—I'm not a murderer. Was I mad at my sister? You bet I was. But I would never have killed her." His lips twisted into a grimace. "I figured Efram must have. And I bet he killed his old man, too, when he found out he'd been talking to the FBI. That guy—he's batshit crazy. I could tell that just from living with him for the time we were in the slammer together. I could see him killing his father, and Jane too."

"Yeah, well . . . I didn't."

I twisted my head to see a figure emerge from the shadows—Jake. Or rather, Efram. My gaze dropped to the shiny .45 he held in his hand. "You always were careless, Tom. Next time make sure the door actually closes behind you."

Thomas rose and looked at Efram. "Hey, Ef, take it easy. We can work this out, just between the two of us. There's no reason why we can't split the bounty fifty-fifty, once we convince the little lady here to give us the book."

"You've got to be kidding," said Efram. "You needn't act

all buddy buddy with me. I know that you never intended to split the profits from selling that formula with me. Riley told me everything."

"What? Riley told me that you were the one who wanted to get your hands on the formula first—*you* were going to cut *me* out. That's why I was going around, trying to locate another copy of the book. I was going to pull another switch on you."

I looked at the two of them. "It would seem, gentlemen," I said, "that the two of you have been played."

"Riley would never do that to me," sputtered Efram. "We planned to run away together to the Far East after we got the money for the formula."

"Riley bought Knight's journals," I said. "The woman at Left for Dead Books said it was a blonde woman with a purple streak in her hair. At first I thought it was your sister Jewell who'd gotten them."

"I told Ree-Ree to get rid of that streak," growled Efram. "But she said that it would cast suspicion on Jewell, and I guess she was right at that."

"Is her name even Riley?" I asked.

"No, it's her mother's maiden name. Her real name is Marie Carson. She did two years for participating in an armed robbery. She used to do some cooking in the prison café. That's how we met." Efram smiled reminiscently. "She makes a mean grilled cheese."

"She knew how to cook up a separation between you two fellows, that's for sure," I said. "What makes you think that Riley hasn't been working against the two of you all this time, trying to get that book for herself?"

The two men stared at each other, then at me. "Riley wouldn't do that," said Thomas.

Efram shook his head. "No, she wouldn't."

Both their tones lacked conviction, so I jumped in. "Wouldn't she? Did you trash my store? Break into my friend's house? Leave a threatening note on my back door?"

Efram jerked his thumb at Thomas. "I assumed he did it."

"I thought you did," growled Thomas. "And I was pissed I didn't think of it first."

"Well, someone did it," I said. "And if neither of you are responsible, that leaves . . ."

"Me."

I glanced up as another figure melded out of the shadows. "My, my, you really are quite the sleuth, aren't you," said Riley.

"Honey Bunch, we need to clear up a few things," said Efram. He pointed at me. "She seems to think you were working with Tom, here, to screw me out of my cut."

"She also thinks you were doing the same with him to me," put in Thomas.

Riley clucked her tongue. "I was right about you, Charley," she said. "Your deductive powers are nothing short of amazing." She raised her hand, and I saw the glint of blue steel as she leveled her .45 at Efram. "Put your gun down on the ground, Efram, and kick it over here. I won't hesitate to shoot you, believe me."

"Oh yeah?" Efram swaggered a bit as he took a step toward Riley. "I won't hesitate to shoot you either, baby. I don't like double crossers. Dammit, I think I *will* shoot you!"

I flinched as Efram pulled the trigger—but nothing happened. Riley barked out a laugh. "You should always check your gun, Ef, make sure that there are bullets in it," she said. "Mine does, and I'm just itching to pull the trigger, too, so—just kick your gun over here, please."

Efram hesitated, then set his gun on the ground and gave it a hard kick toward her. She bent, picked it up, and tucked it in the waistband of her pants. When she raised her head toward me I said, "It was you who trashed my store and all the rest, wasn't it? I remember how conveniently you appeared at every incident."

"That's why I took the cover of a reporter. It never occurred to me that you'd actually try to call me at the newspaper office," she said. "Thank goodness I was there in the guise of making a late-night delivery. You'd be surprised what one can learn, hanging around a newspaper office late at night. Making deliveries to the police station too. For example, that's how I found out that you turned the Poe book over to the FBI." She raised an eyebrow. "Detective Grant really should lower his voice. One never knows who might be lurking in the dark hallways."

"What!" Both Efram and Thomas chorused. "The FBI has the book?"

"Yes, but from what I was able to gather, there's something missing from it. A certain page?"

I looked at Riley. "And you have the decoding key. I'm thinking it's in notebook number eleven?"

"Yes, on page eleven." She smiled at Thomas. "Your sister was right, Tom. Knight was obsessed with those numbers. But like he and Effy's papa said, can't do anything without seventy-seven. Seventy-seven and eleven go together."

"It was you that Jane was supposed to meet at my store that day, wasn't it?" I said. "She kept looking out the window, and I could tell she was nervous."

"She tried to cancel the meet," said Riley. "But I wouldn't let her. I told her I'd be there to pick up the package, but then that darned tour bus stopped at your shop and threw our schedule off. She took advantage of that confusion to slip out, but she hid the book in your store just in case. She admitted it when I went to her hotel room and confronted her. She said that she couldn't go through with it, and then she tried to offer me some jewelry she'd taken from Efram's aunt. I got so mad I took off the scarf I was wearing and strangled her with it. I have to admit, she didn't put up much of a fight. It was as if she were resigned to dying."

Thomas stared at Riley. "You killed my sister! You let me think Efram did it!"

"She told me you killed your sister in a rage," said Efram.

Riley laughed. "The two of you were so easy to play. I have to admit, Efram, your father wasn't as easy. He flat out refused my offer of a cut if he divulged the location of the book. He just said that I'd be lucky to get away with life—after all, what we were planning basically amounted to treason." She raised her gun. "He never saw it coming. His death was swift. Charley knows. She saw his poor, dead body."

Efram's lips thinned. "I confess, I never got along with my family, but . . . I probably could have gotten along with my father, if he hadn't been such a spineless twit. If only he'd stood up to Aunt Maddie, maybe things might have been different—my life might have been different. Instead he did nothing while she treated me like a miscreant, a second-class citizen. She sent me away to New York and told me I'd never see a penny of my mother's money."

Riley knelt down beside me. "Come on, Charley. I really don't want to waste time trashing your store again. Jane had to have hidden that page here, and I'm betting you figured that out and found it. Just hand it over, and there'll be no reason to hurt you."

Oh yeah, like I believed her. I looked her straight in the eye. "Sorry, Riley. I don't have the page."

Riley clucked her tongue. "Do you think I believe you, Charley? Because I don't, not for one second. I know you've got that page. Your end will be a lot less painful if you just hand it over."

"Look," said Thomas. "Why don't we all put our differences aside and work together, as we originally planned? We'll get more than enough from the sale of the formula to ensure we'll never want for anything for the rest of our lives. Why be greedy?"

"Why indeed," said Efram. "OK, I'm in."

"Well, I'm not," huffed Riley. "Why should I share anything with you two losers? It seems to me that I've taken most of the risks here. *I*'ve killed two people over that formula. It's only right that I should get the whole thing and you two . . . well, you two will be going back to prison."

"What?" cried Efram. "You're going to leave us behind to take the heat while you sail off to the Far East?"

"I was thinking more along the lines of Venezuela," she said. "They have no extradition treaty with the US, and to be honest, I like enchiladas much better than sushi."

Suddenly my pocket started to buzz. Riley leaned over and snatched my cell phone. She looked scornfully at her two companions. "What, you didn't take her phone?" She glanced at the screen. "You've got a text from Detective Grant," she said. "He says, Can't get to the station for a while. Can this wait till tomorrow?" She looked at me. "You were going to tell him about the page. You *do* know where it is." Without waiting for me to answer, she started typing a reply. "'Sure can. See you tomorrow.' That should do it." Riley tossed the phone onto a nearby table and then said, "OK, Charley, you and I are going to start moving. But before that, I've got to take care of my friends here."

Like a snake uncoiling to attack, her arm shot out and she clocked Efram on the side of the head with the gun. He let out a low moan and slumped to the floor.

"Christ, Riley, what did you do?" Thomas cried. He moved to bend over Efram, and as he did so, Riley pulled the other gun out of the waistband of her pants and hit him on the back of the head. He went down like a sack of bricks, right beside Efram. "That takes care of them," she said. She tossed the other gun aside and turned back to me. "Now let's get down to business, Charley. Where's that page?"

"I—all right," I said. "I think I know where Jane hid it. You're right, I was going to tell Detective Grant. It's upstairs, in my store."

Riley's lips curved into a smile. "OK, now we're getting somewhere. You are going to show me just where this page is." She leaned over, untied my ankles, and then grabbed my arm and jerked me to my feet. I wobbled a bit but managed to straighten. I held out my hands. She shook her head. "Oh, no. I'm not freeing your hands."

"I'll need them to get the page—if it's where I believe it is," I said.

"You lead me to it, and I'll take care of that," snarled Riley. She gave me a push toward the stairs. "Come on now. Up we go."

I started up the stairs. I could feel Riley's gun jabbing into my ribs. I'd barely taken two steps when Efram let out a loud groan.

"You've got to be kidding me," growled Riley. "I clocked him hard enough to keep him out for an hour. He must have a real hard head."

She turned and I saw my chance. I kicked out and managed

to jab her in the shin. She wobbled, her arms flailing, and then she dropped the gun and fell the few steps down to the floor. I turned and raced up the steps to the door and twisted the knob—the door wouldn't budge! Too late, I remembered I'd locked it from the outside before I left to go to Left for Dead Books.

Riley still lay at the bottom of the steps, stunned. I hurried down the steps and jumped over her, heading toward the corner where I'd seen her gun fall. She reached out and grabbed my ankle, and I went down hard, right beside the table where she'd put my phone. I reached up to grab it, but she recovered and sprang forward, knocking it out of my hand. The phone skittered to a stop near an overturned box. A black paw snaked out from the box and swatted the phone inside. While I was trying to decide if I'd really seen that or if I was hallucinating, Riley grabbed me around the shoulders and jerked me up. She'd also recovered her gun, which she jabbed painfully into my ribs.

"OK, enough funny business," she growled. "Try something like that again and it'll be the last thing you do."

She shoved me against the table and then turned her attention back to the two men. Efram's eyes were shut, but he was groaning. Thomas was out like a light. Riley bent over Efram and gave him another swift whack on the head. He stopped moaning and his head lolled to one side. I hoped the second blow hadn't killed him.

Riley now turned her attention back to me. "OK, that settles it. You're not going upstairs. You're going to tell me exactly where you think Jane hid that page, and I'm giving you five seconds to do it. Five—four—three—two—"

"OK, all right," I said. "I think she might have hidden it in the john. I remembered her asking me if we had one for public use."

"The john? Really?" Riley snorted. Her hand shot out and patted at the waistband of my pants. "I'd be more inclined to think you'd keep it close to you—very close. Ah, what's this?"

Her hand had settled over the tiny lump just below my belly button. With a cry, her hand dipped inside my pants, and a second later she had the page in her hand. "What do you know?" she said gleefully. "Seventy-seven, all right." She turned her gun around and waved the butt in the air. "Now, it's your turn to say night-night, my dear. By the time you and the fellows wake up, I'll be far, far away."

I flinched as she raised her gun, but then we both heard a loud voice shout from upstairs: "Police! Charley, where are you?"

I gave Riley a push and shouted, "I'm down here, in the basement. The door's locked from the outside!"

With a strangled cry, Riley leapt toward me. As she did so, a black form streaked forward and whizzed past her, knocking the page out of her hand. Startled, she dropped the gun and jumped back. Thinking quickly, I thrust out my leg and kicked the gun into the far corner of the room just as the storeroom door burst open and Ian Grant, David Trent, and two other officers appeared on the threshold, brandishing guns.

"Don't make a move," Grant called out as Riley's head angled toward the gun. The two officers came down and quickly cuffed her.

"Her two accomplices are over there," I said, nodding in their direction. "Thomas Radcliffe and Efram Winchell."

"Winchell? You don't say." Grant helped me to my feet and shook his head. "So once again, Charlotte, you put yourself in a position where you nearly got yourself killed."

"I wasn't trying to, trust me. In my defense, I was on my way to the station with the missing page when I was accosted," I said. I looked at him. "And what are you doing here? I thought you texted that you couldn't get down to the station tonight?"

"That was my fault," said Trent. "I'd gotten some information, and I wanted to share it with Grant."

"We'd just started our meeting when your call came in," said Grant. "I couldn't hear too clearly at first, and then I heard sounds of a scuffle and a woman's voice I didn't recognize. I figured something was going down, so I called for backup, and Trent and I came right here. Thank goodness we weren't far away."

I looked at him, puzzled. "I didn't call you, Grant. The only time I called you I got your voicemail. Riley took my phone away from me, and—"

I looked over at Poe, who was sat with the page clamped firmly between his paws. Grant looked at me. "If you didn't make that call, Charlotte, then who did?"

I shook my head, and my face broke into a slow grin. "You wouldn't believe me if I told you," I said.

TWENTY-FIVE

October 31st

"Trick or treat, trick or treat, give me something good to eat."

I smiled at the three figures in front of my counter—a witch, a fairy, and a goblin. I reached beneath the counter and pulled out three foil bags that I'd filled earlier today with bite-size Hershey bars, Reese's cups, and gummy worms. "Happy Halloween," I said. "Have fun trick or treating!"

"Oh, we will," said the goblin as he put the sack of candy into the large plastic bag he carried. A grinning jack-o'-lantern was on one side, a skull on the other. "We're off to the Frozen Spoon now. The Milkshake Lady has Halloween witch ice cream sundaes! I'm getting a strawberry one!"

"Chocolate peanut butter for me," said the fairy, and the witch nodded in agreement.

As the trio of ghosties scampered off, I let out a chuckle. "To be honest, a Halloween witch ice cream sundae sounds pretty good right about now."

The door opened and Phyllis sailed in, a long red cloak trailing behind her. She had on tight black pants and a white blouse open at the collar. When she leaned over and smiled at me, I saw two pointy fangs. "Countess Dracula, I presume?"

"In the flesh." She made a sweeping bow. "I'm glad I extended the Jumpin' Bean's hours today. What I lack in trick or treating kids, I'm making up for with parents sadly in need of caffeine to keep up with the little buggers."

"I heard the goblin call Betty 'the Milkshake Lady,' so I'm assuming she decided on the chocolate shake costume?"

"Actually, it ended up being chocolate chip mint milkshake." Phyllis chuckled. "She had a lot of green material left over from last St. Paddy's Day. Oh, and she said for me to tell you that she'll be in tomorrow to pick up that book for her brother. She thought she could get away, but apparently business is booming over there." Phyllis leaned in closer to me and whispered, "You know, this latest escapade of yours would make a great cozy mystery! Maybe you should contact some publishers."

I raised an eyebrow. "Are you suggesting I write it?"

Phyllis waved her hands in front of her. "Oh gosh no. I know you're not a writer, Charley. But you could pitch the story, and I bet an editor could get a pro to do it, maybe Miranda James or Laura Childs?"

I chuckled. "I'm sure they could. Who knows? Maybe someone will do a book about it someday."

"Well, if they do, I hope they give my character a juicy part." Phyllis glanced around my crowded store. "Anyway, it looks like you're doing a brisk business."

"Having a kid's story hour was a brilliant idea that I must thank Braedon for," I said. "He, Anna, and Mandy have been taking turns reading to the kids. And much like the parents in your shop in need of caffeine, the parents here are not only browsing while they wait for the story time to end, but they end up buying books either for themselves or their kids."

"All in all a stroke of genius," agreed Phyllis. "Makes you wonder how we'll top it next year."

The door opened again, and Ian Grant entered the store. "Detective Grant," said Phyllis. "What are you supposed to be? A law enforcement officer? A keystone cop?" She turned her head slightly and gave me a broad wink.

"Actually I'm just about to start my shift." Grant looked Phyllis up and down. "Countess Dracula, I presume?"

Phyllis bowed. "None other. Well, I guess I'd best get back to my store. See you later, Charley." She breezed out the door.

Grant walked over and rested a hip against my counter. He gave me a once-over, taking in my red pigtails, blue and white checked dress, and the red ballet slippers on my feet. "Let me guess. Dorothy from Oz?"

"Actually Dorothy's from Kansas, but yes," I said with a grin. I pointed to the basket next to the register where Poe lay sleeping. "Instead of Toto, though, I guess you call him—Poeto?"

"Cute." He angled his head toward the reading nook. "Is that the scarecrow I see, reading to the kids?"

"Yep, that's Braedon. We decided to have an Oz theme for our first Halloween. Anna is dressed as a munchkin, and Mandy dug out her old pink prom dress to be Glinda the Good Witch."

He nodded. "The kids seem to like it."

"They do. We're working our way through the Oz books. Some of them make their parents bring them back for the next story hour. We had one at eleven, then two, and now this one at four—the final one will be at six."

"You'll probably get an older crowd for that one," he observed.

"Probably—but who doesn't like Oz?"

"No argument there." He cleared his throat. "I come bearing news from Special Agent Trent. Knight's formula has been decoded and is now in the hands of NASA—thanks to you. He wanted to convey them personally, but unfortunately he couldn't get back here to do so."

I laughed. "Well, if you hear from him again, tell him it was my pleasure. So, was that all? Or are you really here because you heard we're giving out treats?"

"Well, there might be another reason I came here, but I wouldn't turn down a treat," he said with a wide grin. I dug a bag of candy out from under the counter and dangled it in front of him. He reached for it, and I jerked my hand back and held it out of his grasp. "Sorry, Detective. No treats for you until you spill your guts. Does this other reason have something to do with Riley and those two saps she conned?"

"Saps being the operative word." Grant chuckled. "Man, they couldn't wait to turn on her once we got them in interrogation. According to them, they were iffy about the whole plot to steal the formula, but Riley convinced each of them that it was a good plan. Of course, they had no idea that she'd already contacted someone who could sell the formula. She'd already made a reservation on a flight to Venezuela for last night, as a matter of fact. She expected everything to be tied up all nice and tidy by then—until poor Jane Radcliffe threw a monkey wrench into everything by backing out."

"So I was right? Riley was the real brains behind everything?"

He shot me what I could only describe as an indulgent smile. "Yes, Nancy Drew, you were right. Before her arrest, Riley had a rap sheet as long as my arm, mostly petty stuff, but she aspired to the big time. She got acquainted with Thomas Radcliffe first. The two of them struck up a relationship, although Thomas was more smitten than she. Apparently Jane used to call her brother and confide everything Gordon Knight said to her when he thought, in his delusion, that she was his late sister. He told Jane that he'd perfected the rocket fuel formula, but he didn't trust anyone and so he'd written it in invisible ink on page seventy-seven of the book he'd written to honor his two idols—Edgar Allan Poe and Vincent Price. And just in case enemy agents found it, the formula was encrypted, and one needed the key to decode it. He'd written that on page eleven of his eleventh journal—the notebook that had his notes on the Poe book."

"Seventy-seven eleven," I murmured. "Do go on, Detective."

"Thomas Radcliffe was the first to get out on parole. He'd told his sister to wait to switch the book until he could get there so he could forge the signatures. In the meantime, Efram and Riley had become rather tight themselves. Thomas had told Efram about the plan, and he was all for it. Even gave Thomas tips on his aunt's habits that he could pass along to his sister. But Riley saw a golden opportunity to play those two and get the formula and money for herself. She'd heard about Derek Proust leaving and his replacement not arriving for a few weeks, so she decided to pass herself off as a reporter, figuring it was a good cover to get information." He paused and eyed the trick or treat bag. He made another swipe at it, but I once again held it out of his grasp. "Riley was the one who trashed your store. Efram, aka Jake, was out that night with Mandy, and Thomas was, as he put it, drowning his sorrows in a bar after his sister informed him she wasn't going along with his plan. Riley is also the one who broke into Zane's house, and she also left you that note. She deliberately wore size-twelve shoes to throw you off track. Her buyer for the formula was getting impatient, so she was getting desperate to find the book. She'd disguised herself as a pizza delivery person in order to snoop around the station and the news office. She happened to hear me telling Donaldson about turning over the book to Trent, and about a page being missing, and then she really started to panic. She was at the news office delivering pizza when she overheard the receptionist talking about no one named Riley May Connor working there. That was when she figured she had to speed things up a bit. She was pretty sure you knew more than you let on and she planned to get you to give up that page—no matter what she had to do."

A mental picture of Riley waving her gun entered my head, and I shivered. "I'm assuming she's lawyered up?"

"I think they're going to try for temporary insanity, but I doubt that will stick," said Grant. "She'll be back in prison, serving a nice long sentence—if the DA doesn't try for the death penalty. If they can prove she was going to sell that formula to a country considered a foreign enemy, it could qualify as treason."

I shook my head. "She has to be a little unbalanced to take such a risk—not that I'm defending her," I added. "And what about Thomas and Efram?"

"Oh, they'll serve time again, and I wouldn't be surprised if the sentence included the possibility of no parole—ever." He leaned an elbow on the counter. "When I told Maddie Elster, all she said was she was glad that Efram wouldn't get the death penalty, but to quote, 'the boy is getting what's coming to him,' unquote. She didn't seem a bit surprised by his involvement in this at all."

"In a way that's a shame," I said. "Maybe if she had been a bit more understanding to both Efram and his father, things for all of them might have been different."

Grant shrugged. "You can't change people, as much as you might like to. Take you, for instance."

I turned my finger inward toward my chest. "Me?"

"Yes, you. Even though Agent Trent and I told you to halt

your investigation, you went ahead with it anyway and put yourself in a life-threatening situation. And as much as I'd like for you to stop being an older version of Nancy Drew, I somehow think that's impossible. It's like it's in your blood." He placed both elbows on the counter and leaned forward so his face was only inches from mine. "And in spite of all that, your stubbornness and your recklessness, I find you fascinating."

"Fascinating, huh? You know, you're not the first person to say that about me," I said with a grin.

"I bet not. So—remember that Thai restaurant I told you about? The Pad Thai Café? As it happens, I've got Saturday night off, so I thought I'd go there for dinner. I was hoping that you might agree to accompany me."

I batted my eyelashes at him. "Detective Grant—are you asking me out on a date?"

"As a matter of fact I am." His eyes twinkled. "I think it's time we stopped beating around the bush, don't you? After all, we have so much in common. A love of making good food, eating good food—"

"Solving mysteries," I put in.

"Or getting into trouble. And frankly, Charlotte James, I'd really like to date you before I have to end up arresting you for disrupting evidence, or something like that."

"I couldn't agree more." I grinned back at him.

"Good. So what do you say? Saturday night around seven? Maybe we can discuss that recipe exchange while we're at it."

"I'll have to check my calendar," I said demurely. "But I think I can rearrange my schedule."

Poe lifted his head, turned toward Grant, and let out a loud meow.

I dangled the bag in front of Grant again, and this time I let him catch it. He opened it, looked inside, and smacked his lips. "All my favorites." He slid the bag into his jacket pocket, then looked at his watch. "I should get going," he said. "I've got to relieve Detective Donaldson. She said something about taking her niece trick or treating."

I chuckled inwardly at the thought of Barbie out trick or

treating. "By all means, don't keep the good detective waiting," I said. "And I'll see you Saturday."

"That you will." He started to turn toward the door, then paused. "There is still one mystery that hasn't been solved, though."

"Oh? What is that? I thought we covered everything?"

"It's the call I got from your phone. I can't figure out how that could have happened, since you insist you didn't make it."

I shrugged. "My phone was on when Riley took it away from me. Maybe some wires got crossed somewhere, or maybe when it fell, the impact triggered your contact button."

"Maybe." His eyes slitted. "You've got me as one of your contacts?"

"Sure. You never know when a good law enforcement official will come in handy."

He shook his head. "You are really something, Charlotte. I look forward to our date Saturday and finally finding out more about you."

I chuckled. "Not too much, Detective. A girl needs some secrets, after all." I wiggled my fingers at him. "See you Saturday."

He left and I angled my gaze toward Poe, who was sitting up in his basket, innocently washing his face. I waggled a finger at him. "Speaking of secrets, Poe, someday you are going to have to tell me how you got into the store, and how you learned to press contact buttons on my phone."

Poe looked up, widened his eyes, and gave his head an emphatic shake.

"OK, keep your secrets. It had better stay between us anyway. Like I said, no one would believe it." I paused and then added softly, "And yes, I am a lucky woman. In more ways than one. Like Edgar Allan was Knight's idol, you, little man, are mine."

Poe gave me a long, catly look. Then he lay down, curled into a ball, closed his eyes, and curved his lips into a contented kitty grin.